Also by Jennifer L. Schiff

<u>Sanibel Island Mysteries</u>

A Shell of a Problem

Something Fishy

In the Market for Murder

Bye Bye Birdy

Shell Shocked

Trouble in Paradise

A Perilous Proposal

For Whom the Shell Tolls

The Crisis Before Christmas

Framed in Naples

<u>Novels</u>

Tinder Fella

Something's Cooking in Chianti

Finding Gemma Lovegood

A Mocktail for Murder

An Obsession with Murder

Jennifer Lonoff Schiff

Shovel
& Pail
Press

An Obsession with Murder
by Jennifer Lonoff Schiff

Published by Shovel & Pail Press. All rights reserved. No portion of this book may be reproduced in any form without permission from the publisher, except as permitted by U.S. copyright law.

Cover design by Dunya Ivanovic

Formatting by Polgarus Studio

ISBN: 979-8-218-85177-4

More information at https://shovelandpailpress.com

Cure for an obsession: get another one.

—Mason Cooley

CHAPTER 1

Wednesday was Percy's favorite day of the week. Not because it was Hump Day, but because that was when she saw Dr. Rob, her therapist, and had dinner with her two best friends, Bonnie and Carlo. She had started seeing Dr. Rob after her husband died two years ago. Jim's death at age 48 had been quite sudden—a heart attack—and it had made Percy's mild OCD worse.

Percy—whose real name was Persephone[*]—had gone into a tailspin and hadn't been able to leave the house for days, constantly cleaning and organizing (or recleaning and reorganizing) everything. Her daughter Lucy had come down from college to be with her mother. And together with Bonnie and Carlo, they eventually convinced Percy to get help.

Bonnie had been the one to recommend Dr. Rob, whose last name was Mankiewicz. But everyone referred to him as Dr. Rob, even the staff at the Wellness Center.

Bonnie's friend Elyse had been a patient of his for years and had raved about him. But Percy, being OCD and a librarian, needed to research him before making a decision.

---

[*] Percy had adopted the nickname in third grade after some boys had taken to calling her Phony-Baloney. Since then, pretty much everyone had called her Percy, except for her mother and a prickly high school English teacher.

As Percy quickly learned, Dr. Rob had received his undergraduate degree from Harvard and earned a Ph.D. in Psychology from Yale. He had then worked at Yale New Haven Hospital before eventually going into private practice.

That sounded impressive, but what did patients (other than Elyse) have to say about him? To find out, Percy went to RateMyTherapist. Nearly all of the reviews and ratings were glowing. And Percy didn't mind the few less-than-glowing ones. That was to be expected. She looked at a couple of other review sites, which painted a similar picture. Dr. Rob was well thought of. However, Percy knew better than to completely trust online reviews.

She next searched for personal information about the psychologist. But she could find nothing. Nothing about a wife, or a husband, or children. And it appeared that Dr. Rob wasn't on social media. Though that didn't surprise her.

She met with Bonnie's friend Elyse, who gushed about Dr. Rob. And finally, after being nagged by her best friends and daughter, Percy made an appointment to see him.

Percy's first impression of Dr. Rob was that he resembled Mr. Rogers, or rather a sexy version of Mr. Rogers. He had the same brown hair with a touch of gray, hazel eyes, and often wore a cardigan sweater and tie, just like Fred Rogers did on *Mr. Rogers' Neighborhood.* But he had a deeper voice and looked like he worked out.

Objectively, he was an attractive man, which was no doubt why Elyse and other female patients liked him. However, that was not the reason Percy decided to continue to see him. It was because he was a good listener and didn't judge her. And she liked the sound of his voice, which had a soothing quality.

And by the end of the first month of therapy, Percy was back at work at the Stonebridge Public Library, where she worked with Bonnie.

Percy had always loved books and information, and after

Lucy had started first grade, Percy began volunteering at Lucy's school library. She had enjoyed volunteering at the library so much that when Lucy entered middle school, Percy decided to get her master's degree in library science. Then she was fortunate to get a part-time job at the Stonebridge Public Library, which eventually led to her becoming a full-time librarian there.

Percy enjoyed helping people find the information they needed or the right book. She particularly liked the more difficult requests. To be a good librarian, you often had to be an amateur detective, sleuthing out information. And Percy loved a good mystery, so much so that she had started a book club for mystery lovers, which met once a month at the library.

It had been nearly two years now since that first visit with Dr. Rob, and Percy still looked forward to her weekly sessions. Even though her OCD was under control, and she was no longer depressed, Percy still craved routine. And Dr. Rob was the one person she knew she could say anything to, and he wouldn't judge her.

It didn't matter that her insurance only reimbursed her a fraction of what she paid him for each session. She had plenty of money, thanks to her and Jim's investments and the money from his life insurance policy. And even if she hadn't been as well off, she probably would have found a way to keep seeing Dr. Rob.

Percy was going over what she planned on discussing with Dr. Rob at today's session as she waited to cross the street to go to the Wellness Center, which was located just a block and a half from the library. (Downtown Stonebridge was only a few blocks long.) Bonnie and Carlo, who ran the local framing store/art gallery, had been encouraging Percy to start dating, or at least dip her toe in the dating pool. But Percy had been resisting the idea and wanted to discuss it with Dr. Rob.

She was lost in thought when she heard sirens and saw

an ambulance pull up in front of the building that housed the Wellness Center. She watched as two paramedics got out, went to the back of the vehicle, and unloaded a gurney. Then they hurried inside.

Percy wondered who was ill or hurt and was anxious to cross the street. However, she waited until the light turned green. Then she hurried across the street and entered the building. The Wellness Center was located on the first floor, and upon entering, Percy saw the paramedics speaking with Carol, the receptionist/office manager. She looked upset.

Percy waited by the door until the paramedics had gone down the hall. Then she approached Carol.

"Did something happen?" Percy asked her. Though, obviously, something had.

"It's…"

Before Carol could finish, the door to the Wellness Center flew open and two men, one in plain clothes and the other in a police uniform, entered.

The one in plain clothes flashed a badge at the two women.

"I'm Detective Russo, and this is Officer O'Brien," he said. "We received a call that someone had been shot."

Percy tried not to stare. Who had been shot? Was it one of the doctors or a patient? She couldn't recall any shootings in Stonebridge, at least that she was aware of. Stonebridge was such a peaceful town, really more like a village where everyone knew everyone.

"Thank you for coming so quickly," Carol said to the detective, her voice quavering.

"You the one who called it in?" the detective asked her.

Carol nodded.

"Can you tell me what happened?"

"Dr. Rob's been shot!"

Percy sat in a chair in the waiting room, stunned. Carol had told the detective that someone had shot Dr. Rob in his office, while she'd been out to lunch, and now he was dead. The detective had gone to see for himself, telling Percy and Carol not to go anywhere while he visited the crime scene.

Percy couldn't believe it. Dr. Rob was dead? Not just dead but murdered?

"I just can't believe it," Carol said, staring back at Dr. Rob's office. "I was gone less than half an hour. Who could have done such a thing?"

"Where did you go?" asked Percy.

"Not far. Dr. Rob's noon appointment canceled. So I thought I'd run an errand and grab something to eat."

"Was there anyone here when you left?"

"Just Dr. Rob."

"Where was Dr. Richardson?"

Dr. Farrah Richardson was the other therapist, who worked mainly with children and young adults.

"She's on vacation this week."

"So there was no one in the office when you left, no patients, just Dr. Rob?"

"Just him. I would never leave if a patient were here."

"Did you tell him that you were running out?"

"I did. I even asked if I could get him something to eat. He often forgets to. Always so busy with work."

"And what did he say?"

"He said he was fine and to take my time."

"And then you left?"

"I asked him if he was sure, and he was about to answer when his phone rang. He told me he needed to get it, so I left."

"Any idea who called him?"

"No. And whoever it was called him on his cell phone, not the office phone, so I figured it was personal."

"So you left and went where?"

"To the dry cleaner and then to the deli."

"And how did you know Dr. Rob had been shot?"

"I went to tell him I was back and…"

Was Carol about to cry? Percy didn't know what to do, so she just waited for Carol to compose herself.

"Sorry," said Carol, wiping her eyes.

"Please," said Percy. "I can't imagine what it must have been like."

"My late husband was a cop, but I never saw a dead body before. And to see Dr. Rob there, sitting back in his chair, a look of surprise on his face, and all that blood…"

"And you were sure he was dead."

Carol gave Percy a look, as though to say it was obvious.

"And you called 911."

"I did."

"Did you touch anything?"

"Just the doorknob."

"Was the door closed when you got there?"

"It was. Which is why I knocked. But he didn't answer. I thought maybe he was on the phone, but I couldn't hear anything. Then again, you know how solid those doors are. You can't hear a thing outside when they're closed, especially with the white noise machine on."

Percy knew.

"So you opened the door and…?"

"I saw him sitting there in his chair, staring at me. I don't think I'll be able to sleep just thinking about it."

"What about the window? Was it open?"

Percy knew that on nice days like today, Dr. Rob liked to keep the windows open a crack.

"I don't remember. Maybe? I wasn't in there for long."

"Did you see anyone by the entrance to the Wellness Center when you left to run your errand or when you got back?"

Percy realized she was asking Carol a lot of questions,

questions Detective Russo would no doubt be asking her, but she couldn't help herself.

"I saw people going in and out of the building, but I didn't notice anyone hovering around the Wellness Center."

"What about the door to the Wellness Center? Did you lock it when you left?"

"No. We don't usually lock it during the day if someone's there."

"So, theoretically, anyone could have come in and shot him while you were out."

"I suppose. But why would anyone shoot Dr. Rob?"

"Perhaps an unhappy patient?"

"His patients loved him."

Percy was about to ask Carol another question when the paramedics emerged from the back with Dr. Rob's sheet-covered body resting on the gurney. As soon as Carol saw it, she burst into tears. Percy felt for the woman but didn't know what to do. She wasn't the best at comforting people.

A few minutes later, the detective and Officer O'Brien came out and went over to the two women. The detective asked Carol the same questions Percy had, and Carol gave him the same answers.

"Surely, not all of his patients loved him," said the detective, sounding skeptical, after asking her if it could have been one of Dr. Rob's patients who had shot him. "There must have been a few who weren't happy with him and had stopped seeing him."

He waited for Carol to reply.

Carol sighed.

"I suppose there were a few. But that's to be expected."

"Could you give me their names?"

"Do you have a search warrant?"

The detective frowned.

"Not on me, but I can get one. Or you could just give me their information, make things go a lot faster."

"At the Wellness Center, we respect our patients' privacy," Carol primly informed him.

Detective Russo looked at Carol for a few more seconds. Then he turned to Percy.

"And you are?"

"Percy Rollins," said Percy. "I'm a patient of Dr. Rob's. I was here for my one p.m. appointment."

"And did you love the deceased?"

Although Carol had said that Dr. Rob's patients loved him, Percy still thought that was a rather impertinent question, but she answered it anyway.

"I wouldn't say *love*, but he was an excellent therapist."

"How long had you been seeing him?"

"About two years now."

"That seems like a long time."

"Clearly, you've never been in therapy, Detective."

"Never needed it."

Percy mentally rolled her eyes. The detective turned back to Carol.

"Did Dr. Mankiewicz ever mention having an issue with one of his patients? Any of them ever threaten him?"

"Dr. Rob never discussed his patients with me."

"You ever hear anyone grumble out here in the waiting room?"

"I don't eavesdrop on patients."

Detective Russo looked like he found that hard to believe.

"What about his personal life? You know of anyone who might have wanted to harm him, an ex-wife or an ex-girlfriend or boyfriend?"

"Dr. Rob didn't discuss his personal life with me."

"What about family?"

"What do you mean?"

"I mean, was he married?"

"He was single."

"What about parents and siblings?"

"His parents died a few years back."

"Any brothers or sisters?"

"He has a younger brother, Edward."

"He live here in town?"

"No."

"You know where he lives?"

"I believe in Beauport."

"You got an address and phone number for him?"

"I do not. But I'm sure you can find him. He's a real estate agent."

"What about Dr. Mankiewicz? He live here in Stonebridge?"

"He does—did," said Carol.

"What about the other therapist, Dr. Richardson?"

"What about her?"

"She get along with Dr. Mankiewicz?"

"She did."

"They ever fight?"

"Not in front of me."

"And where is Dr. Richardson?"

"She's on vacation this week."

"Do you know where?"

"At their place in Beauport."

Beauport was a seaside town about ninety minutes from Stonebridge, on Long Island Sound.

"She shared a place with Dr. Mankiewicz?"

Carol looked confused.

"You said *their* place," said the detective.

"Oh. Sorry. I meant Dr. Richardson and her family."

"You tell her about Dr. Mankiewicz?"

"Not yet."

"And how long have you worked here, Mrs. Fielding?"

"Going on six years. I've been here since the center opened."

"You like your job?"

"I do. Dr. Rob and Dr. Richardson have been very good to me."

"Would you say that you and Dr. Rob were close?"

"Close?"

"You two ever have lunch or go out for a drink after work?"

"Our relationship was strictly professional."

The detective turned to Percy.

"And when did you arrive at the Wellness Center?"

"You mean today?"

Detective Russo nodded.

"A little before one. I saw the ambulance pull up as I was about to cross the street."

"And do you know of anyone who might have wanted to harm Dr. Mankiewicz?"

"I do not."

"You ever hear another patient grumble about him?"

"No."

"And what do you do?"

"I work at the Stonebridge Public Library. I'm a librarian."

"And how long have you worked there?"

"Full-time? Just over six years now."

"And where were you before you came here today?"

"At the library. You can ask my coworkers."

The detective turned back to Carol.

"You ever have a patient become violent?"

"What do you mean?"

"I mean, has a patient ever threatened one of the doctors or tried to harm them?"

"Not that I recall." Though something in Carol's expression made Percy wonder if she was telling the truth.

"Let's say a patient did threaten one of the doctors during a session. What would happen? They have some sort of panic button?"

"They had ones installed, but they never had to use them."

"So Dr. Mankiewicz didn't press his before he was shot?"

"I don't know. I wasn't here."

Percy watched as the detective wrote something in his little notebook. Then she noticed her smartwatch was flashing. She needed to get back to the library. Though a part of her wanted to stay and take a look around. Not that the detective would let her. But she wanted to see the crime scene. She turned to the detective.

"I should get back to the library. Am I free to go?"

"Give me your contact information."

Percy reached into her bag and pulled out a business card.

"You got a cell phone number?"

Percy sighed, took the card back, and wrote down her cell phone number.

"Here," she said, handing the card back to the detective.

"Thank you," he said.

"May I go now?"

"You may. Just don't go disappearing."

"I wasn't planning to."

She turned to Carol. She felt bad about leaving her alone with the detective.

"You going to be okay?"

"I'll be fine," she said. "You go to the library. I don't want you to be late."

"Thanks," said Percy. Then she hurried off.

CHAPTER 2

"You're five minutes late," said Bonnie. "Everything okay?" Bonnie knew that Percy was a stickler for being on time, especially for work.

Percy glanced around to make sure no one could overhear them, then she pulled Bonnie into an alcove, just to be on the safe side.

"Someone shot Dr. Rob."

Bonnie stared at her friend.

"Excuse me. I could have sworn you just said someone shot Dr. Rob."

"I did."

Bonnie continued to stare at her friend.

"When? Is he all right?"

"Just now, or a little while ago. And no, he's dead."

Bonnie continued to stare.

"How can you be so calm?"

"I don't know. Maybe I'm in shock. I think Carol is too. She's the one who found him."

"Hold up. Are you saying someone shot Dr. Rob at the Wellness Center, the place just across the street from us?"

Percy nodded.

"In his office."

"Whoa," said Bonnie. "You think it was a patient?"

"I don't know. The detective who was there asked me

and Carol that, but Carol refused to believe it could have been a patient."

"Did you see the body?"

"Only when the paramedics wheeled him out on the gurney. And he was covered by a sheet."

"Wow. He was so young. And so good-looking."

Now it was Percy's turn to stare.

"What?" said Bonnie. "You didn't think he was good-looking? Didn't you tell me you thought he looked like a sexy Mr. Rogers?"

"I don't recall saying that," Percy primly replied.

"Uh-huh. So who do you think killed him?"

"I have no idea, which is what I told that detective."

"What detective?"

"Russo. He arrived at the scene shortly after I got there."

"Did he question you?"

"He did. But I don't think I was very helpful."

"What about Carol?"

"What about her?"

"Who did she think killed him?"

"She had no idea."

"Hmm. Maybe she killed him."

"What?!" said Percy. "No way. Carol adored Dr. Rob. You should have seen her, Bonnie. She was barely holding it together, and she burst into tears when they wheeled his body out on the gurney."

"Maybe she's a good actress."

"Not that good. Carol could never shoot anyone. Besides, she's a new grandmother."

"So, grandmothers can't shoot people?"

Percy made a face.

"Why would she shoot him? She loved working there."

"Maybe he was planning on firing her."

"Never. That place couldn't run without Carol." Bonnie looked skeptical. "Look, even if he was for some crazy reason, I doubt Carol would shoot him for it."

"Did you shoot him?"

Percy stared at her friend.

"Me?! How could you think I shot him? I didn't even get there until after the ambulance arrived. And what reason would I have to kill him?"

Bonnie shrugged.

"I'm just covering the bases."

"Well, I didn't shoot him. You know how I feel about guns."

"You hate the noise they make."

"And the fact that they kill people."

"There's that too. So, are you going to try to figure out who killed him?"

"What makes you say that?"

"Please. I know how obsessed you are with figuring out mysteries. You even created a book group."

"Yes, well."

"So?"

"I may make a few discreet inquiries, try to learn a bit more about Dr. Rob. Though the man was very good at keeping a low profile. There's next to nothing about him online."

"Hmm. Well, let me know if you need help. Maybe Elyse knows something."

Percy looked down at her watch.

"I should get back to work. I don't want Carmen on my case." Carmen was their boss.

"She's not here."

"Where is she?"

"No idea. I saw her hurry out of here around noon, and she hasn't come back."

Percy's eyebrows went up.

"Don't be ridiculous," said Bonnie. "Why would Carmen kill Dr. Rob?"

"A minute ago, you thought I could have killed him."

"I didn't really think that."

"Well, I doubt Carmen's the killer."

"You never know. Maybe she and Dr. Rob were having a secret affair."

Percy gave her friend a skeptical look.

"Carmen's married and in her late fifties."

"So? Married women in their fifties have affairs."

"Dr. Rob had to have been at least ten years younger."

"Please. Carmen's a good-looking woman. And lots of older women have affairs with younger men."

"Carmen is not a cougar, and I am going back to work."

"You could take the afternoon off. I imagine finding a dead body must be pretty shocking. Though you seem okay."

"I'm fine. And I didn't actually see the body. Besides, work is the best place for me to be right now. If I were at home, I'd just be obsessing about it."

As opposed to now, Bonnie wanted to say but didn't.

"Okay, but if you want to reschedule dinner…"

"No way. You know how I look forward to our Wednesday night dinners."

Percy, Bonnie, and Carlo had been getting together for dinner every Wednesday since shortly after Percy's husband died. It had started as a way to get Percy out of the house. Then it had morphed into a regular thing.

"Okay, but if you change your mind…"

"I won't. I'll see you and Carlo at Annie's at six-thirty."

Percy was greeted at her door by a petite Siamese cat, who immediately began to rub herself against Percy's legs.

"Did you miss me, Minnie?" Percy asked the feline.

Minnie was technically Lucy's cat. But Lucy was at college, and Minnie had always been fond of Percy, who was usually the one who fed, watered, and cleaned up after her, even when Lucy was home.

Lucy had begged her parents to let her have a dog or a cat for years. But it wasn't until she was a freshman in high school and had been pet sitting for several months, to prove that she could take care of an animal, that Percy and Jim had relented. Lucy had wanted a dog, but with everyone gone during the day, Percy thought a cat would be more practical.

They had gone to the local shelter to look for a cat when Lucy had spied Minnie. The woman at the shelter warned Lucy and Percy that although Minnie was small and looked cute, she was feisty. But to Lucy, that only added to Minnie's charm.

Minnie had been more of a fraidy cat when they brought her home. But after a few days, and a lot of treats, Minnie acted as though she owned the place—and would plunk herself in Lucy's or Percy's lap whenever one of them sat down.

After Jim died, Percy was glad to have Minnie. She would often talk to the cat, telling her things she would have told Jim, even though she knew Minnie didn't understand her. But she was comforted by Minnie's warm, purring body on her lap or desk.

Percy headed to the kitchen, and Minnie followed her. Percy gave the cat some food and ran the kitchen faucet for her, Minnie preferring to drink from the sink rather than her water bowl.

"So, what have you been up to today, Miss Minnie?" Percy asked the cat when she was done drinking.

Minnie looked up at her and mewed.

"I see," said Percy. "Well, you will never guess what happened to me."

Minnie tilted her head and waited for Percy to continue.

"My therapist was murdered."

Was it Percy's imagination, or did Minnie's eyes go wide?

"I know," said Percy. "I was shocked too."

Minnie continued to look up at Percy.

"And I'm going to try to find out who did it."

"Mew?" said Minnie.

"Yes, me. I know, you think I should let the police handle it." Minnie didn't say anything. "But I promise to be careful."

Minnie went over and head-butted Percy's arm. Percy scratched the side of Minnie's face, and Minnie purred.

"Now, I have a few things to do, then I need to meet Bonnie and Carlo for dinner," she informed the feline.

"Bonnie told me about Dr. Rob," Carlo said after they had ordered drinks.

Percy had met Carlo shortly after she and Jim had moved to Stonebridge. She wanted to have some of the photographs she had taken on a recent trip to Northern Italy framed, and Carlo owned the local framing store, which doubled as an art gallery.

Carlo had mentioned that his family was from that part of Italy, and that led to a conversation about Northern Italy and eventually a friendship.

Percy had then introduced Bonnie to Carlo, and the three of them had become good friends.

"So, who do you think killed him?" Bonnie asked Carlo. He shrugged.

"Oh, come on. Wasn't he a customer?"

"He was. But it wasn't as though he confided in me."

"Do you think it could have been one of his patients?"

"It's possible. Or it could have been someone outside of work."

"Was he seeing someone?" Carlo took a sip of water. "Come on. Give."

"I don't know anything about Dr. Rob's personal life."

Bonnie and Percy waited for him to go on. "But about a week ago, he came into the gallery with a very attractive woman."

"Someone from Stonebridge?" Percy asked him.

"No. She's new in town."

"How do you know that?" Bonnie asked him.

"Dr. Rob told me."

"And does this mystery woman have a name?"

Carlo took another sip of water.

"This is like pulling teeth," Bonnie said to Percy. Then she turned back to Carlo. "Well?"

"I'm not sure I should say."

Bonnie rolled her eyes.

"You're not her doctor or lawyer. Did she tell you not to tell anyone?"

"No," he said slowly.

"Then tell us," said Bonnie.

Carlo looked around before speaking.

"Her name is Miranda Yates."

"Do you know what she was doing with Dr. Rob?"

"They seemed like old friends."

"Could they have been more than friends?" Bonnie asked him.

"I couldn't say for sure."

"Were they all touchy-feely?"

"I saw her put a hand on his arm at one point, but…"

"Aha!" said Bonnie.

"That doesn't mean anything," Percy told her friend.

"Or it could mean they were a couple." She turned back to Carlo. "Do you think they were a couple?"

"I don't know. I didn't get that impression."

"Do you think she could be his killer?"

Percy looked at her.

"Seriously? We know nothing about this woman."

Bonnie turned to Carlo.

"What did this Miranda Yates look like?"

"She was tall, maybe five-nine? And in good shape. Like she worked out. And she had long dark hair and big brown eyes."

"She sounds a bit like Dr. Rob," said Percy. "Maybe they're related. Though Carol just mentioned a younger brother, nothing about a sister."

"I'm sticking with lover," said Bonnie stubbornly.

Their drinks arrived, and they took a moment to sip them.

"So why are you two so interested in Dr. Rob?" Carlo asked the two women.

"Hello?" said Bonnie. "It's not every day that someone gets murdered in Stonebridge. And Percy was a patient of his. And you know how obsessed with murder she is."

"I am not obsessed with murder," Percy replied.

Bonnie gave her a look.

"Not real murders. Just ones in books."

"Didn't you say you wanted to solve the case?"

Carlo's eyebrows went up.

"Is that a good idea?"

"I just want to do a little investigating," Percy told him. "See what I can find out about Dr. Rob."

"And who might have wanted to kill him," added Bonnie.

"Just be careful."

"I will."

"I can help," said Bonnie. "I can talk to Elyse, see what she knows. You know how she loves to gossip. And you should see what Carol knows."

"I doubt she'll tell me much."

"You won't know unless you ask."

"I suppose."

"What about the other doctor?"

"You mean Dr. Richardson?"

"Unless he had some other partner."

"No, just her."

"What did she have to say?"

"I don't know. She wasn't there."

"Where was she?"

"On vacation."

"Where?"

"In Beauport. Her family has a home there."

"Very nice. Though Beauport isn't that far. You should meet with her, ask her about Dr. Rob."

Percy opened her mouth to reply, but the server had come over, asking them if they were ready to order.

"You know what you're going to have?" Bonnie asked Percy, who had not picked up her menu like the others. "Wait. Let me guess: You're going to have the rotisserie chicken and fries."

"What can I say? I like their rotisserie chicken and fries. And it's not like I can rotisserie a chicken at home."

"What are you going to have?" Bonnie asked Carlo.

"I'm still deciding. I was thinking either the pork chop or the tagliatelle Bolognese."

"I was thinking of getting that too. You want to get the pork chop, and we can share?"

"Fine. Though last time you said we should share, you didn't want to after taking a bite of your pasta."

"That's because it was so good."

Carlo made a face.

"If you want to get the tagliatelle, get the tagliatelle," said Bonnie. "There's no law that says we both can't have it."

Carlo sighed.

"No, you get the tagliatelle; I'll get the pork chop."

Percy couldn't help smiling. She loved her friends.

They spent the rest of the evening talking about work, books, art, and other things. And Bonnie did share her tagliatelle with Carlo.

And even though they all said they were full when they were done with their main course, they couldn't resist sharing a slice of Annie's famous chocolate cake with vanilla ice cream for dessert, which Percy carefully split three ways before anyone took a bite.

When they were done, they got separate checks—and promised to share any information they uncovered about Dr. Rob.

CHAPTER 3

As soon as Percy got home, she went to her office and got on her computer. She typed *Dr. Robert Mankiewicz* into her browser and waited as the screen began to populate.

At first glance, there didn't appear to be anything new. It would probably take a day or two until news of his murder trickled out. Maybe then there would be some new information. However, in the meantime, it wouldn't hurt to review what was there.

Percy clicked on Dr. Rob's profile on the *Psychology Today* website. It looked the same as the last time she had looked at it, two years before. There was a bit about his philosophy and where he had gone to school and worked, but not much else. She returned to the search list and clicked on a few more links. However, none of the links told her anything new.

She continued to scroll, hoping to find something she might have overlooked two years ago or something new, but she didn't see anything beyond what she already knew about him. She even checked LinkedIn, TikTok, Instagram, Twitter, Bluesky, and Facebook to see if Dr. Rob had a profile on any of those sites. But he didn't appear to have a social media presence. She sat back and sighed. Then she leaned forward again.

What about his brother, Edward? Maybe Edward was on social media and had posted something about his brother.

Percy typed *Edward Mankiewicz* into the search box. There was a link to a real estate agent named Edward Mankiewicz on LinkedIn. Percy clicked on it.

It had to be Dr. Rob's brother, she thought, looking at the profile photo. And he was based in Beauport. She wondered if he knew Dr. Richardson and/or had sold the Richardsons their house.

Percy scrolled down and saw that Edward had gone to Wesleyan undergrad, majoring in Sociology. Probably a useful degree for a real estate agent. Though she doubted he was planning on becoming a real estate agent when he was in college.

According to the date he received his degree, he was a couple of years younger than Dr. Rob.

She clicked on the link to his website and scrolled through the listings. Beauport Realty had several very nice-looking beachfront homes for sale, as well as some more modest homes a few blocks or miles from the shore.

Percy and Jim had talked about purchasing a beach house or summer place when Lucy was little. They had even looked at a few places in Beauport. However, nothing in their price range had grabbed them. Maybe she would reach out to Edward, tell him she was interested in purchasing a summer home. Then, while he was showing her around, she could ask him about his brother.

The more she thought about it, the more it seemed like a good idea. If nothing else, Percy would enjoy a day in Beauport, especially as the forecast for that weekend was supposed to be good. Though in New England, the weather could change several times over the course of a day.

Percy clicked on the Contact Us link and filled in the form. She would have called, but it was late. She read over what she had written, then hit *Submit*. A few seconds later, she received a notification that her message had been received.

She took a closer look at the two houses she had

mentioned she was interested in. One of them was right on the beach; the other was just a couple of blocks away. She thought Jim would have liked both of them. Though they were both well above their original budget. But Percy could afford them now. How ironic.

Her heart ached thinking about it—and Jim. If only they had bought a beach house when he'd been alive to enjoy it.

Well, maybe she'd buy one now, a place where Lucy could bring her friends over the summer—and Percy could watch her grandchildren grow up. But that was putting the cart before the horse. Lucy had just turned 20 and, as far as Percy knew, wasn't seeing anyone, at least not seriously.

Percy clicked on the About Us section. There was a photo of Edward, who went by Ed. He looked a lot like his older brother. Though he wasn't as good-looking. Per his bio, Ed had grown up in Connecticut and had spent summers in Beauport before moving there with his wife, Josie, and two sons.

If Ed had grown up in Connecticut and had spent summers in Beauport, Dr. Rob must have too, Percy reasoned. She looked again at Ed's photo and wondered if he and Dr. Rob had been close. She would ask him.

Percy yawned and looked at the time. It was nine-thirty. She thought about getting ready for bed, as she liked to be in bed by ten, but she had one more person she wanted to look up first: Dr. Farrah Richardson.

She returned to her browser and typed Dr. Richardson's name into the search box.

Percy had seen Dr. Richardson in the office a few times, while she was waiting to see Dr. Rob. But she had never had a conversation with her. She was an attractive woman in her forties, of medium height and slim with ash-blonde hair. Percy wondered if Dr. Richardson, who had been born in the late 1970s, had been named after Farrah Fawcett. She even looked a bit like her.

Just as with Dr. Rob, Percy didn't find a lot of information about Dr. Richardson, although she did find a wedding announcement. She clicked on it and quickly scanned it. Dr. Richardson looked pretty much the same as she had at 30. She must have good genes, Percy thought.

Percy felt she had aged ten years in the two years since Jim died. That was partly because her hair had started to turn gray. She had thought about coloring it, but decided to let it go.

She clicked on Dr. Richardson's *Psychology Today* profile next. However, it didn't reveal more than what she already knew: that Dr. Richardson had received a Ph.D. in Psychology from Yale, like Dr. Rob, and worked mainly with children and young adults.

Percy sighed and sat back. Time to stop looking at her computer and get ready for bed. She brushed her teeth and changed into her pajamas. Then she set her alarm for six-thirty as she planned on going for a run before work.

Percy had run track when she was in high school and college and had continued to run since. It had become part of her daily or near-daily routine. Though when Jim died, she had stopped running. That was because she had barely been able to get out of bed those first few awful days. And when she did get out of bed, she spent all day cleaning and organizing. It was only when she started therapy that she started running again. And now she rarely missed a day.

Percy got into bed, and Minnie curled up beside her. Then she picked up her book. It was about a group of senior citizens who tried to solve cold cases. Percy found the book engrossing and could have kept reading until she had finished it. However, she forced herself to put the book down at ten-thirty and turned off the light.

The next morning, the alarm went off at six-thirty, startling Percy. She had had trouble falling asleep, no doubt due to the book and Dr. Rob's murder, and then had slept fitfully.

She thought about hitting the snooze button, but she forced herself to get up, dislodging Minnie. The cat mewed in protest, then closed her eyes and went back to sleep. Or so Percy thought, for as soon as Percy headed downstairs to the kitchen, Minnie was right beside her.

Percy gave the cat some food and water. Then she drank a large glass of water herself, did a few stretches, and headed out the door. It was a beautiful spring day, albeit on the cooler side. Perfect running weather. Percy did one last stretch, then she was off.

The entrance to a trail was just a couple of blocks away. Percy headed toward it. She typically ran two to four miles, depending on the weather and how she was feeling. Today, she planned on doing three miles.

As she ran, she thought about Dr. Rob. *Who had killed him and why? Was it a disgruntled patient or someone from outside of work?* Then she remembered what Carlo had said, about seeing Dr. Rob with a woman. What was her name again? It took Percy a minute to remember. It was Miranda, Miranda Yates. Percy would look her up when she had time.

She got home half an hour later and checked her phone. There was nothing from Ed Mankiewicz, but it was early yet. If she hadn't heard from him by the afternoon, she would call him. She scratched Minnie's chin and then went to take a shower.

Percy arrived at the library a little before nine. Carmen was there, waiting for her.

"I'm sorry I wasn't here yesterday afternoon," she told Percy. "Bonnie told me about what happened. If you need to take some time off…"

"Thank you," said Percy. "But this is the best place for me to be."

Carmen studied her.

"If you're sure. You haven't taken any personal days this year."

"That's because I'm saving them for when I actually need them."

"Very well." Carmen looked around, then returned her focus to Percy. "So," she said, keeping her voice low. "Any idea who killed him?"

"Not yet," said Percy. "The man is a bit of a mystery."

"And I know how much you love a good mystery."

Percy didn't comment.

"I didn't know him, but I'd heard good things about him," said Carmen. "I'm sure he'll be missed."

"I'm sure he will. Was there anything else?"

"No. I just wanted to make sure you were okay."

"Thank you. As I said, I'm fine."

Carmen glanced at her watch.

"I should probably unlock the door. It's a minute after nine, and you know how patrons are."

Percy did.

Percy couldn't stop thinking about Dr. Rob all morning, the same thoughts replaying over and over again in her brain. She wanted to reach out to Carol, but she didn't know how to. Of course, she could just call over to the Wellness Center. Though, would it even be open? She wished she had Carol's email address or phone number. Then again, she could probably find them online. Even so, what would she say or write to her? Then Percy had an idea.

Percy knew Carol was a big fan of romance novels. She had discovered this early on, having seen one on Carol's desk and then asked her about it. So she decided to go to the Village Bookshop during her lunch break and get Carol a couple of books.

Even though she worked in a library, Percy was always buying books. It was her way of supporting authors. And the Village Bookshop was just a couple of blocks from the library, at the other end of town. She entered the shop and saw Suzi, one of the two women who regularly worked there, helping a customer. Suzi was in her twenties and an avid reader. (The other woman who worked there, Ginny, was in her sixties and also loved to read, no doubt a requirement for working in a bookstore.)

Percy waited for Suzi to finish with the customer and then went up to her.

"So, what can I help you with today?" Suzi asked Percy. "You looking for a new mystery?"

"Actually, I'm looking for something for a friend who likes romance novels."

"Do you know what sort of romance novels your friend likes?"

Percy frowned.

"Does she prefer historical, contemporary, paranormal, clean, or romantasy?"

"I'm not sure. She's in her fifties, so maybe not paranormal or romantasy."

"Don't be so sure. Romantasy books are very popular with women of all ages right now."

"I think she's more of a traditionalist. Maybe something historical and/or something contemporary?"

"Spicy or not-so-spicy?"

Percy thought. She remembered seeing a book on Carol's desk that pictured a handsome man in a kilt embracing a voluptuous redheaded woman.

"Do you have something mildly spicy?"

Suzi smiled.

"Let me show you a few books she might like. And if she doesn't like them, she can return them and get something else."

"How long does she have to return them?"

"Seven days. And they need to be in good condition. No dropping them in the bathtub."

"Do people drop books in their bathtubs?" Percy asked.

"You'd be surprised."

"Huh."

Percy would never read in the bathtub. Besides, she mainly took showers as she considered bathtubs too germy.

Suzi took out several books from the Romance shelf and handed them to Percy. Another customer had come in, and Suzi told Percy to take her time.

Percy read the back covers of each book. She wasn't familiar with any of them, Romance not being her preferred genre. (Contrary to popular belief, librarians aren't familiar with every book that's ever been published, though they tend to be more well-read than the average person.)

She continued to stare at the books.

"Can't decide?" said Suzi, returning a few minutes later.

"Can you just pick for me?"

"I'd get her these two," said Suzi, plucking two of the books from Percy's hands.

"Fine. Let's go with those."

"And like I said, she can always return them if she's already read them or wants to get something else."

"Great."

"Would you like me to gift wrap them?"

Percy looked down at her watch.

"I can do that later. Do you maybe have a little bag?"

"Of course," said Suzi.

She rang Percy up and placed the books in a little bag.

"Thanks!" said Percy, taking the bag.

"I hope your friend enjoys them!" called Suzi.

Percy exited the bookstore and looked out across the street at the building that housed the Wellness Center. There was no telltale yellow police tape, at least outside the building. Could the Wellness Center be open? Percy decided to cross the street and find out.

She entered the building and headed to the suite that housed the Wellness Center. But there was a sign on the door saying the center was closed until further notice, with a number to call for assistance. Percy wrote it down and then tried the door. It was locked.

She entered the number into her phone. There was a recorded message, saying the center was closed, that if this was a true medical emergency to call 911, and to otherwise leave a message. She didn't bother leaving a message.

Percy returned to the library, getting her lunch out of the refrigerator in the staff room. She had a few minutes to eat her sandwich before she needed to return to work.

She checked her phone as she chewed. Someone had just left a voicemail. It was Ed Mankiewicz, saying he'd be happy to assist her in her house hunt and to give him a call. Percy was tempted to phone him right then, but she needed to eat. So Ed would have to wait.

As soon as she got off work, Percy gave him a call. He answered on the third ring.

"Ed Mankiewicz."

"Hi, Mr. Mankiewicz. This is Percy Rollins returning your call."

"Ah, Ms. Rollins. I saw your note, and both houses are still for sale."

"Wonderful. Any chance I could see them this weekend?"

"I'm a bit busy this weekend, but I'm sure I could squeeze you in. Was there a particular day and time you were thinking of?"

"Whenever you can squeeze me in. I'm just in Stonebridge."

"Stonebridge is lovely. Been there many times. Let me take a look at my calendar. Can you hold for a minute?"

"Sure," said Percy.

The real estate agent returned a short time later.

"Could you come here Saturday around noon? I have appointments that morning and later that afternoon, but I should be free between twelve and two. And I know the couple who own the first house you are interested in. They're away this weekend, so there should be no problem getting in. And I believe the other house should also not be a problem."

"Great!" said Percy. "I'll be there."

"I just need you to sign some paperwork first."

"Not a problem."

"I also have a couple of other properties I'd like to show you while you're in town if we have time."

"That would be great."

"Is the email you put on the form the best email?"

"It is."

"Very good. I'll send you the paperwork to sign, and I'll see you Saturday at noon. Do you know where my office is?"

"I do."

The call ended, and Percy was putting her phone away when it began to ring. It was Lucy.

"I just heard about Dr. Rob! Are you okay?"

"I'm fine. What did you hear?"

"That someone shot him! I can't believe someone would do that! Do you think it was one of his patients?"

"I don't know. Who told you about Dr. Rob?"

"Cassie."

Cassie was one of Lucy's best friends from Stonebridge.

"Cassie told you Dr. Rob had been shot? How did she know?"

"Charlie told her."

"Charlie?"

"Cassie's little sister, Charlotte."

"Right. And how did she know?"

"She overheard her parents talking about it. Are you sure

you're okay? I know how fond you were of Dr. Rob. Should I come home?"

"No!" Percy said. "You need to stay there and take your finals."

"But if you're not okay…"

"I'm fine, Lucy. Yes, it was a bit of a shock. But I won't be okay if you skip school and miss taking your finals."

"I could come home Saturday, spend the weekend with you."

"You should be studying, and I'm going to Beauport on Saturday."

"Oh? What are you doing in Beauport?"

"I thought I'd take a look at some houses there."

"You're not planning on selling the house and moving there, are you?"

"No. I was just thinking of maybe getting us a summer place. You know how your father always wanted a beach house."

"Though it wouldn't be the same without Daddy."

Percy felt her heart clench. She knew Lucy missed her father. And it wouldn't be the same without Jim. She thought about telling Lucy the real reason she was going to Beauport, but she didn't want to worry her. Her daughter definitely wouldn't approve of her mother investigating a murder.

"I'm just taking a look. Good for me to get out of the house."

"You going to take Bonnie or Carlo with you?"

Percy hadn't thought about that. Should she ask her friends to go with her? But would Ed Mankiewicz open up about his brother with Bonnie and Carlo around? Probably not.

"They're busy," she lied.

"Okay. Just don't buy anything without consulting me first."

"I promise," said Percy. "And I'll see you when finals are over."

"Yes, you will," said her daughter. "I've got to go. I'll check in with you over the weekend."

"Okay," said Percy. "Love you."

"Love you more," said Lucy. Then they ended the call.

CHAPTER 4

The next morning, it seemed as though everyone had heard about Dr. Rob. Indeed, the librarians had to shush several patrons who were loudly discussing the murder.

"Do you think it was one of his patients?" Percy overheard one patron tell another.

"I bet it was a jealous lover," said the other.

"What makes you say that?" said the first patron.

"He was a good-looking man. And I heard he was shot through the heart."

"That doesn't mean anything. Besides, I heard he was gay."

"And gay people can't have jealous lovers?"

That was when Carmen had come over and told the two women that gossip had no place at the library and to keep it down. That had made Percy smile as Carmen often indulged in a bit of gossip.

Percy was checking in a pile of books when she saw Carol enter the library. She was surprised to see her there.

"Carol," said Percy.

Carol smiled and went over to her.

"What brings you to the library?"

"I thought I'd get a couple of books."

"Of course. Why else would you be at the library? Did the Wellness Center reopen?

"Not yet. Hopefully, Monday."

"And you came all the way to Stonebridge to get a book?"

Percy knew that Carol lived in Kenwick, which was about twenty minutes from Stonebridge.

"It's not that far. Besides, I'm meeting with Dr. Richardson at ten-thirty and got here a little early. Figured I'd get some new reading material."

"A new romance novel, perhaps?"

"I'm taking a break from romance novels. Thought I'd try something else, maybe some historical fiction or a cozy mystery."

"Oh," said Percy. She made a mental note to return the two romance novels she had just purchased.

"What do you recommend?"

"Hmm," said Percy. "Let's go over to the Staff Picks table."

Percy examined the dozen or so books the librarians had chosen to feature and pulled out *The Briar Club* by Kate Quinn.

"Have you read this?" she asked Carol, handing her the book.

"No, I haven't," Carol replied, looking at the cover. "What's it about?"

"A group of women who live in a Washington, D.C., boardinghouse during the McCarthy Era. I guess you could say it's a work of historical fiction-slash-murder mystery. But it's really about the power of female friendship. I really enjoyed it."

"Sounds interesting. I'll take it. Thanks."

"Take a look at some of the other books while you're here. They're all quite good. And the New Fiction and New Nonfiction sections are just over there."

"Thanks," said Carol.

A few minutes later, she went over to the desk with several books to check out.

"I always liked this library," Carol told Percy. "I can use my Kenwick library card to check these out, yes?"

"Yup. We have reciprocity. Have you checked out books from us before?"

"I have, but not in a while."

"If you would just give me your card…"

Carol handed Percy her library card.

"None of my friends are big readers," Carol said as Percy checked out her books. "Though I probably read enough for all of them."

"You know," said Percy. "I'd be happy to chat about books with you. Maybe over coffee or a drink?"

"Really? That would be wonderful. Though, to be honest, I feel a bit intimidated discussing books with you."

"Why?"

"You're a librarian. You read and talk about books for a living."

"So? I love talking about books," which wasn't strictly true, but Carol didn't need to know that. "So, how are you doing? I can't imagine what the last two days have been like for you."

"I still can't believe he's gone. He was there smiling at me one minute, and the next… Thank goodness for family. My daughter and my new little grandbaby have been staying with me. Hard to be sad around her."

Percy smiled.

"How old is she?"

"Almost two months now."

"Here you go," said Percy, handing Carol her books. "They're due back in three weeks."

"I'll probably finish them before then. Well, I should go. Don't want to be late for my meeting."

"Where are you meeting Dr. Richardson? I thought you said the Wellness Center was closed."

"Over at the Morning Grind." That was a coffee shop near the Wellness Center.

"She's back from vacation, I take it."

"Oh, yes. She hurried back as soon as she heard."

"Were you the one who told her about Dr. Rob?"

"I was. Poor thing. She was devastated."

"Did you also phone Dr. Rob's brother?"

"Dr. Richardson notified him. Anyway, I should go. Thanks again for your help."

"Any time. And text or call me if you want to grab a coffee or a drink."

"I'll do that," said Carol. Then she left.

Percy thought about going over to the Morning Grind to get a coffee while Carol and Dr. Richardson were there, so she could eavesdrop. But that would look suspicious. She wondered what they were discussing. It probably had to do with the Wellness Center. Had Carol and Dr. Richardson informed all of Dr. Rob's patients about what had happened? Would Dr. Richardson see them now? How many patients did Dr. Rob have? Would Dr. Richardson hire another therapist to take Dr. Rob's place?

"A quarter for your thoughts," said Bonnie.

"It's a penny," said Percy.

"Not with inflation."

Percy couldn't help smiling.

"What were you thinking about? You seemed distracted."

"Carol from the Wellness Center was just here."

"Oh? Did the center reopen? That was fast."

"No, it's closed until further notice. Carol's in town to meet with Dr. Richardson. She got here early, so she figured she'd get a couple of books. Apparently, she's a big reader."

"Ah. How's she doing?"

"She seemed good. Probably because her little granddaughter has been visiting her."

"Maybe. Or maybe it's because she's glad that Dr. Rob's dead."

"I doubt that. I told you, she adored him."

"Maybe it's an act."

Percy looked at her.

"Anyone tell you that you have a suspicious mind?"

"My ex-husband, all the time. Though I was right to be suspicious of him."

Bonnie's ex, Marv, had cheated on her with a woman he worked with, a much younger woman. Oldest cliché in the book. When Bonnie found out, she divorced him.

"So, how's the sleuthing going? You find out anything?"

"Not yet. But I'm meeting with Dr. Rob's brother, Ed, in Beauport tomorrow."

"Oh?"

"He's a real estate agent. I told him I was interested in looking at some houses there."

"And when were you planning on telling me?"

"I'm telling you now. I only made the appointment yesterday afternoon. You want to tag along? I'm heading there around ten-thirty and should be back by dinnertime. My appointment's at noon."

"Thanks, but I've got plans. Harry and I are having lunch with his daughter."

Harry was the man Bonnie had been dating for the last four months.

"Things must be serious if he wants you to meet his daughter. Was it your idea or his?"

"Oh, his. I thought it was too soon, but Harry said she'd been asking about me, and he figured, let's get it over with."

"When did his wife die again?"

"Four years ago now? His daughter took it pretty hard. Though Cecile, that's his wife, had been sick for a while."

"How old's the daughter?"

"Thirty. She does something in finance in New York."

"Well, I hope the three of you have a good time."

"I'm sure we will. I mean, who wouldn't love me?"

Percy smiled.

"Just let me know if you get anything out of the brother."

"I will."

The next morning, Percy went for a long run. Then she showered, put on a pair of capris and a cute top, and had breakfast before heading to Beauport. She figured she'd get there a little early and walk around town before her appointment.

Percy hadn't been to Beauport in ages. She and Jim used to go there for the day, either on their own or with Lucy. But she hadn't been there since Jim died. And the thought of being there without him felt wrong. But it was a beautiful spring day, getting up to 70 degrees by noon, and she was on a mission.

Unfortunately, many other people had decided to go for a drive that morning, and Interstate 95 crawled. So Percy didn't arrive in Beauport until fifteen minutes before her appointment. And by the time she found a place to park, she only had time for a quick stroll down Main Street.

She walked into Beauport Realty and went over to a woman seated at a desk near the front of the office. The woman was staring intently at her computer, seemingly unaware of Percy.

"Excuse me," said Percy.

The woman looked up at her.

"May I help you?" she said.

"Yes, I have an appointment with Ed Mankiewicz at noon. Percy Rollins."

"He's not here," said the woman. Percy looked confused. "He's with a client, but he should be back any minute," the woman clarified. "Have a seat."

Percy took a seat on a nearby chair. On the coffee table

in front of it were several magazines. She picked one up and started to flip through it.

Ed came in ten minutes later. He saw Percy and immediately went over to her.

"Ms. Rollins?"

Percy nodded.

"I apologize for my tardiness. I tried to tell my client I had someone waiting for me, but…"

"It's all right," said Percy. Though she didn't like it when people were late.

"Just give me a few minutes to freshen up, then we can head out. I have several places for us to look at. Be right back."

Ed returned a short time later, quietly spoke with the woman at the desk, and then went over to Percy. Percy wondered who the woman at the front desk was. She didn't think she was an agent as her photo wasn't on the website. Maybe she was Ed's assistant?

"So, are you ready to look at some houses?" Ed asked Percy.

"I am," she replied.

"Shall we take my car? It's just in back."

"That's fine," said Percy and followed him out of the office.

The first house Ed took her to was a little cottage near the beach. It was cute but needed a lot of work. Then Ed took her to see the beach house she had seen online. It had three bedrooms, two and a half bathrooms, and a view of Long Island Sound.

"Wow," said Percy, looking out the sliders that led to a deck. "Jim would have loved this."

"Jim?" said Ed.

"My late husband. He always wanted us to get a beach house."

"Why didn't you?"

"Half a dozen reasons. We looked at a bunch of places over the years, but none of them were quite right."

"When did he pass?"

"Two years ago. He had a massive heart attack. We had no idea there was an issue. Jim was only forty-eight and seemed so healthy."

"I'm so sorry. I just lost someone very close to me unexpectedly too."

"Oh?" said Percy, feigning ignorance.

"My brother," said Ed. "It was very shocking, actually. I still can't believe it."

"Oh?" said Percy again. "If you don't mind my asking, what happened? Did he have a heart attack?"

"No. Someone shot him."

"Someone shot him?"

Percy knew she was probably laying it on a bit thick, but Ed didn't seem to notice.

Ed nodded.

"I wish I could say I was surprised, but honestly, I always thought Rob's high and mighty attitude would get him into trouble one day."

"High and mighty attitude?" That didn't sound like the Dr. Rob Percy knew. Though what did she really know about her therapist? "You thought he was arrogant?"

"Rob thought he was better than everyone, or at least smarter."

"Was he?"

"Was he what?"

"Smarter than most people?" Percy had always thought that Dr. Rob seemed very smart. After all, he had gone to Harvard and Yale, which tended to admit and graduate smart people. Though, of course, there were exceptions.

"If you think going to Harvard and Yale made you smarter than most people."

Percy didn't comment.

"So you two weren't close."

"What makes you say that?"

Percy wanted to say, *Well, you just spent several minutes dissing him, telling me how stuck up he was.* But she held her tongue.

"We were actually quite close as children. We just grew apart in college. But I still loved him, and cared about him, and was upset when I heard what happened."

"Any idea who might have shot him?"

"Probably some woman he used and dumped."

"He used women?" That didn't sound like the Dr. Rob she knew. Then again, how well did she know him?

"All the time. Women were always throwing themselves at him. God knows why. Rob would sleep with them a couple of times, then ghost them."

"Was he married?"

"Married? Rob?" Ed snorted. "Rob was married to his work. I think he thought of himself as some kind of savior."

"Any children?"

"Why are you so interested in my brother?"

"Curiosity, I guess. You know us librarians."

"You're a librarian?"

"Didn't I say?" Ed shook his head. "I work at the Stonebridge Public Library."

"You don't look like a librarian."

Percy wanted to ask him what he thought a librarian should look like, but she decided not to go there.

"So, shall we have a look upstairs? There's a fantastic view of the Sound from the master."

Percy nodded and followed Ed up the stairs.

"What did I tell you?" he said, looking out the big picture window, which had a window seat.

"Wow," said Percy. "You were right. I could spend all day here."
Ed smiled.

"The bathroom is just across the hall."

Percy went into the bathroom. It was a good size, with a claw-foot tub and a large shower.

"Is this the only bathroom upstairs?"

"It is. But as you can see, it's quite roomy."

Ed took her to see the other upstairs bedroom. Then they went back downstairs to look at the third bedroom, another full bathroom, and a little powder room. Then they went back to the open living area.

"So, what do you think?"

"It's a great house," said Percy. "I like the open kitchen, though it's a bit on the small side."

"The owners don't cook much," Ed explained. "But what about that view!"

"It is pretty special." Percy couldn't help staring out at the Sound.

"And there's a private path down to the beach. Shall I show you?"

Percy nodded, and Ed led her out onto the deck and down a few steps through a gate and onto a little path that led to the beach.

"Pretty sweet, eh?"

Percy stared out at the water. She and Jim had dreamed about owning someplace like this, but they couldn't have afforded it back then.

"It's a wonderful house."

"And it's sure to sell quickly."

Percy was tempted to make an offer, but she knew Lucy would kill her if she did.

"I need to think about it. And you said you had two more places to show me."

"I do, but as I said, this place is likely to be scooped up fast. It only came on a few days ago."

Percy said she understood, but she wasn't ready to put in an offer just yet.

The two other houses Ed showed her were nice, but not as nice as the beach house. When they got back to the office, Ed again said that the beach house was likely to sell quickly. And Percy again said she realized that, but she wasn't ready to put in an offer. Then she thanked Ed for his time and headed down the block to a little café.

As she ate, she texted Bonnie.

I think I found a house, she wrote, sending her a few of the pictures she had taken of the place.

It's gorgeous, Bonnie replied a minute later. *Can you afford it?*

If I'm careful. How was your lunch?

Very nice. We just finished.

You get along with Harry's daughter?

Like she was my own.

You don't have a daughter.

You know what I mean.

So it went well.

It did. And what did you think of Dr. Rob's brother?

I'll tell you later.

Percy's phone rang. It was Bonnie.

"Tell me now."

"I can't. I'm in a restaurant, having lunch."

"Fine. Call me when you're done."

After lunch, Percy took a walk around Beauport. She could easily see herself spending time there. She stopped in a little park to call Bonnie, filling her in on Ed. Then she drove to the beach house. It was only a mile from downtown. You could easily walk to Main Street from there or ride a bike.

As she looked at the house, she thought she saw Jim standing by the upstairs window, or his shadow.

"Should I get it, Jim?" she asked the shadow. But the

shadow didn't respond. And Percy realized the shadow was just the reflection of a tree.

She sat there for another minute, then she put the car into drive and drove home.

CHAPTER 5

There was traffic on the drive back to Stonebridge, so Percy didn't get home until nearly five-thirty. She wasn't hungry as she had had a late lunch, but Minnie was clearly starving, judging by the way she was meowing.

"Come," said Percy, heading to the kitchen. Though Minnie didn't need to be commanded. She raced ahead of Percy, meowing for Percy to hurry up.

Percy gave Minnie some food and fresh water. Then she got a glass of water for herself. She looked out the kitchen window at the backyard. Percy had tried multiple times to grow vegetables, herbs, and flowers back there, but she didn't have a green thumb. So she had eventually given up. But it was still nice to sit on the patio on warm summer days, enjoying an iced tea or lemonade.

As she stared out the window, she kept thinking about the house in Beauport. What would Lucy think? Well, there was only one way to find out.

She sent her daughter a text, along with a few pictures of the house she had taken.

Nice house! Lucy replied.

I thought so, wrote Percy.

Are you going to buy it?

I'm thinking about it.

Can I see it?

It may not be available by the time you get home.

Then it wasn't meant to be.
I suppose.
Hey, I've got to go.
Where are you off to?
Going to a concert.
Have fun.
Love you.
Love you more.

Percy went up to her office to take a look at the listing for the house on her monitor, along with the pictures she had taken. It really was a special place. Maybe she should put in an offer, before someone snapped it up. No, she would wait until Lucy got home next weekend, and she could show her the place.

She glanced down and saw a note she had written to herself next to her computer. On it was the name *Miranda Yates*. Right. Percy had forgotten about her. Good thing she had left herself a note.

She opened her browser and typed *Miranda Yates* into the search box.

That was interesting. Miranda Yates was a psychologist. Was she a former colleague of Dr. Rob's, a friend, or something more?

She clicked on the link to Miranda Yates's *Psychology Today* page. Dr. Yates had a very impressive CV. She had gone to Stanford undergrad and then earned a Ph.D. in Psychology from Yale, just like Dr. Rob and Dr. Richardson. Did the three of them know each other? They were all around the same age, so it was likely.

Her professional credentials were also impressive. According to her profile, she had spent the last seven years working in Chicago at Northwestern University's Feinberg

School of Medicine's Department of Psychiatry and Behavioral Sciences.

Had she left there for a new job in Connecticut? Carlo had said she had just moved here. But there was nothing listed on her *Psychology Today* profile about a position in Connecticut or New York, which wasn't far away. Maybe she just hadn't updated her profile.

Percy stared at Miranda's profile picture. She had long brown hair and big brown eyes, just as Carlo had said. Had she dated Dr. Rob back in graduate school, or had she been seeing him when he died?

Percy returned to the list of links and saw that Dr. Yates had a LinkedIn profile. She clicked on it. But there wasn't much there, not even a profile pic.

Percy wondered: Had Miranda Yates come to Stonebridge to be with Dr. Rob?

Her head started to hurt. What she needed was to go for a walk. Walking, or running, always helped her feel better.

She checked the temperature, grabbed a sweatshirt, and headed out. Before she knew it, she was in front of Carlo's frame shop/art gallery. The shop closed at six on Saturdays, but the lights were still on. No doubt Carlo was still there. (He often worked late.) Though the door was locked.

Percy rapped on the door. No answer. He was probably in back, listening to music as he worked. Carlo loved opera and would often listen to one as he framed works of art.

Percy knocked again, louder this time. Still no sign of Carlo. She got out her phone and sent him a text. A minute later, he appeared, a smile on his face. He came to the door and unlocked it.

"Sorry, I was listening to *Tosca*. Is everything okay?"

"Everything's fine. I was just out for a walk. May I come in?"

Carlo ushered her inside.

"Working late again?"

"It's not work when you love what you do."

Percy smiled at that.

"And I get to listen to whatever I like when customers aren't around."

"Which, in this case, is *Tosca*? Remind me what that one's about." Percy wasn't an opera buff like Carlo and was always getting the plots confused.

"It's a story of love, lust, murder, betrayal, and political intrigue, set in Rome in eighteen hundred. Tosca is a diva, in love with a painter and republican, Cavaradossi, and lusted after by a corrupt chief of police, Baron Scarpia. Scarpia wants Tosca for himself and arranges to have her lover arrested for assisting an escaped political prisoner. Then he tells Tosca that if she does not give herself to him, he will have Cavaradossi killed."

"Wow. Heavy. So what does Tosca do?"

Carlo smiled.

"She refuses, of course. At least initially. But then she agrees, only to stab Scarpia as he embraces her."

"So do she and Cavaradossi live happily ever after?"

"Not quite. Scarpia had told Tosca there would be a mock execution, that Cavaradossi would not really be killed and would go free if she gave herself to him. But he lied. And when Tosca finds Cavaradossi shot to death and the soldiers come to arrest her, she kills herself."

"And you find this music relaxing?"

Carlo smiled.

"It is music that stirs the soul."

"If you say so."

"You should listen sometime."

"You know I'm not a big opera fan."

"You just haven't listened to it enough. So, you just happened to find yourself outside my shop at six-thirty on a Saturday?"

"I needed to go for a walk."

"Something on your mind?"

"It's about that woman you told me about, the one who was here with Dr. Rob, Miranda Yates."

"What about her?"

"Did you know that she was a psychologist, like Dr. Rob?"

"I might have heard Dr. Rob refer to her as Dr. Yates, now that I think about it. But I didn't know she was a psychologist."

"They talk about anything while they were here?"

"You mean other than the pieces she wanted to have framed?"

"Yes."

"I don't make it a habit to listen in on my customers' conversations."

"You heard him refer to her as Dr. Yates. Did she say why she was here in Stonebridge?"

"I believe it was for a job."

"You believe? You're not certain?"

Carlo sighed.

"I may have overheard them saying something about work as I was measuring."

"Like what?"

"Like Dr. Rob saying he thought she would like working here."

"Here, as in Stonebridge?" He nodded. "Do you think she was moving here to work at the Wellness Center?"

"That I don't know."

Percy sighed.

"And you don't think they were a couple?"

"More like old friends. So, how was your visit to Beauport?"

"How do you know about that?"

"Bonnie told me."

"Of course she did."

"So? You speak with the brother?"

"I did. And I may have found a house."

"Oh?"

Carlo's smartwatch was flashing. He looked down at it and frowned.

"Is everything all right?"

"It's a text from Gianna." Gianna was a young woman who worked for Carlo part-time.

"Is she okay?"

"She's fine, but her *nonna*, her grandmother, is very ill, and Gianna took time off to be with her."

"That was good of her."

"It is, but now I have to frame all of these pieces, including the ones for Dr. Yates, myself. And I was already behind."

"I could help you."

Carlo gave her a look.

"Do you know how to frame works of art?"

"No, but you could teach me."

"I don't have the time. And don't you have a job?"

"I do, but I have personal days."

"Save them. Besides, Gianna said she should be back Monday or Tuesday."

"Well, if you need me…"

"Thank you, but I'll be fine. I just need to get back to work."

"Of course. Though… Could you let me know if Miranda Yates stops by?"

"Why?"

"I'd like to meet her."

"You mean interrogate her."

"I would never interrogate her. I just want to ask her a few questions."

"What sorts of questions?"

"Like how well she knew Dr. Rob."

"Mm."

Percy saw Carlo looking back at the workroom.

"I'll let you go. Just shoot me a text if Miranda Yates stops by."

"And you'll what, run over here from the library?"

Percy could tell that Carlo was in a tetchy mood.

"Go listen to your opera. I'll see you Wednesday. Unless you're too busy to have dinner with us."

"I'm never too busy for that. And if Dr. Yates happens to stop by, I'll try to let you know."

Percy grinned.

"Thank you. And if you hear anyone else mention Dr. Rob, let me know."

"I told you, I don't eavesdrop on my customers."

"No one's asking you to eavesdrop. Just let me know if you happen to overhear something."

Carlo sighed.

"Good night, Percy."

CHAPTER 6

Monday, Percy received a call from Dr. Richardson. That didn't surprise her. She figured Dr. Richardson would be reaching out to Dr. Rob's patients. The message—Percy was working at the time, so the call had gone to her voicemail—simply asked that Percy get in touch with her.

As soon as Percy was able to take a break, she stepped outside to return Dr. Richardson's call. Dr. Richardson was unavailable, Carol informed her, but would Percy like to schedule an appointment to speak with her? There would be no charge.

Percy was more than happy to speak with Dr. Richardson and asked Carol when the doctor was free. As it turned out, she was available at the same time Percy normally went to the Wellness Center, at 1 p.m. on Wednesday. Percy took the appointment and asked Carol how she was doing.

Carol said it was hard being back at the Wellness Center with Dr. Rob gone, but that she felt it was important to be there for Dr. Richardson and their patients.

Percy admired her loyalty and work ethic.

"Is she thinking of hiring someone to take Dr. Rob's place?" Percy asked her.

"As a matter of fact," Carol began. But she was interrupted by another call coming in. "I have to go," she told Percy. "I'll see you Wednesday at one."

Percy stayed outside for a couple more minutes, staring

across the street at the Wellness Center. A part of her was surprised that it was open so soon after Dr. Rob's death. Then again, Dr. Richardson may have been worried about patients leaving the center if she didn't act quickly. Though that may have been a cynical view.

Maybe, like Percy, Dr. Richardson felt work was the best cure or panacea for grief. Or maybe she wanted to be available for her and Dr. Rob's patients, who were no doubt feeling a range of emotions. Or it could have been all three. In any case, Percy would find out in a couple of days.

Bonnie intercepted Percy as she reentered the library.

"Did you make an appointment to see Dr. Richardson?"

Percy had mentioned to Bonnie that Dr. Richardson had phoned her.

"I did. For this Wednesday at one."

"When you usually met with Dr. Rob. Won't that be weird?"

Percy thought for a second.

"A little, I guess. Then again, that's when I'm used to going there."

"Frankly, I'm surprised they reopened so quickly. Dr. Richardson must be worried about losing patients."

"That's rather cynical of you," said Percy. Though she had had the same thought.

"Maybe. But it's not like there's a shortage of therapists around here."

"True, but there aren't that many that take insurance like the Wellness Center does. And she probably wanted to make sure Dr. Rob's patients were okay, let them know the center was there for them."

"So, are you going to ask her about Dr. Rob when you see her?"

"I was planning to."

"And you'll let me know what she says?"

"I will. Did you talk to Elyse? Does she know about Dr. Rob?"

"Thank you for reminding me. I left her a message, but she hasn't gotten back to me. I think she was away this weekend. I'll shoot her a text."

"Okay. Let me know if she replies. I'd love to speak with some of Dr. Rob's patients, find out if they know anything."

"You could always put up a post on Facebook, in the Stonebridge group."

"I don't know."

"Oh! Or better yet, you could create your own page, a Dr. Rob memorial page, where people could leave their thoughts. I bet a bunch of his patients would follow it."

"And how would people even find out about it?"

"You could post something on the Stonebridge page, say you created a page for current and former patients, and friends of Dr. Rob, to share their thoughts and memories."

"Hmm. It sounds like a good idea, but would patients really post something there? Not everyone wants to admit they've been in therapy."

"You could make it a private group, just for current and former patients."

"But how would I know if people really were patients?"

"You could ask them. Lots of groups have you answer questions before letting you join. You had to prove you lived in Stonebridge before joining that group."

"True. But I don't want people to feel uncomfortable."

"Just post a list of rules for participating."

"I guess I could do that."

"And as the moderator, you could make sure people followed them."

Percy looked thoughtful.

"How much time would that require? I do have a full-time job."

"I doubt it would require a lot of time. Just check the page in the morning and then again at night."

"Okay. I'll think about it."

"Don't take too long. You've got to strike while the iron is hot. And who knows? Maybe someone will confess to killing him!"

"I doubt that." Percy looked down at her watch. "I should get back to work."

Percy thought about Facebook all afternoon. Should she create a Dr. Rob memorial page or shouldn't she? And if she did create one, would anyone follow it? She was still undecided by the time she left work. However, she was leaning towards setting up the page, just to see what would happen.

As soon as she got home and had paid attention to Minnie, who acted as though Percy had been gone for days, not hours, Percy went to her office and got on her computer. She looked up how to create a page to honor someone and read about memorial accounts, where a family member could keep the account of a deceased loved one active, so people could share memories. But Dr. Rob didn't have a Facebook account. At least one that she could find. So she would need to create a group.

But what should she call it? *In Honor of Dr. Rob? Current and Former Patients of Dr. Rob? In Praise of Dr. Rob? Remembering Dr. Rob?*

She decided on the last one, liking the way it sounded. Then she needed to select the privacy setting. She was going to make it private, but then she wondered if it should be public. A public page might get more people. Then again, it might scare away patients. After going back and forth for several minutes, she decided to make the page private.

Now she needed to write the page description. Percy wrote that she was a patient of Dr. Rob's and had created this page as a way for fellow patients to eulogize him and/or connect.

Percy was about to hit the button to make the page live when she thought she should add a photo of Dr. Rob. She did an image search, but there weren't many photos of him—and most of them looked the same. It was probably best to use the one on the Wellness Center's website, assuming his bio hadn't been deleted.

Percy went to the Wellness Center website to check. Dr. Rob's profile was still there. And it didn't say anything about his death. Whoever maintained the website hadn't updated it or taken it down.

Percy saved the photo of Dr. Rob to her computer and then uploaded it to the Dr. Rob Facebook page. She hoped Dr. Richardson wouldn't mind. Then again, how would she know? She didn't appear to be on Facebook. Though one of Dr. Rob's patients might tell her about it. Percy would deal with that if or when it came up.

Satisfied with her handiwork, she tapped *Create*. Now to the Stonebridge Facebook group, to let people know about the Dr. Rob page.

Percy wasn't sure what to say and must have rewritten her post a half-dozen times before she was satisfied with it. The post wasn't very long, but she hoped it would lead to people joining her group.

Hi, she wrote. *I created a Facebook group to honor the late Dr. Robert Mankiewicz, known to his patients as Dr. Rob. The group is called* Remembering Dr. Rob *and is private. If you would like to share a memory or connect with fellow patients, of which I am one, please consider joining. Note: All comments will be moderated, and bad behavior will not be tolerated.*

She read what she had written one last time and then hit *Post*. Although Percy was tempted to sit there and see if anyone replied to her post, she thought it best to close Facebook and not look again for at least an hour.

Percy had resisted checking Facebook until she was sitting down to eat her dinner. And when she did check, she was surprised by how many people had commented on her post.

What a lovely idea! one person had written.

He was the best, wrote another.

I miss him, wrote a third.

I heard he was murdered, wrote someone else. *Anyone know who killed him?*

I heard it was a patient, someone replied.

I heard it was the mafia, wrote a different person.

That one caused Percy to raise her eyebrows.

There were more comments, many of them saying that her page was a great idea, others speculating on who might have killed him, with responses ranging from the rational (a patient or a lover) to the irrational (the U.S. government or the Russians).

Apparently, Percy wasn't the only one in Stonebridge with an active imagination or an interest in Dr. Rob's murder.

Next, Percy checked the *Remembering Dr. Rob* page, to see if anyone had requested to join and was delighted to see that over a dozen people had answered the questions and were awaiting membership in the group. Percy quickly reviewed their answers and then checked their Facebook profiles before admitting them.

She recognized some of the names but not all of them. Still, everyone who had requested membership in the group seemed legit. She finished her dinner and went to clean up. Although she had a dishwasher, she usually just washed her plates, glasses, and flatware by hand as she lived alone and didn't like running the dishwasher unless it was full, which could take a week or longer. And by then it would have started to smell or get moldy.

She went into the living room to stream something. Then at nine-thirty, she checked Facebook again before going upstairs to get ready for bed. There were a few more comments on her post in the Stonebridge group, as well as more people requesting membership in the Dr. Rob group, along with a few comments from the people who had already joined.

Percy went through all of the comments and then went upstairs to change into her pajamas, wash her face, and brush her teeth. When she was done, she got into bed, turned off her phone, and shoved it into the drawer in her nightstand.

The next morning, Percy took out her phone, turned it on, and was immediately flooded with Facebook notifications. She opened the app and started to look at her messages, but she was quickly overwhelmed. If she continued to read them and took the time to respond to each one, she wouldn't have time for her pre-work run. So she put her phone on silent, turned it over, got dressed in her running clothes, did a few stretches, and headed out.

Over breakfast, Percy reviewed the new requests to join her group. Over thirty people had requested to join now, with only a couple looking suspicious. And there were more comments. Mostly typical things you'd expect someone to say on a commemorative page, about how Dr. Rob would be missed, how he had helped so-and-so during a difficult time, how they couldn't believe someone would want to harm him.

Percy also checked the comments people had left on her Stonebridge post. They seemed to be equally divided between people mourning Dr. Rob's passing, worried about violence in their small town, and wondering or theorizing who killed him. Percy had to stop herself from reading all of them; otherwise, she would be late for work.

As she walked to the library, she wondered if she had bitten off more than she could chew. She had a full-time job, after all, and she couldn't spend all day on Facebook. Though Bonnie had said she should limit checking and responding to posts and comments to once in the morning and once at night.

However, Percy hadn't considered that library patrons would have seen her Facebook post and would want to ask her about Dr. Rob. It got so bad that Carmen told Percy she could work in the back, which Percy was grateful for. She had never been bombarded with so many questions, and none of them about books.

As she added protective covers to books, Percy wondered if she should hire someone to help her moderate the Dr. Rob group. But who? She didn't want to hire some college or high school student. No, she needed someone who knew Dr. Rob, who would be sensitive. She immediately thought of Carol. Though Carol also had a full-time job. But who better to moderate comments about Dr. Rob? She would ask her tomorrow.

That evening, Percy was so busy reviewing and responding to Facebook comments that she didn't realize someone was calling her at first. It was Ed Mankiewicz.

"This is Percy," she said, answering her phone.

"Hi, Ms. Rollins. This is Ed Mankiewicz. I'm just calling to let you know there's been an offer on the house you liked."

"Oh," said Percy. She had been meaning to call Ed to arrange an appointment for that weekend, to take Lucy to see the place. But she had been distracted. "Did the sellers accept it?"

"Not yet. At least as far as I know. So if you're still interested, now's the time to act."

"I've actually been meaning to call you, to arrange a second viewing for this weekend, when my daughter will be home. She's at college, taking finals, but she'll be home Friday."

"That might be too late."

Percy bit her lip. She wasn't one to make hasty decisions. If anything, she tended to overthink and second-guess things. But she had really liked that house.

"What do you think I should offer?"

"It's a very desirable house, and the Beauport market is only going to get hotter over the summer."

"Do you think I should offer asking? Is that what the other people offered?"

"I don't know what the other people offered."

"What if I offered a bit under asking but could pay cash?"

Percy couldn't believe she was actually, seriously thinking of putting in an offer on the house. It was kind of exciting but also a bit scary.

"I'd say, why don't we give it a shot? What were you thinking?"

Percy had pulled up the listing and was staring at the asking price. She subtracted five percent and said the number to Ed. Ed thought it might be too low, but he would write it up and send the offer to her to review and sign.

"Great," said Percy. "So could I see the place this Saturday with my daughter?"

"I'll ask Sheila. She's the listing agent. What time were you thinking?"

Percy thought. Lucy would probably be tired when she got home on Friday and would want to sleep in the next morning.

"Would noon work, or else early afternoon?" Percy was thinking she and Lucy could have lunch in Beauport, make a day of it.

"I'll let you know."

"Thanks. Hey, Ed," Percy said, realizing she hadn't asked him about Dr. Richardson.

"Yes?"

"Do you happen to know the Richardsons, Farrah and Tom?"

"I sold them their house. Why?"

"So you know them well?"

"Farrah worked with my brother."

"She must be devastated."

"She is. She and Rob go way back."

"Oh?" said Percy, feigning ignorance again.

"They were at graduate school together. Even dated briefly."

"Dr. Richardson dated Dr. Rob?"

"As I said, briefly. My brother wasn't big on commitment."

"So he dumped her?"

"Actually, she dumped him. Found out he was seeing someone else, and that was it."

"Ouch. That must have hurt. But she wound up working with him."

"Farrah's a very forgiving woman."

"She must be a good therapist."

"I imagine so. She's the breadwinner in that family. Hey, I need to go. I've got a bunch of stuff going on, but I'll send you the offer to review tomorrow, and I'll let you know if Saturday at noon works."

"Great. Thanks, Ed."

CHAPTER 7

Percy returned to Facebook. She had comments to approve, as well as more requests to join the Dr. Rob group. But she couldn't stop thinking about her conversation with Ed Mankiewicz.

So, Dr. Richardson had dated Dr. Rob in graduate school. That was interesting. Was she still carrying a torch for him? And had Percy really just made an offer on the Beauport house? That was so not like her.

She finished approving the requests to join and comments, most of which were benign. Mainly people mourning Dr. Rob, saying what a great therapist he was and how he had helped them. Then she closed Facebook and sent Bonnie a text.

I've created a monster, she wrote.

??? Bonnie replied.

The Dr. Rob Facebook group.

Lots of people requesting to join?

And leaving comments.

That's good though, right?

I guess.

Anyone admit to killing him?

Percy made a face.

Not yet. It's mostly people mourning him, saying what a great therapist he was.

You could always ask people if they knew of anyone unhappy with him.

I guess. Right now, I'm too tired. Oh, and I also put in an offer on that house in Beauport I told you about.

A second later, Percy's phone rang. It was Bonnie.

"You did what? I thought you were going to wait until Lucy saw it."

"I was, but Ed phoned a little while ago and said someone else had put in an offer. So I needed to act."

"You're just full of surprises, aren't you? So, did they accept your offer?"

"Ed hasn't submitted it yet. He needs to write it up first and then have me review it and sign."

"Well, keep me posted. You still going to bring Lucy there?"

"If I can. I asked Ed if we could see the place Saturday."

"Did Ed have anything else to say?"

"As a matter of fact, he did."

"Well, don't keep me in suspense. Spill."

"He said that Dr. Rob and Dr. Richardson used to date."

"When?"

"In graduate school."

"Huh. How long did they date for?"

"Not long. Per Ed, Dr. Richardson found out Dr. Rob was cheating on her and dumped him."

"Good for her. Though they must have kissed and made up if she went into business with him."

"I don't know about the kissing part, but yeah. Ed said Dr. Richardson was a very forgiving woman."

"She must be. No way could I go into business with my ex."

Percy let out a yawn.

"I'll let you go," said Bonnie. "I'll see you tomorrow at the library."

"See you tomorrow."

The next morning, Percy checked Facebook as she was eating breakfast. More people were waiting to join the Remembering Dr. Rob group, and there were more comments awaiting moderation. She approved the new people who wanted to join and began reading the new comments. The third one made her stop.

Dr. Rob was not a good man, read the comment. It was left by a woman named Arianna Cardinale at 2 a.m. Percy didn't know Arianna, though she had approved her admission to the group. Percy bit her lip. Should she approve the comment or delete it? She decided to do nothing for now. She needed to finish her breakfast, brush her teeth, and get to work. But the comment nagged at her as she got ready and then as she walked to the library.

Should she message the woman, ask her what she meant? She didn't think it was fair to delete the comment without an explanation. On the other hand, Percy wasn't a fan of censorship. And the woman hadn't written anything inappropriate. She was just expressing an opinion.

Percy entered the library and saw Bonnie speaking with one of the volunteers. She greeted the two of them and then asked Bonnie if she could speak with her.

"Is everything all right?" Bonnie asked her.

"I just need your opinion on something."

The volunteer looked curious.

"It's a private matter," Percy clarified.

"I'll be right back," Bonnie told the volunteer.

They went into a nearby alcove.

"What's up?" Bonnie asked her.

"I received a new comment this morning, and I don't know how to handle it."

"What did the comment say?"

"That Dr. Rob was not a good man."

"Who left it?"

"I know the person's name, obviously, but I don't know her personally."

"So it's a woman. Did you look at her Facebook profile?"

"It's private."

"So you don't know anything about her."

"I know her name and that she lives in Stonebridge."

"You didn't do an online search?"

"Not yet. I just saw her comment while I was having breakfast."

"Hmm. Is she attractive?"

"What's that got to do with anything?"

"Maybe they had gone out and he dumped her."

Percy hadn't thought of that.

"If her profile photo is really her, I'd say she was attractive."

"You don't think the photo's legit?"

"It could be old."

"Well, give me her name, and I'll get the goods on her."

Percy hesitated.

"I don't know, Bonnie."

"At least tell me her name."

"The group's private."

"Fine. So what do you want me to tell you?"

"Whether I should approve her comment or not."

"You should definitely approve it. Why wouldn't you?"

"She left it at two a.m. Maybe she wasn't thinking."

"Maybe, but it's not like she said anything inappropriate, just that she didn't think Dr. Rob was a good man. Aren't you curious why she said that?"

"Of course I am."

"Then publish the comment!"

"What if people attack her?"

"You're the moderator. You can tell them to back off and/or delete any inappropriate comments."

"I suppose."

"Look, she left the comment for a reason. Maybe she wants to find out if other people thought the same thing."

That hadn't occurred to Percy.

"Oh. I hadn't thought of that."

Bonnie tried not to look smug.

"So, are you going to publish it? Who knows? Maybe Dr. Rob wasn't the saint people thought him to be."

"I don't know if people considered him a saint."

"Well, from the comments I read in the Stonebridge Facebook group, some people seem to think so. And he did help you with your depression and OCD."

"Yes, but I don't consider that a miracle. He's just a good therapist."

"Publish the comment and see what transpires."

"Okay. I will. Thank you."

"And let me know what happens."

"You know, you can always join the group."

"I wasn't a patient of his."

"I'd still let you join."

"Thanks, but it would feel weird. Much as I'd love to read what people are saying, I'll pass."

"Speaking of patients, you hear back from Elyse?"

"I did. She's away, as I thought."

"Did she know about Dr. Rob?"

"She did."

"And?"

"She said she was shocked."

"She say anything else?"

"Not really. She's on vacation. We'll talk when she gets back. In the meantime, ask your new Facebook friends about him."

"Wouldn't that be weird?"

"Isn't that why you created the group, to find out more about him?"

"I guess, but I wasn't planning on directly asking people about him."

"If not you, who?"

Percy didn't say anything.

"As my late father used to say: don't ask, don't get. Besides, what have you got to lose?"

"I suppose."

"Look, I need to go help that volunteer. Are you going to be okay?"

Percy nodded.

"Okay, I'll check in with you later. You want to have lunch?"

"I'm seeing Dr. Richardson at one."

"Right. I forgot. Well, you can catch me up on everything at dinner tonight. You sure you're good trying that new Italian place?"

"I said I was."

"Just confirming. In the meantime, if you need to talk, you know where to find me."

CHAPTER 8

Percy went to her locker after speaking with Bonnie, removed her phone from her bag, and published Arianna Cardinale's comment before she could second-guess her decision. Then she put her phone back in her bag and put her bag back in her locker.

She didn't check her phone again until it was time for her to go to her appointment with Dr. Richardson. She glanced at her phone before leaving the staff room. There were notifications from Facebook, but she didn't have time to read them. There was also an email from Ed Mankiewicz, but she didn't have time to read that either. She needed to get to the Wellness Center.

Percy was curious about what Dr. Richardson would say to her. Was she planning on taking on Dr. Rob's patients? Well, Percy would soon find out.

She crossed the street and headed down the block to the Wellness Center. Carol greeted her and told her that Dr. Richardson would be with her in a minute. She was just finishing up with another patient. Percy said that was fine. Then she asked Carol if she had a minute.

"What's up?"

"So," Percy began. "I don't know if you heard, but I created a Facebook group for people who knew Dr. Rob."

"One of the patients mentioned something."

"And I was wondering…" Carol waited for her to go. "The

thing is… I could really use another moderator, someone to vet comments and people wanting to join. And I thought… I thought maybe you could help me? That is, if you had the time."

Percy had checked to see if Carol was on Facebook. She appeared to be, but her account was private, and it seemed as though she hadn't posted anything in a while.

"Thanks for thinking about me, but I have to turn you down. Dr. Richardson has a strict policy regarding social media."

"But don't you have a Facebook page?"

"I do, but it's private. And I rarely post on it. And I'm not supposed to post anything having to do with work."

"Dr. Richardson not a fan of social media?"

"She is not. She feels it's harmful to adolescents."

"I don't disagree with her. It can be harmful, and not just to adolescents."

"So have you been getting a lot of comments?"

"I have, which is why I need help. I just don't have the time to deal with all of them."

"What have people been saying? Anything you think Dr. Richardson or the police should know about?"

"Not yet." Percy hadn't thought about the police wanting to know about the Dr. Rob group. "Speaking of the police, have you heard anything? Do you know if they have any suspects?"

"If they do, they haven't told me."

Just then a man came down the hall. Percy thought he looked familiar. She had definitely seen him before. Had he been a patient of Dr. Rob's? He looked deep in thought and didn't stop by the desk, just left.

"That man, was he a patient of Dr. Rob's?" Percy asked Carol. "I'm pretty sure I've seen him here."

Carol glanced around and lowered her voice. "I probably shouldn't be telling you this, but he's the one who canceled his noon appointment that day."

Several thoughts simultaneously popped into Percy's head, including whether he could be the killer.

"Ms. Rollins?"

"Hmm?"

Percy realized Dr. Richardson was calling her.

"Sorry," said Percy. "I guess I was preoccupied."

Dr. Richardson smiled at her.

"No worries. We all have a lot on our minds these days. Would you like to come back to my office?"

Percy nodded and followed her.

"Please, have a seat," said Dr. Richardson.

Percy took a seat on a comfortable-looking couch.

"You're probably wondering why I've asked to meet with you."

"I assume it has something to do with Dr. Rob no longer being available. Are you taking on his patients?"

"Unfortunately, I'm not able to add more than a few people. As you probably know, I mainly work with adolescents and young adults."

Percy waited for Dr. Richardson to go on.

"We were actually in the process of hiring another therapist before Dr. Rob…" Dr. Richardson paused, no doubt looking for the right words.

"Was murdered?" Percy supplied.

Dr. Richardson looked pained.

"I was going to say died. But I suppose there's no sense in candy-coating it."

"Do the police know who shot him?"

"If they do, they haven't informed me."

"But you've spoken with them."

Dr. Richardson nodded.

"Do they have any suspects?"

"Probably, but again, they haven't shared that information with me. Anyway, I asked you here to chat about you, about your therapy, not to discuss who may have shot Dr. Rob."

Though Percy was far more interested in discussing who may have shot Dr. Rob than in whether she would continue therapy.

"As I started to say, we were in the process of hiring another therapist, someone Dr. Rob and I knew and felt would be a good fit with the Wellness Center."

"And did you hire this person?"

"We did."

"And does this person have a name?"

Dr. Richardson smiled indulgently.

"Dr. Miranda Yates."

"From Chicago?"

Dr. Richardson tilted her head.

"She is from Chicago. Do you know her?"

Percy didn't want to reveal how she knew Miranda Yates.

"No. I just heard someone say that she had recently moved here from Chicago."

Percy inwardly winced as she said it. *She heard someone say that she had recently moved here from Chicago?* She just hoped Dr. Richardson wouldn't ask who she heard it from.

"I often forget what a small town Stonebridge is, with everyone knowing everyone else's business."

"When does she start?" Percy asked her.

"Next week. And I was hoping you would agree to meet with her. She has a most impressive resume. Most recently, she worked at Northwestern University's Feinberg School of Medicine's Department of Psychiatry and Behavioral Sciences. And one of her specialties is helping people with OCD."

"She sounds very impressive. I'd be happy to meet with her, but I can't promise anything. I really enjoyed working with Dr. Rob, and I feel like my OCD's mostly under control."

"I understand. I know many of Dr. Rob's patients feel the same way. But I think you'll like Dr. Yates. Her approach to therapy is similar to Dr. Rob's."

"As I said, I'd be happy to talk to her"—*and find out more about her relationship with Dr. Rob*, Percy silently added.

"Excellent. Carol can arrange an appointment. And if you have any questions or concerns, you can always speak to me."

"Thank you. May I ask you a question now?"

"Of course."

"It's about Dr. Rob." Dr. Richardson waited. "Do you think it could have been a patient who killed him?"

Dr. Richardson frowned.

"I don't think…"

"What about the man who was just here?" said Percy, interrupting her. "Carol said he was the one who had the noon appointment but canceled last minute."

Dr. Richardson looked annoyed.

"Carol shouldn't have said anything."

Percy suddenly felt guilty.

"Please don't blame Carol. I was asking her about him as I thought he looked familiar and…"

"Yes, well, I doubt Mr. Barnes was the killer."

Percy secretly smiled. Now she had his name.

"Oh? How come?"

"He was at the vet."

"The vet?"

Dr. Richardson was frowning again. She must have realized she had said too much.

"May I ask you another question?"

"Is it about Dr. Yates?" Dr. Richardson asked hopefully.

"It's about Dr. Rob's brother, Ed. I understand he helped you purchase a house in Beauport."

Dr. Richardson looked confused.

"He's helping me buy a house there, and he mentioned

he sold you your house." Dr. Richardson didn't say anything. "Do you think he's trustworthy?"

"Trustworthy?"

"As in, can I trust him to do right by me? It's a big purchase."

"Ed's a good real estate agent."

That didn't answer Percy's question.

"Did he and Dr. Rob get along?"

"Why do you ask?"

"Just curious."

"They were brothers."

"Meaning? I'm an only child, so…"

"They loved each other, but they were very different people. And now, Ms. Rollins, I'm afraid our time is up."

"Okay," said Percy. "Thanks again for seeing me. I'll ask Carol about scheduling an appointment with Dr. Yates."

"Excellent. Please let me know how it goes."

"I will."

Percy made an appointment to meet with Dr. Miranda Yates the following Wednesday. She had hoped to see her sooner, but that was the first appointment she could get with the new therapist.

"So, have you met Dr. Yates?" Percy casually asked Carol.

"I have."

"And?"

"She seems very nice."

"As nice as Dr. Rob?"

"Dr. Rob was one of a kind."

"Dr. Richardson said that Dr. Yates was a lot like him. Or that her approach to therapy was."

"She would know. The three of them were in graduate school together."

"Oh really?" said Percy. Though she already knew that.

Carol nodded.

"Dr. Richardson told me that people used to call them the three musketeers."

"So I guess they spent a lot of time together."

"Sounded like it."

"What else do you know about her?"

"Not much. I saw her resume. It's very impressive."

"She married?"

"Divorced. I think that's why she took the job here. She wanted a fresh start."

"Interesting. And what do you know about the patient who was here before me? Mr. Barnes, was it?"

Carol grinned.

"You interested? He's quite good-looking. And single. He's a widower. Lost his wife to cancer a couple of years ago."

Was Carol trying to play matchmaker?

"I'm not ready to start dating. I was just curious about him. Dr. Richardson said he canceled his appointment that day because he had to go to the vet."

Carol nodded.

"He felt terrible about canceling last minute, but Fluffy hadn't been feeling well, and he promised his daughter he'd take Fluffy to the vet."

"Fluffy?"

"His daughter's cat."

"Ah. So had Mr. Barnes been seeing Dr. Rob long?"

"He started around the same time you did."

"Anything else you can tell me? He looks so familiar. Though that's probably because I've seen him here."

Carol smiled.

"He's an author. That's probably why he looks familiar. He writes romantic thrillers."

"I don't think I've read any romantic thrillers by someone named Barnes."

"That's because he doesn't write under his own name."

"Have you read any of his books?"

"I've read all of them. But he stopped writing after his wife died. She was his inspiration."

"That's so sad."

"It is. But with Dr. Rob's help, he's started writing again."

"That's wonderful!"

"I just hope he doesn't stop now that Dr. Rob's not here to help him. He was pretty shaken up by Dr. Rob's death."

"Do you think he feels guilty about not being here? Though if he had been, he could have been shot too."

"Oh my gosh! You're right! I didn't think about that. He really dodged a bullet."

"He did, literally and figuratively."

Percy was going to ask Carol another question, but a woman had entered the Wellness Center and was heading over to them. So Percy said goodbye to Carol and left.

CHAPTER 9

Percy had ten minutes before she had to be at the circulation desk. She had packed a lunch and was looking over the offer agreement Ed Mankiewicz had sent her as she ate. Everything seemed to be in order. She just couldn't believe she was actually going to put in an offer on a house, especially one that cost that much money.

Percy was about to e-sign when she changed her mind. She should wait until after work and read through the document one more time before signing it. She still had a couple of minutes, so she checked Facebook. More comments had come in, including several in reply to Arianna's post. She was reading through them when she noticed Carmen.

"I hate to interrupt, but I need you to help one of the volunteers. She's having trouble putting protective covers on the paperbacks, and you're the expert."

"No problem," said Percy. "I'll be right there. Is there someone at the circulation desk?"

"Mary Beth's there."

"Would you tell her I'll be there in a few?"

Carmen said that she would and left.

Percy closed her salad container, put it back in her insulated lunch bag, and put the bag back in the refrigerator. Then she went to help the volunteer.

Percy was off at five, but she stayed a few extra minutes to help a patron. She had wanted to check Facebook all afternoon, but she had a rule about not checking her phone while she was working, and she hadn't had time during her afternoon break.

However, as soon as she stepped outside the library, she checked her phone. Ed had texted her twice. The first text asked if she had received the offer document. The second, left half an hour ago, said she needed to act quickly if she still wanted the house.

Percy sent him a text saying she had received the offer document, but she had had a busy day and hadn't been able to look it over. It was a lie, but only a small one. She had been busy.

As soon as she got home, Percy opened the offer agreement on her computer, reviewed it one more time, and, sending up a prayer to Jim, hoping she was doing the right thing, signed and submitted it. Immediately, she began to second-guess her decision to sign without talking to her financial advisors or her friends. But what was done was done. The sellers would probably reject her offer anyway.

Now to review the comments people had left in the Remembering Dr. Rob group.

Several people had replied to Arianna's post. The first was from a woman Percy knew from the library but didn't personally know.

What do you mean he wasn't a good man? The man helped dozens of people, including my husband.

The second reply, from a man who had been a counselor at Lucy's high school, said he was sorry that Arianna felt that way and asked why she thought Dr. Rob wasn't a good man.

It was a good question, and Percy hoped that Arianna would reply.

The third reply was from another woman Percy didn't personally know, who also wanted to know why Arianna thought that.

Percy approved all three comments and then read

through the rest of the comments awaiting moderation. As before, they were mostly people mourning the loss of the therapist. However, a couple of people asked if anyone knew about the new therapist the Wellness Center had hired to replace Dr. Rob.

Percy was interested to hear what people had to say and immediately approved the two comments. All of the comments finally taken care of, she announced to Minnie that she had to get ready for her dinner with Bonnie and Carlo. Of course, at the mention of dinner, Minnie began to mew.

"I'll give you your dinner on my way out," she told the cat.

"So, how did your meeting with Dr. Richardson go?" Bonnie asked Percy as soon as they had sat down. "Did you learn anything?"

"Actually," Percy began. But she was interrupted by their server, asking if they'd like to order drinks.

"I'll have an Aperol spritz," said Carlo.

"Make that two," said Bonnie. She looked over at Percy.

"I'll have a glass of Pinot Grigio." Percy usually ordered a glass of white wine. Though in the summer she would sometimes order rosé.

The server went to fill their order, and Bonnie turned back to Percy.

"So...?"

"So, I didn't learn anything new about Dr. Rob, but I did learn something interesting."

Bonnie and Carlo leaned in.

"Miranda Yates is going to be working at the Wellness Center!"

"The woman Carlo saw Dr. Rob with at his shop?" said Bonnie.

"The same," said Percy.

"What's she going to do there?"

"She's a therapist. Attended graduate school with Dr. Rob and Dr. Richardson."

"Huh. Well, that was fast."

"Not really. According to Dr. Richardson, they were in the process of hiring her before Dr. Rob was killed."

"Hmm…" said Bonnie.

"Hmm, what?" said Percy.

"Didn't you say that this Miranda Yates was very attractive?" Bonnie asked Carlo.

"I don't know about *very*, but…"

"And didn't you say that she and Dr. Rob seemed quite familiar, touching each other and…"

"I just saw her lay a hand on his arm. It wasn't as though they were making out."

Bonnie made a face.

"I'm just saying, maybe they were more than colleagues."

"What's your point?" Carlo asked her.

"My point is…" But she was interrupted by their server, who had arrived with their drinks.

Carlo raised his glass, and the others followed suit.

"*Salute!*"

"*Salute!*" said Bonnie and Percy.

After they drank, Percy put down her glass and looked at her two friends.

"There's something I need to tell the two of you."

Bonnie and Carlo waited, a look of concern on their faces.

"Is everything all right?" Bonnie asked her. "Did something happen after you left the library? Is Lucy okay?"

"Lucy's fine. It's… I submitted an offer on that house in Beauport I told you about."

"I thought you already did," said Bonnie.

"I hadn't signed the offer agreement when I spoke to you."

"So it's a done deal?" said Carlo.

"Not yet. I'm waiting to hear if the sellers accepted my offer."

"How much did you offer?"

Percy told him, and Carlo whistled.

"That's a lot of money."

"I know, but… It was Jim's dream to own a beach house in Beauport."

"Are you sure about this?" Bonnie asked Percy.

"No, but if it's meant to be, it's meant to be."

"Since when did you become a fatalist?"

"I think I've always been one, to a degree. Anyway, the sellers will probably reject my offer."

"There's the Percy I know and love!" said Bonnie.

"I think we should do another toast," said Carlo. He raised his glass. "To Percy and her new house. May it make her happy."

"It's not mine yet," said Percy. "But thank you."

"Can we still drink?" asked Bonnie.

"I think it's all right," said Percy.

"So, when do you find out if the sellers accepted your offer?" asked Bonnie after they had put down their drinks.

"I don't know. Hopefully, soon. Do you think I should check my phone?"

"You know the rule," said Carlo. "No phones during dinner."

"I think we can make an exception this one time," said Bonnie.

Carlo gave her a stern look.

"We made the rule for a reason."

Bonnie rolled her eyes.

"Fine. But can she look after we get the check?"

Carlo sighed.

"I suppose. But first, we need to decide what we're getting."

Percy had been torn regarding what to get. She had never been to this restaurant before, as it was new. Though she had her go-tos when she ate Italian food: chicken cacciatore; linguini with clams, if clams were in season; or a Margherita pizza. The restaurant had all three, and she was having a tough time deciding.

"I heard the fish here is very good," said Carlo. "Maybe I'll get the branzino. What about you, Bonnie?"

"I was thinking the veal Milanese. Percy?"

"I can't decide. Do I get the chicken cacciatore, the linguini with clams, or a pizza?"

"What are you in the mood for?"

Percy frowned.

"I like all three."

"Get the linguini," said Carlo.

"Did you hear it was good?" asked Percy.

"I was just thinking it would be different. You always get chicken at Annie's. And you can get pizza anywhere."

"Though not Neapolitan-style pizza. And their pizzas look good."

"Then get a pizza."

"I don't know."

Their server came over and asked if they were ready to order. Carlo and Bonnie looked at Percy.

"Are you ready?" Bonnie asked her.

"You guys order. I'll decide by the time you're done."

Carlo ordered the branzino, and Bonnie ordered the veal Milanese. Then the server turned to Percy.

"I'm going to have the prosciutto and arugula pizza," she announced.

Bonnie and Carlo stared at her.

"What?" said Percy.

"I did not see that coming," said Bonnie.

"Would you like anything to start?" asked the server.

"I'd be good with some fried calamari," said Bonnie. "You guys good with that?"

Carlo and Percy nodded.

"Very good," said the server and left.

"A prosciutto and arugula pizza," said Bonnie. "You're just full of surprises this evening. First, you make an offer on a beach house. Then you order a non-traditional pizza."

"It's not that big a deal," said Percy, suddenly feeling self-conscious. "Besides, it's good to try new things."

"I agree, but you usually stick to what you know."

"Well, I thought it was time for a change."

Bonnie and Carlo exchanged a look.

"What?" said Percy.

"Nothing," said Bonnie.

"So, how is your Facebook page?" asked Carlo. "Any interesting comments?"

"As a matter of fact," said Percy. "A woman left a comment saying Dr. Rob was not a good man."

"Did you approve the comment?" Bonnie asked her.

"I did."

"Anyone reply?"

"Several people."

"And?"

"They wanted to know why she thought that."

"And? Did she reply?"

"Not yet."

"Can you tell us her name?" said Carlo.

"The group is private. So I don't know if I should."

"Come on," said Bonnie. "It's not like we're going to tell anyone." Percy didn't budge. "Just tell us her first name."

Percy hesitated.

"Come on, Percy."

"Fine, it's Arianna."

"Arianna," said Bonnie.

"By any chance, is her last name Cardinale?" said Carlo, pronouncing it *car-dee-NAH-lay*.

Percy stared at him.

"How do you know that?"

"She's a customer."

"But," Percy began.

Carlo looked at her.

"How many Ariannas do you think there are in Stonebridge?"

He had a point.

"What do you know about her?" Bonnie asked him.

"Not much."

"Is she married? Single?"

"Pretty sure she's single."

"And was she a patient of his?" Bonnie asked Percy.

"Maybe? To be honest, I haven't been checking that carefully."

Bonnie turned back to Carlo.

"This Arianna Cardinale, is she attractive?"

"Very," he replied.

Bonnie turned back to Percy.

"You think she could have dated Dr. Rob?"

"I hope not if she was a patient."

"Maybe that's why she said he wasn't a good man. Maybe she was a patient, and he hit on her."

"I can't imagine Dr. Rob ever hitting on a patient. It would be unethical."

They were silent for a few seconds.

"Well, let us know if she replies," said Bonnie.

"I will," said Percy.

CHAPTER 10

They finished dinner, sharing a tiramisu for dessert, and paid. As they were leaving, Percy spied Mr. Barnes, the man she had seen earlier at the Wellness Center, seated near the bar and stopped.

"Everything okay?" Bonnie asked her.

"That man," Percy said in a low voice, looking over at Mr. Barnes. "He's the one who canceled his appointment with Dr. Rob the day Dr. Rob was shot."

"How do you know that?"

"I saw him this afternoon at the Wellness Center. He was just leaving. And Carol let slip that he was the one who had the noon appointment the day Dr. Rob was shot, but he canceled, supposedly to take his cat to the vet."

"Cute and a cat lover," said Bonnie, looking over at Mr. Barnes. "Is that his wife?"

"No, she died."

"He doesn't look happy."

Percy looked over at the table.

"You think that's his date?" Bonnie asked her.

"It could be a business meeting."

"Hmm. You say his wife died?"

"A couple of years ago."

"Then I'm thinking date. What do you think, Carlo?"

"I think we should leave."

Just then, Mr. Barnes looked over at them.

"Let's go!" said Percy.

She hustled her companions out of the restaurant.

"Really, Percy. If you plan on solving Dr. Rob's murder, you need to get better at spying on people," Bonnie told her.

"I wasn't spying."

"What do you call it then?"

"Observing."

"Whatever. In any case, you need to be more casual about it and not act guilty when you're caught."

"You think he knows who I am?"

"It's possible if he's been to the library. He looks familiar. Is he a member of your Facebook group?"

"I don't think so. I think I would have recognized him or his name. But I'm pretty sure no one named Barnes asked to join. But I'll double-check when I get home."

"Of course, he could be using an alias."

"I need to go," announced Carlo.

"Oh?" said Bonnie. "Where are you off to? You got a date?"

"With a canvas. It's my busy season. Lots of college diplomas and Father's Day gifts to frame."

"You need to hire more help."

"I've tried but…" He shrugged.

"I thought Gianna was back," said Percy.

"She is, but she's only part-time. It's all right. I don't mind framing."

"It's an excuse to listen to opera," Percy informed Bonnie.

"Whatever floats your boat," Bonnie replied. "Or helps you work. Hey, you want to check your phone, see if Dr. Rob's brother got back to you about the house?"

Percy had forgotten all about the house.

"Do you think I should?"

"Go on."

Percy looked at Carlo.

"The pictures can wait a few more minutes. Go on."

Percy retrieved her phone.

"Nothing from Ed." She frowned. "Is that a good thing or a bad thing?"

"He probably just hasn't heard back from the seller's agent," said Carlo. "I'm sure he'll text or call you tomorrow. And now, I must be off."

"Happy framing!" called Bonnie. Then she turned to Percy. "You all right?" Percy was staring down at her phone.

"Sorry. More Facebook stuff."

"People leaving comments and wanting to join?"

Percy nodded.

"It's a bit overwhelming."

"Did you ask Carol if she would help?"

"I did, but she said Dr. Richardson had a rule about employees being on social media."

"I guess I can understand that. But there must be someone else who could help you. Maybe another patient?"

"I don't know any of Dr. Rob's patients."

"What about that cute Mr. Barnes?"

"You think he's cute?"

"You don't?"

"I didn't notice."

Bonnie sighed.

"You should reach out to him."

Percy gave her a suspicious look.

"Don't you want to know if he really took his cat to the vet?"

"I suppose. But I don't know his first name."

"Please. He probably has a library card. Look him up in the system."

"I don't know. That doesn't seem ethical."

Bonnie rolled her eyes.

"You are never going to solve Dr. Rob's murder if you're not willing to bend the rules."

"I'm willing to bend them, just not break them."

Bonnie huffed.

"You could always do a Google search. That wouldn't be bending or breaking any rules."

"True. And Carol said he was a writer. So he should be relatively easy to find."

"There you go. Let me know what you find out."

"I will."

"And let me know as soon as you hear something from Ed."

"I will, but I'm guessing that the sellers rejected my offer."

"You're such a pessimist."

"I prefer to think of myself as a realist. Ed said they had another offer."

Just then, the door to the restaurant opened.

Bonnie grabbed Percy.

"Don't look, but Mr. Barnes and his date just left the restaurant."

Of course, Percy looked—and watched as Mr. Barnes shook hands with the woman he had been dining with. He turned and headed their way—and Bonnie let go of her handbag.

"Oh, how clumsy of me!"

"What do you think you're doing?" Percy hissed as Mr. Barnes bent to pick it up.

"Here you go," he said, standing up and handing Bonnie her bag.

"Thank you," said Bonnie. "Good to know that chivalry isn't dead."

He smiled at her and then noticed Percy.

"Do I know you?" he asked her.

"Percy works at the Stonebridge Library," said Bonnie, before Percy could answer. "You've probably seen her there."

"That must be why you look familiar," replied Mr.

Barnes. "My daughter loves the library. I'm Hugh," he said, extending his hand.

Percy stared at it. She wasn't one for handshakes.

"I'm Percy," she said. "Percy Rollins."

"Nice to meet you, Percy Rollins."

"And I'm Bonnie," said Bonnie. "I work at the library too."

"Nice to meet you both," said Hugh.

"Actually," said Percy. "I have a confession to make."

Bonnie and Hugh looked at her.

"I saw you earlier, at the Wellness Center. I had the appointment right after you. And I've seen you there before. I'm a patient of Dr. Rob's, or was."

"Ah," said Hugh. "I knew you looked familiar. I was a patient of his too. Awful what happened. I was supposed to see him that afternoon, but my daughter's cat, Fluffy, hadn't been feeling well, and Madison made me promise to take him to the vet."

"Your cat's named Fluffy?" said Bonnie.

"My daughter named him. He's a Maine Coon."

"And no doubt quite fluffy," said Percy.

"Exactly," said Hugh, smiling at her.

Percy had to admit, he had a nice smile.

"I should go," he said. "I told Madison I'd be home by eight-thirty."

"Well, we won't keep you," said Percy.

Bonnie nudged her and mouthed *Facebook group*. Percy shot her a look.

"Is everything all right?"

"Percy manages a Facebook group dedicated to Dr. Rob. It's a place where his patients can connect and post remembrances."

"What a nice idea," said Hugh.

"You should join," said Bonnie.

"I'm not really on Facebook. I just have an account so I

can keep tabs on Madison. I worry about the effects of social media on people her age."

"How old is she?" asked Bonnie.

"Fourteen."

"An impressionable age."

"You have kids?" he asked her.

"No, but I have nieces and nephews."

A cellphone was ringing. It was Hugh's.

"That's probably Madison, wondering how my date went." He removed his phone from his pocket and answered. "I'm on my way home," he told the caller. "I'll tell you about it when I get there." He ended the call and put his phone back in his pocket.

"Was that your daughter?" Bonnie asked him.

"It was. I should get going. Nice to have met you both."

They watched as Hugh got into a silver SUV.

"I should go too," said Bonnie. "I told Harry I'd call him after dinner."

"Have a good night," said Percy.

"You too."

As soon as Percy got home, she went on her computer and did a search for *Hugh Barnes*. It turned out that he wrote under a pen name, William Darcy. She had seen his books but hadn't read any of them. Probably because she didn't usually read romantic thrillers. But now that she knew him, maybe she would check one out of the library.

She clicked on his website and went to the About page. The photo must have been taken quite a few years ago, as Hugh's hair was dark brown in the photo and it was now tinged with gray. However, he looked the same otherwise. She wondered if he had chosen the pen name because of the character in Jane Austen's *Pride and Prejudice*. He even looked like she imagined Fitzwilliam Darcy looked.

His bio mentioned his late wife, Elizabeth, who was the inspiration for Sophie, one of the two main characters in his books. There was even a photo of her. Percy thought she was very pretty. No wonder Hugh hadn't been able to write since she died. Though didn't Carol say that he had recently started a new book?

That reminded Percy: she had meant to ask Carlo if Miranda Yates had picked up her pieces. But surely Carlo would have texted her if she had stopped by. He had said that he would. Then again, he had been so busy. Maybe he forgot.

Percy decided to text him. But he didn't reply. He was probably listening to opera and didn't hear his phone ping. She would text him again in the morning if he didn't get back to her. And there was still nothing from Ed Mankiewicz. Should she text him? No, she would wait until tomorrow to follow up with him too.

She looked back at her monitor, staring at the photo of William Darcy, aka Hugh Barnes. He didn't look like a killer. Then again, what did a killer look like? And what was his motive?

Percy let out a yawn. It was nearly nine-thirty. She put her computer to sleep and got ready for bed.

CHAPTER 11

The next morning, Percy went for a long run. When she got back, she turned on her phone and checked her messages. There was still nothing from Ed, but it was still early. If she hadn't heard from him by noon, she would text him.

Carlo, however, had gotten back to her. He had finished framing Miranda Yates's pieces and was going to let her know she could pick them up whenever.

Would you let me know when she stops by? Percy texted him back.

Aren't you seeing her next week? Carlo replied.

Percy was surprised he was up, considering he had texted her around midnight. Did the man not sleep?

Yes, but I'd love to speak with her before then.

Percy watched as the three dots danced on her screen.

OK, he finally wrote.

Thank you! Percy replied, adding a kiss emoji. Then she jogged up the stairs to take a shower.

Percy reviewed comments left in the Facebook group as she ate breakfast. There was nothing more from Arianna Cardinale, though she hadn't deleted her post, which had received more replies, mainly people wondering why she thought Dr. Rob wasn't a good man. Percy wondered too.

She looked at the time. She needed to get to the library. She quickly washed her bowl and spoon and put them in the drying rack. Then she went upstairs to brush her teeth.

Minnie followed Percy to the door as she was leaving, giving a plaintive mew. Percy felt bad leaving the cat, although she knew Minnie would be fine. And soon Lucy would be home for the summer.

"I'll be back this afternoon," Percy told the feline and leaned down to scratch Minnie's chin. Then she left to go to the library, which was less than a mile away.

One of the reasons she and Jim had chosen the house was its proximity to town and a trail where you could run or ride your bike.

It was another beautiful day, and Percy enjoyed the short walk. Bonnie was already there, and she immediately went over to Percy.

"So, any news about the house?"

"Not yet," said Percy. "I'll text Ed at lunchtime if he hasn't reached out by then."

"What about Facebook? Any new developments?"

"Nothing of note."

"Nothing more from Arianna Cardinale?"

"No."

"Do you think something could have happened to her?"

That hadn't occurred to Percy.

"Do you?"

"You said she hasn't replied to any of the comments."

"But that doesn't mean something happened to her. Do you think I should reach out to her, make sure she's all right?"

Before Bonnie could reply, Carmen came over.

"I need your help," she said.

"What's up?" said Bonnie.

"I need the two of you to set up the lecture room."

"Where's Miguel?" said Percy.

Miguel was in charge of maintenance, which included setting up rooms for talks or events.

"He had a family emergency and had to take a personal day."

"I hope everything's okay."

"I do too," said Carmen. "But in the meantime, we need to get the Stonebridge Room set up for today's talk."

"Why not get some of the volunteers?" said Bonnie.

Carmen gave her a disapproving look.

"Victor has a bad back, and you can't expect me to ask Mrs. Peabody," who was in her eighties and frail but had an encyclopedic memory.

"No problem," said Percy. "But the talk isn't until noon. Why the rush?"

"Better to do it now, before the library opens, than pull people away to do it later when we could be busy."

"The usual setup?" asked Percy.

"Put out some extra chairs," said Carmen. "We're expecting a full house for Diana Love."

Diana Love was a popular romance author who lived near Stonebridge and had recently released her tenth book. Percy had heard of her, of course, and had read one of her early books, but she wasn't a fan.

"We're on it," she said.

"Have you read any of her books?" Percy asked Bonnie as they were setting up the room.

"A couple."

"And?"

"They're quite racy. Have you read her?"

"I read one of her early ones. However, I'm not a big fan of romance authors, especially ones who take liberties with history, turning historical figures into sex symbols. John Adams was clearly brilliant, but to depict him as simmering with sex appeal…" Percy shook her head. "Just no."

Bonnie chuckled.

"Yeah, that one was a bit of a stretch. But you should read

the one she wrote about Thomas Jefferson." She grinned.

"No, thank you. The cover alone turned me off. Did we really need to see Jefferson's bare chest? And I doubt Sally Hemings was that voluptuous."

Bonnie chuckled.

"I agree: It was a bit much. But you know what they say: You can't judge a book by its cover."

"In this case, I think you can. If I want to read about major historical figures, I'll stick to well-researched biographies."

"Diana does her research. She just likes to spice things up."

"Mm."

They finished setting up the room and stood back.

"Looks good to me," said Bonnie.

"You really think we'll have this many people?"

"There's a waiting list."

"Huh." Percy looked at her watch. "The library opened ten minutes ago. We should go."

Percy was working at the circulation desk when she saw Hugh Barnes.

"Can I help you?" she asked him.

"I'm here for the talk."

"The Diana Love talk?" Though there were no other talks scheduled that day.

"She was one of Elizabeth's favorite authors. Other than me, of course," he added with a self-deprecating smile.

"Elizabeth?" said Percy, pretending she didn't know who Elizabeth was. "And you're an author?"

"Sorry. Elizabeth was my late wife. She died two years ago. That's why I was seeing Dr. Rob. Lizzy was my soulmate and the inspiration for one of my characters. And when she died, I just couldn't write. I felt…"

"Uninspired? Bereft? Like part of your soul had died?"

Hugh looked at her.

"Did you lose someone?"

"My husband, Jim. He died two years ago too. Heart attack. We had no idea there was anything wrong. He was only forty-eight."

"I'm so sorry. That's awful."

"And Lizzy?"

"Cancer. She had been ill for a while, but we didn't realize it was cancer until it was too late."

"I can't imagine what that must have been like. And you said you had a daughter."

"Madison. I got her Fluffy when Lizzy was ill, to help her cope. Though nothing can replace a mother."

"That's why she was so worried when Fluffy got sick."

"Exactly."

"But Fluffy is okay now."

"He is. He just ate something he shouldn't have."

"Well, you should get to the Stonebridge Room if you want a good seat. I hear the talk is sold out."

Hugh hesitated.

"I realize this is very forward of me, but would you like to get a drink after work or a coffee sometime?"

Percy stared at him. No one had asked her out since Jim had died. Well, no man on a date. Not that Hugh was asking her out on a date.

"Sorry, I…"

"I'd like that," said Percy, cutting him off.

She smiled at him, and he smiled back at her. Percy thought he had a nice smile.

"I should get to the talk, but I'll stop by on my way out."

Percy continued to smile as Hugh walked away.

"I knew it!" It was Bonnie.

Percy turned to face her.

"Knew what?"

"That there was a spark between the two of you."

"Don't be ridiculous."

"Did he not just ask you out on a date?"

"He asked if I'd like to get a drink or a coffee sometime."

"Sounds like a date to me."

Percy made a face.

"So, anything from the real estate agent?"

"My phone's in my bag in my locker."

"You want to go check it?"

"I said I would give him until noon."

"It's almost noon. Go check."

Percy hesitated.

"I'll watch the desk," Bonnie told her. "Go check."

"Fine."

Percy hurried to the staff room and reached into her bag for her phone. There was a voicemail. It was Ed. He had left a message saying he hadn't heard back from Sheila, the seller's agent, and would phone her at three if he hadn't heard anything by then. Percy frowned. Didn't they work in the same office?

She went back to the circulation desk.

"So?" said Bonnie.

"Ed left a message saying he hadn't heard back from the seller's agent, but he would follow up with her at three if he hadn't heard from her by then."

Just then, Percy saw Carol. Was she there for the talk?

"Are there any seats left?" Carol asked her and Bonnie, sounding a bit out of breath. "I meant to get here earlier, but I got stuck at the office."

"Are you here to hear Diana Love?" Percy asked her.

Carol nodded.

"She's one of my favorite authors."

"Did you register?"

"I did. As soon as I heard about it."

"Then you should be fine," said Bonnie. "The Stonebridge Room is just over there."

"Thanks!" said Carol and hurried off.

"I should get going too," said Bonnie.

"Where are you off to?"

"To hear Diana Love!"

Percy waited for Mary Beth to replace her so she could grab a bite to eat. Was she listening to Diana Love too? The talk was supposed to end at one, but it was now ten after. A few minutes later, a steady stream of people began passing by the circulation desk, and Percy saw Mary Beth hurrying towards her.

"Sorry I'm late," she said. "The talk ran long, what with all of the questions."

"No worries," said Percy, trying not to sound annoyed. "You're here now."

She headed to the staff room to get her bag and nearly collided with Hugh Barnes.

"I was just coming to see you, to say goodbye," he said.

"Oh," said Percy. "Did you enjoy the talk?"

"Her books aren't really my thing. Not a fan of turning historical figures into sex symbols, but Lizzy found them amusing. And Love's a good speaker. You didn't want to listen to her?"

"I'm not a fan of her kind of historical fiction. And someone needed to check people out and answer questions. But I'm glad you enjoyed the talk."

Hugh didn't move.

"Is there something I can help you with?"

"Have you eaten, lunch, that is?"

"I was just heading out to grab a bite."

"Would you mind if I joined you?"

Percy stared at him.

"You want to have lunch, with me?"

"Unless you have other plans. I'm always looking for suggestions about what to read."

Ah. So that's why he wanted to have lunch with her, to pick her brain about books.

"I was just going to get a sandwich and sit outside. It's such a nice day."

"Sounds perfect. So, may I join you?"

"If you like. I just need to grab my bag. Why don't you wait for me outside?"

Hugh said that he would, and Percy went to get her bag.

"So, you're not a fan of historical fiction," Hugh said to Percy as they ate.

"I wouldn't say that. I'm just not a fan of authors who twist history. But there are many good works of historical fiction out there I do like."

"Such as?"

Percy named several books and authors.

"I like Kate Quinn's books too. Have you read Hilary Mantel's *Wolf Hall* trilogy? I highly recommend them if you haven't."

"I've read them. Mantel clearly does her research."

"So, what other sorts of books do you like?"

"All sorts. I'll read pretty much anything if it's well written. But I suppose mysteries are my favorite genre."

Hugh smiled.

"What?" said Percy.

"My books are mysteries."

"I thought they were romantic thrillers. That's how they're described."

He gave her a look.

"I thought you didn't know I was an author."

Uh-oh. Busted.

"Okay, I may have looked you up. But I didn't know who you were when I met you."

"So you haven't read any of my books?"

"Not yet. To be honest, I'm not a big fan of romance novels."

"Why not?"

"They seem so contrived, not at all realistic."

"You'd be surprised. Some are quite realistic."

"Are you saying yours are? Aren't your main characters spies? Wait. Don't tell me: You're actually a spy."

Hugh smiled again.

"If I told you, I'd have to kill you."

"Then I guess I'd prefer you didn't tell me."

"Anyway, I consider my books more thriller than romance novel. It was someone in the marketing department's idea to call them romantic thrillers."

"I see. And how did you come up with your pen name? Are you a fan of Jane Austen? Though Darcy's first name is Fitzwilliam, not William."

"I was inspired by my late wife. Elizabeth's maiden name was Bennet, and she always said I was her Mr. Darcy."

"You must miss her."

"I do. But Dr. Rob helped me deal with my grief. Thanks to him, I was even able to start writing again. He was actually helping me with my new novel. And I felt terribly guilty when I heard someone had killed him when I was supposed to be there."

"Though if you had been there, you could have been shot too."

Hugh looked thoughtful as he took a bite of his sandwich.

"I heard you were there right after it happened."

Percy wondered how he knew. Then again, Stonebridge

was a small town, and it wasn't exactly a secret that she had been there.

"Any idea who shot him?"

"Not yet. What about you, Mr. Romantic Thriller Writer? Any theories?"

"My money's on it being either patient or a lover."

"What makes you say that?"

"They're the two most obvious choices."

"But in most mysteries, it's usually the least obvious person. And, according to Carol, all of Dr. Rob's patients loved him."

"Yes, but this isn't a book or a made-for-TV movie, Percy. And I doubt everyone loved Dr. Rob. He wasn't a saint."

"Oh? Do you know something, about Dr. Rob?"

"I probably know as much about him as you do. He didn't really talk about himself. But I was thinking of making the main character in my new book a therapist who fancies himself an amateur sleuth. So I asked him what it was like, being a therapist and listening to people tell you their problems day in and day out."

"And what did he say?"

"That it wasn't always easy. And that people often gave therapists too much credit. He said therapists weren't saints. They were just doing their job. And that they were often flawed."

"Do you think he was speaking from personal experience?"

"I do. I pressed him on it, but he wouldn't explain. He also told me that some people couldn't or wouldn't be helped, and that he sometimes felt like a failure."

"Huh." She was seeing a whole different side of Dr. Rob.

"Do you know if Dr. Rob was seeing someone? You said you thought that his killer could have been a lover."

"I don't know. But he's an attractive man."

"Did you know that Dr. Rob and Dr. Richardson had dated?"

Hugh stared at her.

"They dated? When?"

"Back in graduate school."

"Ah. Well, it must have been an amicable split if they decided to work together."

"Mm. So, are you going to meet with Dr. Yates?"

"I agreed to, but I'm not sure I'll continue with therapy. I was really just seeing Dr. Rob the last few weeks because of my book. I wanted to get some insight into what it was like being a therapist."

"I'm sure Dr. Yates could give you some additional insight, from a woman's perspective."

"Hmm."

"Did you know that Dr. Yates attended graduate school with Dr. Rob and Dr. Richardson?"

"I did not."

"And it's possible she and Dr. Rob were seeing each other, romantically."

Percy didn't know why she was telling Hugh all of this. She didn't usually gossip. Maybe it was because she found him easy to talk to. Or maybe she wanted to impress him.

"How very interesting. Well, now I'm glad I made an appointment to see her—and invited you out to lunch. You librarians are full of useful information." He looked down at his smartwatch. "I'm afraid I need to get going."

"What time is it?" Percy looked down at her watch. "Oh! I didn't realize we had been here so long! I need to get back to the library."

They got up and went to throw away their sandwich wrappers. Then they stood awkwardly by the trash receptacle.

"Could I have your phone number?" Hugh asked her.

"Why?"

He smiled.

"I'd like to see you again."

"Why? Is there a librarian in your new novel?"

Hugh continued to smile.

"No, but there's one I'd like to check out."

Percy winced.

"Sorry. I was never good with puns."

Percy gave him her phone number.

"Thanks. I'll shoot you a text, so then you'll have mine."

"Great!" she said, feeling her face grow warm. "Good luck with your book!" Then she turned and hurried to the library.

CHAPTER 12

Percy was finding it hard to concentrate. She kept thinking about Hugh and Dr. Rob. She never thought Dr. Rob was a saint, but… She wondered what his flaw was. And who did he think he had failed? Was it a patient? Or maybe it was someone in his personal life.

That made Percy think of Arianna. She still hadn't reappeared on Facebook. Percy decided she would message her later, when she got off work.

"So, how was lunch with the handsome Mr. Barnes?" said Bonnie.

"Hmm?" said Percy. She had been lost in thought and hadn't heard or seen Bonnie approach.

"I asked how your lunch with Mr. Barnes was."

"How did you know we had lunch?"

Bonnie gave her a look.

"It was fine."

"Just fine?"

"What's wrong with fine?"

"Did he ask to see you again?"

"He asked for my number."

"And, did you give it to him?"

"I did."

Bonnie grinned.

"What?" said Percy. "He just wants to pick my brain, Bonnie."

"Uh-huh. Trust me, it's not just your brain he wants to pick."

"You have a dirty mind. Hugh's working on a new thriller involving a therapist, and we were discussing Dr. Rob."

"He writes thrillers? Do we have any of his books? I don't recall seeing anything by him."

"That's because he writes under a pen name: William Darcy."

"Oh my God! Hugh's William Darcy?!"

"I take it you've heard of him."

"Are you kidding? All of his books were bestsellers. Though he hasn't published one in a while. Must be two or three years now."

"That's because his wife, who was his inspiration, died two years ago."

"Right. I think I read about that. But I didn't connect your Hugh with William Darcy. Though I should have. I knew he looked familiar!"

"Ahem. He's not *my* Hugh."

"Uh-huh. So is that why he was seeing Dr. Rob, to get his mojo back?"

"Something like that. In any case, Dr. Rob must have helped him because Hugh said he's been working on a new book."

"How exciting! Do you know what it's about?"

"He said it involves a therapist. But please don't say anything. I think he told me about it in confidence."

"My lips are sealed. Did Dr. Rob know about the book?"

"Hugh said he did. And here's the weird thing: He told me that Dr. Rob made a point of telling him that therapists weren't saints. That they were often flawed and failed people."

"Huh. Do you think Dr. Rob was talking about himself?"

"Quite possibly."

"Do you think he failed someone and that person killed him?"

"That's what Hugh thinks."

"So it must be a patient."

"Or someone he was involved with outside of work."

"Was he seeing someone?"

"Not that Hugh or I know of, but his brother Ed told me that Dr. Rob was famous for breaking hearts when he was younger. Maybe he had broken one more recently."

"Like, maybe, that Arianna woman?"

"Maybe."

"Hey, speaking of his brother, any word from him about the house?"

"Not when I last checked. I'll check again when I leave."

"Okay. Make sure to find me if you hear something."

"I will."

Percy went to the staff room to get her bag. She pulled out her phone and checked for messages. She saw there was a voicemail. It was from Ed. She thought about waiting until she left to listen to it, but she was feeling too anxious, so she pressed *Play*. He said the sellers had made a counteroffer and to give him a call.

Percy frowned.

"What's up?" said Bonnie.

"Ed left me a voicemail. The sellers countered."

"I'd have been surprised if they didn't."

"What should I do?"

"What's the counter?"

"I don't know. Ed said to call him."

"So, call him and find out."

"I don't want to do it here."

Two more people had entered the staff room.

"Call him outside."

"I should probably wait until I get home."

"Fine. But let me know what he says."

"I will."

Percy called Ed as soon as she got home. He picked up after only two rings. The sellers' counteroffer was only five thousand dollars below their asking price.

"That's not much of a counter," Percy grumbled.

"The only reason they're even considering your offer is because it's a cash deal, and you don't have to sell something," Ed replied.

"So the other buyers do and need a mortgage?"

"That's my guess, but they offered close to full price. If you really want the place, I'd offer them asking."

"But their counter was a few thousand below asking."

"Yes, but if you offered asking, that would pretty much guarantee the house was yours."

Percy didn't know what to do. What would Jim say? She looked up at the ceiling. Was there a crack?

"Hello?" said Ed. "You still there?"

"Sorry," said Percy. "I need time to think."

"Don't take too long."

"Don't I get at least twenty-four hours? And did you ask Sheila if I could take Lucy there on Saturday?"

"Sheila hasn't gotten back to me on that. I'll ask her again when I deliver your response."

"Give me twenty-four hours. But please ask her about Saturday before then."

"Okay. And if you want to discuss it, give me a call anytime."

"Thanks."

Percy didn't know what to do. She thought about calling her friends, but what did they know about Beauport real estate? And it was probably too late to phone her financial advisor, who would probably tell her she was crazy to pay cash for a house, even though interest rates were currently high.

While she was mulling over what to do, she received a notification from Facebook. Someone had left a comment in the Dr. Rob group. Percy opened the app and read the comment. The person wanted to know what was taking the police so long to find Dr. Rob's killer.

Percy wanted to tell the woman that in real life murders weren't usually solved in a week, unless the killer was caught in the act. But that hadn't been the case. Unless… Unless there was a closed-circuit TV that had caught someone suspicious entering or leaving the building around the time Dr. Rob was shot.

But did the building that housed the Wellness Center, or the surrounding ones, even have CCTV cameras? She would check tomorrow. Yet even if they did have CCTVs, she doubted the killer would be dumb enough to enter or leave the building waving a gun.

She approved the woman's comment but didn't reply, much as she was tempted to. And there was still nothing from Arianna Cardinale. So Percy decided to send her a message.

Hi, Arianna, she typed. *I hope you are okay. I'm the administrator of the Remembering Dr. Rob group and also a former patient of his. I posted the comment you left about Dr. Rob not being a good man, and I was curious why you thought so. If you'd like to talk about him, I promise not to judge. And anything you tell me would be confidential.*

Percy read over what she had written. It was a bit awkward, but she had already edited the message twice. "Good enough," she finally said, and then hit *Send.*

Percy checked her messages as soon as she got up the next morning. There was nothing from Arianna Cardinale or from Ed, just a message from Lucy, saying she would text when she was leaving school that afternoon.

Do you want me to make something special for dinner? Percy asked her.

Could you make your roast chicken with potato roasties? Lucy wrote back.

You're up early! Percy replied. She hadn't been expecting Lucy to be up.

Doing some last-minute cramming for my final final. So, chicken?

Sure. I'll go to the supermarket after work. Just let yourself in if I'm not back.

Lucy sent her a thumbs-up emoji.

And I'm hoping we can go to Beauport tomorrow, so I can show you the house.

I'm getting together with Cassie and the gang tomorrow night. Will we be back by 6?

I'll make sure we are.

Thanks. Hey, I've gotta go. See you later!

Percy thought about texting Ed about Saturday, but she stopped herself. She would go for a run first.

She tried to clear her head as she ran, but she kept thinking about the house and Dr. Rob. And before she knew it, she found herself by the Wellness Center. She didn't usually run through town, but clearly her subconscious had guided her there. Percy jogged around the building. There didn't appear to be any closed-circuit TV cameras on it. But there was a delivery entrance in the back that she hadn't noticed before. Could Dr. Rob's killer have slipped out the back?

She jogged around the building a second time, but she still didn't see any cameras on it or on the neighboring buildings. Though as she ran down the block, she noticed a camera on a jewelry store. However, the camera was pointed away from the Wellness Center.

Percy ran until she got to the little stone bridge that had given the town its name. Then she turned around and headed home.

She checked her phone before heading to the library. Still nothing from Arianna or Ed. She would wait for Arianna to reply, but she sent a text to Ed, asking again about Saturday. Then she put her phone in her bag, grabbed her car keys, as she would drive to the supermarket after work, and headed out.

Bonnie was waiting for her at the entrance to the library.

"Did you make a decision?"

Percy had texted her the night before about the house, saying she didn't know what to do.

"No. I wish I knew someone in real estate who could advise me."

"You should talk to Mary Beth's husband. He runs one of the real estate offices here in town. I'm sure he'd be happy to give you some advice." Bonnie spied Mary Beth entering the library and called her over.

"Is everything all right?" Mary Beth asked them.

"Percy needs some real estate advice, and I thought Bruce could help her."

"What kind of advice do you need?" Mary Beth asked Percy.

"I put in an offer on a house in Beauport, and the sellers countered for basically the asking price. It's a great house, but I'm not sure I'm ready to spend that much money. And there's a competing offer."

"Hmm... Are you moving to Beauport?"

"No. This would be a place to spend weekends and then summers when I retire. Jim always wanted a beach house."

"I see. Well, I'm sure Bruce would be happy to chat with you. Just call over to his office and make an appointment. He's at Stonebridge Realty."

"The problem is, I'm on a bit of a deadline. I need to tell

my agent if I'm going to move forward by this evening."

"Ah. Well, in that case…" Mary Beth pulled out her phone and began typing. Percy waited. "He has a few minutes now if you're free. His office is just across the street if you want to run over there."

Percy was about to say she couldn't when Bonnie said, "Go! We'll cover for you."

"You sure?"

"Go. I doubt you'll be gone long. And it's not like there's a line to get in here."

"Okay," said Percy. "I'll be quick."

She hurried out of the library and ran across the street. The door to the real estate office was locked, but Percy saw people inside and knocked. A woman came over and opened the door.

"Hi, I'm here to see Bruce."

"Did you have an appointment?"

"His wife just arranged it. I'm Percy, Percy Rollins. I work with Mary Beth at the library."

"I've got it," said Bruce, coming over to the two women. "You must be Percy."

Percy nodded.

"I only have a few minutes, but Mary Beth said you could help me."

"Why don't we go to my office?"

He led her upstairs and told her to have a seat.

"Mary Beth said you had a question about a house you're considering in Beauport?"

"Yes. I put in an offer five percent below asking, but I offered cash and a fast closing, no contingencies, well, other than an inspection. And the sellers rejected my offer. I guess technically they didn't reject it. They just came back with a counter that was only a few thousand below their asking price, and now I don't know what to do. My agent thinks I should accept their offer or offer asking since there's another bidder, but they need a mortgage and to sell their place first."

Percy knew she was rambling, but she was in a hurry.

"And who's your agent in Beauport, if you don't mind my asking?"

"Ed Mankiewicz. Dr. Rob's brother."

Bruce frowned.

"Do you know him?"

"I do."

"Do you not like him?"

He sighed.

"Ed worked here briefly before moving to Beauport."

"He did?"

"He did."

"But just briefly? Was that because he moved to Beauport?"

"Something like that."

Percy got the distinct feeling that Bruce was withholding information.

"If there's something I should know about him, please tell me."

Bruce looked thoughtful.

"I liked Dr. Rob. Sold him his home here. So when he asked me if I could help out his brother, I said yes."

Percy waited for him to go on. When he didn't, Percy asked him if there was a problem.

"Ed was a decent agent. Got a bunch of listings and worked as a buyer's broker. But apparently that wasn't enough for him."

"What do you mean?"

"I mean that he must have thought he wasn't making enough money as he started charging buyers a fee for his services."

"I thought buyer's brokers got a fee, usually from the seller, when their clients purchased a house."

"They do in most cases. But Ed had buyers pay him a fee upfront, whether he found them a house or not."

"Is that legal?"

"I don't know if it's technically illegal, but it's not something we do here."

"How did you find out that he was charging buyers a separate fee?"

"People started to complain."

"What did you do?"

"We fired him. But he already had a job lined up in Beauport and didn't care."

Percy was a bit stunned.

"Did Dr. Rob know about this?"

"I felt I had to tell him."

"How did he react?"

"He was very professional. Said he would reimburse any client who wanted their fee back."

"That was very generous of him. So did anyone ask for their money back?"

"A couple of people. Did Ed ask you to pay a fee upfront?"

"He did not." But Percy made a mental note to check her paperwork that evening.

"I'm glad to hear it. Maybe he's reformed."

"So, what do you think I should do about the Beauport house?"

"What's the address?"

Percy told him and watched as he typed on his keyboard.

"Very nice," he said. "Beauport is quite hot right now. Has been since Covid. I'm not surprised the sellers think they can get asking or close to it. Of course, I don't know the condition of the place, but I think the sellers' counter seems fair considering the market. Just make sure to have an inspection done—and I wouldn't use someone Ed recommended."

"Why not?"

Bruce gave her a look.

"You think Ed could be in cahoots with the inspector?"

Cahoots? Really, Percy?

"Just find someone you feel you can trust."

Percy looked down at her watch.

"I should go. Just one more question." Bruce waited. "Do you think Dr. Rob and his brother had a good relationship?"

Bruce looked thoughtful.

"I didn't know either of them that well. I got the sense that Dr. Rob worried about Ed, that there was a bit of strain there. Why?"

"Just curious." Percy got up. "Thank you for your time."

"I hope I was somewhat helpful."

"You were."

"And if you're ever looking for a house here…" Bruce said with a smile.

"I'll be sure to give you a call," Percy replied.

"There you are!" said Bonnie as Percy hurried over to the circulation desk. "I was going to send out a search party."

"You knew where I was. And you were the one who told me to go!" Percy replied.

"I just didn't expect you to be gone so long."

"Well, I'm here now. And the library isn't exactly busy."

"So, was Bruce helpful?"

"In more ways than one."

"What does that mean?"

"It turns out, Ed Mankiewicz used to work for him and left under a cloud."

"Oh? Do tell."

"Bruce said that Ed was charging clients a fee for helping

them, whether or not he sold them a house."

"Huh. Did Dr. Rob know?"

"Bruce told him, and Dr. Rob offered to reimburse any clients who wanted their money back."

"Very nice of him."

"Indeed. Bruce also said that he sensed the relationship between the brothers was strained."

"Hmm. And what did Bruce have to say about the house?"

"He said that if I loved it, I should offer full price, but be sure to get a good inspector."

"So, what are you going to do?"

Percy sighed. "I don't know."

CHAPTER 13

Percy had been itching to review the contract she had signed with Ed Mankiewicz all afternoon, but the signed contract was on her computer, and she needed to go to the supermarket right after work.

Finally, it was time to leave.

"You have a hot date?" Bonnie asked Percy as Percy hurried past her.

"With Lucy. She just got home. And I need to run to the supermarket to pick up stuff for dinner."

"Tell Lucy I said hi."

"I will."

"And let me know about the house!" Bonnie called after her.

Percy drove to the supermarket and quickly purchased what she needed. Then she drove home. Lucy was sitting on the couch, stroking Minnie, who was purring in her lap. Percy smiled.

"You two look comfortable."

Lucy looked up and smiled at her mother.

"I forgot how relaxing it can be to just sit and pet a cat."

"I know."

"Do you think Minnie missed me?"

"I know she did."

"Do you need help with the groceries?"

Percy was still holding her reusable grocery bag.

"I'm good. We wouldn't want to disturb Minnie."

Lucy smiled and continued to stroke the cat.

"You hungry?"

"Starving."

"I'll start dinner in a few. I just need to check something on my computer. But first, I could use a hug."

Percy put down the grocery bag, went over to the couch, and leaned over Minnie to hug Lucy.

"I've missed you."

"I've missed you too," Lucy replied.

"How were finals?"

"Exhausting."

"Well, you're home now and can take it easy."

"Until my job starts."

"Well, that gives you ten days to recover. I need to run upstairs to my office, but I won't be long. Then I'll start dinner."

"Everything okay?"

"Everything's fine. Just need to check something. Be back in a few."

Before Lucy could say anything, Percy ran up the stairs. She sat down at her computer and pulled up the buyer's agreement she had signed with Ed Mankiewicz. There was a paragraph about fees, saying that the buyer's agent was entitled to a commission, to be paid either by the seller or the buyer, but there was nothing about her being required to pay him anything upfront or if a deal fell through. She breathed a sigh of relief.

"Okay," said Percy, coming down the stairs. "I'll start dinner."

"Do you need some help?" Lucy called from the living room, where Minnie was still perched on her lap.

"I'm good. Though if you'd like to keep me company…"

Lucy looked down at the cat.

"Sorry, Minnie," she said, gently removing the cat from her lap and placing her on the floor.

Minnie looked up at her and mewed. Then she followed Lucy to the kitchen.

"Okay to give Minnie her dinner?" Lucy asked her mother.

"Go ahead."

Lucy retrieved a can of cat food and emptied the contents into Minnie's bowl.

"So, tell me about school," Percy said as she began preparing dinner. And Lucy did.

"So, are we going to Beauport tomorrow to see that house?" Lucy asked her mother after Percy had put the chicken and potatoes into the oven.

"Good question. I should call Ed."

"Ed?"

"My real estate agent. I thought I mentioned him. He's Dr. Rob's brother."

"Did you know he was Dr. Rob's brother when you hired him?"

Percy hesitated before answering.

"I may have."

Lucy gave her a look.

"What's that look for?"

"Did you hire him so you could ask him about his brother?"

"I may have."

"So...?"

"So what?"

Lucy sighed dramatically.

"So, did you ask him if he knew who might have killed Dr. Rob?"

"I may have."

Lucy gave her mother an exasperated look.

"And?"

"He thinks it could have been someone Dr. Rob dated and dumped. According to Ed, Dr. Rob broke a lot of hearts, at least when he was younger."

"Really? I mean, he's not bad looking, but he's so old."

"He's not that old." He and Percy were both in their mid-40s. "And he's still quite attractive."

"Please tell me you didn't have a crush on him."

"What?! No! I mean, I thought he was nice to look at, but he was my therapist!"

"Don't act like it's such a crazy idea. Lots of women develop crushes on their therapists."

"Well, I didn't." Though there was that one dream… But she would never tell anyone about that.

"So, do you think a spurned lover killed him?"

"I don't know. Hugh thinks it was a patient."

"Hugh? Who's Hugh?"

"Um… He's a patient of Dr. Rob's."

"Did you meet him through your Facebook group?"

"No. I know him from the Wellness Center."

"And you asked him about Dr. Rob? That's very unlike you."

"Yes, well, um…" Percy could feel her face growing warm as she thought about Hugh.

"Is he cute?"

"Cute?"

"You know, good-looking."

"He's not bad to look at."

"Is he single?"

"He's a widower."

"He ask you out?"

"Lucy!"

"What? It's totally obvious you like him."

"I do not! I mean, I don't dislike him. I just hardly know him."

"You didn't answer the question. Has he asked you out?"

Percy balked. He had asked her to have lunch with him. But was that a date? She didn't consider it one.

"Look, Mom. Dad's been gone two years now. And I doubt he expected you to become a nun. If you like this guy, go out with him."

"Your father was the love of my life, Lucy, and I miss him every day."

"I know you do. I miss him too. But that doesn't mean you can't date. Do you like this Hugh person?"

Percy sighed.

"I find him interesting."

"Well, that's a start. And does he have a last name?"

"It's Barnes."

"And do you know what he does?"

"He writes romantic thrillers."

"So he's a single, not-bad-looking author. Sounds perfect! You should definitely go out with him."

"Mm."

"You should ask him out."

"I need to call Ed Mankiewicz."

"Fine, change the subject."

"I'll be back in a few."

Percy went upstairs and waited as Ed's phone rang.

"Percy?"

"Hi, Ed. Just checking to see if I can bring my daughter to see the house tomorrow."

"Have you come to a decision regarding the seller's counteroffer?"

"I have. You can tell them I accept, but I want to do an inspection—and see the house tomorrow with my daughter."

"Great. I'll let Sheila know. And no problem regarding the inspection. What time tomorrow did you want to swing by?"

"Late morning or early afternoon would be preferable."

"Okay. I'll ring you back in a few, but it shouldn't be a problem. Sheila said the sellers are away."

"Thanks," said Percy.

She went downstairs to check on the chicken. She basted

it, and then she went over to Lucy, who was reading on the couch.

"You talk to Ed? We all set for tomorrow?"

"He said he needed to get back to me about the time, but it should be fine."

"I just need to be back by six."

"So you said."

After dinner, Lucy insisted on cleaning up.

"You don't have to," Percy told her.

"I know. But you cooked. It's only fair."

"Thank you, but it's really okay."

Lucy looked at her mother.

"I thought you said your OCD was under control."

"It is."

"Then let me clean up. I promise to do a good job."

She saw her mother hesitate. Percy was a bit obsessive—her family would say more than a bit—when it came to cleaning.

"Fine."

"See? That wasn't so hard."

"Just don't forget to clean the counters."

"I won't."

"And mop the floor."

"Got it, Mom."

Percy watched as Lucy started to clean.

"Go into the living room and watch something on Netflix or BritBox," Lucy commanded. "I'll let you know when I'm done."

Percy reluctantly left the kitchen. Fifteen minutes later, Lucy called to her.

"All done. You can come back now!"

Percy immediately went to the kitchen. It looked clean.

"I'm impressed," she said.

"Well, I was taught by the best. Hey, I need to go."

"Go? Where are you going? You just got home."

"To Jeremy's. He's having a welcome home gathering."

Jeremy was another of Lucy's Stonebridge friends. The two of them had known each other since they were little.

"Fine."

"If you don't want me to go…"

"No, go. We'll spend the day together tomorrow."

"Thanks, Mom! I promise not to be home too late."

She gave her mother a kiss and then grabbed her bag and headed out the door.

Percy kept looking at her phone, waiting for Ed to call or text her. She was starting to get frustrated when she finally received a text from him. They were all set for tomorrow at noon. He hoped that was okay. Percy said that was fine.

She received a notification from Facebook. Someone had left a comment on the Dr. Rob page. It was in reply to the comment asking if the police had any suspects. The commenter, a woman Percy didn't know, suggested the police talk to Arianna Cardinale if they hadn't already. Percy hesitated. Should she approve the comment or contact the woman who had left it?

She hadn't heard back from Arianna, nor had Arianna posted anything in the Facebook group since her original post. Percy hoped she was okay. Should she message her again? She went to Arianna's Facebook page. But as it was private, she couldn't tell if Arianna had posted anything recently. Next, she did an online search for her, but her search came up nearly empty. That was odd. Could *Arianna Cardinale* be a fake name? Or maybe she was in the witness protection program. Or a spy.

Seriously, Percy? said a little voice inside her head. *Hey, it's possible*, she told the voice. She could always do a LexisNexis search on her at the library, but she didn't feel that was ethical. Hmm. Maybe she would ask Hugh about her. After all, he wrote about shady people.

A little before ten, Percy turned off the TV. Lucy still wasn't home, and Percy was still not sure if she should approve the comment the woman had left about Arianna. She thought about messaging the woman but decided to reach out to Arianna one more time instead. She kept the message short and simple: *Please contact me. It's important.* Then she headed upstairs.

She went through her nightly routine and then climbed into bed. She took one last look at her phone. There were no new messages. She sent Lucy a text saying she was about to turn off her phone for the night and turned it off. Then she picked up the book she had taken out of the library that afternoon. It was William Darcy's first novel, titled *Love on the Run.*

CHAPTER 14

Percy hadn't heard Lucy come home. Had she come home? In a panic, Percy leapt out of bed and went to Lucy's room. The door was ajar. Percy peeked in and saw Lucy, curled up in her bed, Minnie curled up beside her. She smiled. Then she quietly backed away.

She put on her running clothes and went downstairs to the kitchen to make a pot of coffee. Minnie appeared a few seconds later.

"I thought you were asleep," Percy said to the cat.

Minnie gave her a look, one that said, *Well, I'm awake now.*

"Would you like some food?" Percy asked her.

Minnie mewed.

"I'll take that as a yes."

Percy got out the bag of dry food and shook some into Minnie's bowl.

"Oh, I left my phone upstairs. Be right back."

She hurried up the stairs and retrieved her phone, turning it on. As it was booting, she went back downstairs. She saw that she had messages and opened her texting app first. There was a message from Hugh Barnes, asking if she was free for brunch tomorrow. She smiled.

Then she checked Facebook Messenger. There was a message from Arianna Cardinale, left late the night before.

Sorry to have worried you, she had written. *I deleted my post.*

"What?!" said Percy. She went to the Dr. Rob page.

Arianna's post about Dr. Rob was gone. Percy frowned. Then she went back into Messenger and began to type.

Was it something someone said or wrote? Please know that if you'd like to talk about Dr. Rob with someone who won't judge, I'm available. I work at the library and could meet you for an early morning coffee or a drink after work. Just shoot me a text at… She typed her phone number and, before she could second-guess herself, hit *Send.*

She left Lucy a note by the coffee maker, saying she'd be back soon and to help herself to coffee. Then she did a few stretches and left. The coffee pot was full when Percy got back. Lucy must still be sleeping. Percy quietly went upstairs and looked in Lucy's room. Yup, still asleep.

She went to take a shower and get dressed. She would wake Lucy at nine-thirty if she wasn't up by then, as they needed to be on the road a little after ten. However, when she returned, Percy found Lucy in the kitchen, sipping coffee from a large mug.

"You're up. What time did you get home?"

"Around midnight?"

"You have a good time?"

"It was all right."

Percy wanted to ask if something had happened, but it could wait.

"Well, we need to be on the road a little after ten."

"Okay."

"Would you like me to make you some breakfast?"

"I'm good."

"Have you eaten?"

"I'm not really hungry."

Something was definitely up.

"You should eat something before we go. You know, breakfast is the most important meal of the day."

"Have you eaten?"

"I was about to."

Percy looked in the cabinets and then in the fridge.

"Can't decide?" said Lucy. "What do you usually have?"

"It depends. Maybe I'll just have a protein bar as we're going to have lunch in Beauport. Would you like one?"

"Sure."

Percy got out the box of protein bars and held it out to Lucy. Lucy took one, and then Percy did the same.

"So, did something happen at Jeremy's last night?" Percy asked Lucy as they ate.

"Why do you ask?"

"You seem to be in a bad mood."

"I'm just tired."

Percy didn't push it.

"Well, you can take a nap in the car. We just need to be on the road a…"

"Little after ten. I know."

Percy saw that Lucy kept glancing at her phone.

"I'm going to go brush my teeth and finish getting ready," Percy said when she finished her protein bar. "Unless you want to talk."

"I'm good," said Lucy.

"Okay," said Percy. Then she headed upstairs.

They left the house at five after ten. It was a beautiful May morning, and traffic heading to Beauport wasn't too bad. Though it still took them over an hour and a half to get there.

They didn't speak during the first part of the drive. Lucy was busy typing on her phone most of the time. And Percy had put on her favorite jazz station.

"So, Lucy…" Percy began, after they had been on the road for just over half an hour. Lucy stopped typing and looked over at her mother. "Would you be okay entertaining yourself tomorrow afternoon?"

"No problem. What's up? Wait. Did that guy you mentioned ask you out?"

Percy often wondered if Lucy could read her mind.

"As a matter of fact…"

"I knew it! You should totally go out with him. Please tell me you said yes."

"I haven't said anything yet. I wanted to talk to you first."

"You don't need my permission to date, Mom."

"It's not a date, Lu. He just asked if I was free for brunch. He probably just wants to discuss Dr. Rob."

"Uh-huh."

"So, you're okay if I tell him yes?"

"Absolutely. Do I get to meet him? Tell him to pick you up at the house."

"I think it's a bit soon for that. I don't want you grilling him."

"I would never grill someone you liked."

"I don't know if I like him yet."

"Please. You wouldn't agree to go out with him if you weren't interested."

"I'm interested in hearing what he has to say about Dr. Rob. That's all."

Lucy rolled her eyes. "Whatever." Then she turned her attention back to her phone.

They arrived in Beauport a little before noon. Parking was more difficult than the last time Percy had been there, but she eventually found a spot.

"It's cute," said Lucy.

"Do you remember it at all? Your father and I used to take you here when you were little."

"Vaguely. I can see why you like it."

"The real estate office is just a couple of blocks away. We

can have lunch and walk around town after we show you the house.”

As they headed to Ed's office, they passed an ice cream shop with a line out the door.

“Can we get ice cream later?” Lucy asked her mother. “I read about this place online. It's supposed to be really good.”

“Sure,” said Percy.

They entered the real estate office. The same woman that Percy saw the last time was seated at a desk near the front, looking at her computer.

“Hi,” said Percy, trying to get the woman's attention. “Is Ed here?”

“He's in back,” said the woman, not removing her eyes from her computer monitor.

“Could you let him know there are people here to see him? I have an appointment at noon to look at a house with him, Percy Rollins.”

The woman continued to look at her screen, as though she didn't hear Percy, and Lucy looked at her mother, as if to say, *What the heck?* Percy was about to say something to the woman when Ed emerged from the back.

“Percy! So good to see you again! And this must be your daughter.” He extended a hand to Lucy. “Ed Mankiewicz.”

“Lucy,” said Lucy, not taking his hand.

“Nice to meet you, Lucy. Are you excited to see the house?”

“Sure.”

Either her daughter was in a bad mood or she didn't have a high opinion of Ed. Percy would ask her later what she thought of the real estate broker.

“Do you want to follow me, or should we take my car?” Ed asked them. “Where are you parked?”

“I got a spot a couple of blocks away. Parking was a bit tough this morning.”

“Why don't we take my car then. That is if you don't

mind being in a convertible. It was such a nice day, I couldn't resist."

Percy looked over at her daughter.

"Whatever," she said.

They followed Ed out the back and got into his convertible.

"So, if you don't mind my asking, how old are you, Lucy?"

"I'm twenty."

"I have a son who's twenty. He's been in England, doing a semester abroad. Going to travel a bit when he's done. You go abroad?"

"No, I didn't want to be that far away from my mother."

"Aw. Your mother told me about your father. I'm very sorry for your loss."

"Thanks," said Lucy.

"You know, I would have been fine with you going abroad for a semester," Percy said to her daughter in a low voice.

"You're going to love the house your mother picked out!" Ed said to Lucy. "You can invite all your friends and have parties on the beach!"

Neither Lucy nor Percy said anything.

"Here we are!" Ed said a couple of minutes later. "As you can see, it's not far from downtown."

They got out, and Ed went to unlock the front door. He showed them around the first floor and then took them up to the second floor.

"Check out the view!" he said to Lucy. "You can see the Sound from here."

"Nice," she said.

"Shall we go see the beach?"

Lucy shrugged. Something was definitely up with her, Percy thought.

They followed Ed back down the stairs and out to the deck. Then they followed him through the gate and onto the walkway that led to the beach.

"Behold! Your own private beach!"

"It's not technically private, is it?" said Lucy. "I mean, I see other people."

"Not technically, no. But the walkway belongs to you. And you would have the beach to yourselves in the off-season."

"What about the neighbors?" asked Percy, looking around. "Do they live here year-round?"

"I know the ones to your left, the Hatfields. They're very nice. Older couple."

"And the other neighbors?"

"I don't know them. But I'm sure they're nice too. Beauport's a very friendly place."

"Do you want to take one more look around the house?" Ed asked them.

"Lucy?" said Percy.

"I'm good."

Ed led them back up the walkway.

"As you can see, there's an outdoor shower, so you don't bring sand into the house," he said. "So, what do you think of the place, Lucy?"

"It's nice," she replied. "Can we go, Mom?"

Something was definitely up.

"I'll just lock up and then I'll drive you back to the office," Ed told them.

"Could we walk?" Lucy asked her mother. "I'd like to get a feel for the neighborhood."

"An excellent idea!" said Ed. "You two go ahead. Percy, I'll be in touch. I'm just waiting to hear back from Sheila."

"You told her that I agreed to the sellers' counteroffer, yes?"

"I did, but she hasn't gotten back to me. She's actually away, but she checks her messages regularly. I'll follow up with her if I haven't heard anything by this afternoon."

"Okay," said Percy.

"Let's go, Mom."

Percy followed Lucy to the street.

"Is everything all right?" Percy asked her daughter as they walked back towards town. "You've seemed off all morning."

Lucy sighed. "It's Jamie."

"What about Jamie? Did something happen to him?" Jamie was one of Lucy's college friends, who she had met freshman year.

"We sort of got together just before school ended, and now he's acting all weird."

"Ah," said Percy. So it was boy trouble.

"And I don't know what to do. He hasn't been replying to my texts. And I'm worried he doesn't want to be friends anymore after what happened."

"What happened?"

Lucy gave her mother a look.

"Ah."

"Do you think I ruined things by sleeping with him?"

"I'm sure you didn't. You've been friends with him since freshman year. He's probably just been busy with finals."

"That's what most of my friends say, but I don't know. Finals are over now, and he still hasn't gotten back to me."

"So was this the first time the two of you…"

Lucy sighed.

"It was. But it felt right, you know? But maybe he didn't feel the same way."

"Tell me what happened."

"We were studying for finals together in my room. It was late, and we were listening to music. And this song we both really liked came on, and he leaned over and kissed me."

"Had you been drinking?"

"No. We both had finals the next day."

"So, he leaned over and kissed you and… did you kiss him back?"

"I did."

"And?"

"And one thing led to another and, you know."

"And did you enjoy it?"

"I did. I know this will sound corny, but it was like he and I were meant to be. I mean, I always thought Jamie was attractive, and smart, and kind. But I never really thought of him *that* way until he kissed me. And since then, I can't stop thinking about him."

Percy saw how confused and hurt her daughter was and felt for her.

"I don't think that sounds corny at all. I felt the same way the first time your father kissed me."

"You did?"

Percy nodded, and Lucy sighed.

"I'm sure you'll hear from Jamie eventually."

"You really think so?"

"I do. He's young, and he's probably confused."

"He's the same age I am. Actually, he's nearly a year older."

Percy smiled at that.

"That's still young. Boys don't mature as fast as girls do. But I'm sure you'll hear from him when he's ready. Just give him some space."

"But we were supposed to meet up in Boston over the summer."

"I'm sure you'll hear from him before then."

Lucy didn't look convinced.

"So, where shall we have lunch?" Percy asked as they approached town.

"I don't care," said Lucy. "You pick."

CHAPTER 15

Percy and Lucy found a cute café to have lunch. After they placed their orders, Percy texted Hugh, saying yes to brunch the following day. Hugh immediately wrote back, saying he would pick her up at noon. Percy frowned.

"What is it?" Lucy asked her.

"It's Hugh. I told him I'd have brunch with him tomorrow, and he said he'd pick me up."

"So? What's the problem?"

"I'd rather meet him someplace in town."

"Oh, come on. He's being chivalrous. Let him come get you."

"You just want to meet him."

Lucy grinned.

"I do, but that's not why you should let him pick you up."

"Fine. I'll tell him that's all right."

Their food arrived, and after they'd had a few bites, Percy asked Lucy what she thought of the house.

"It's really nice," she replied. "But how often are you going to use it?"

"What do you mean?"

"I mean, I can't really see you spending summers there. What about the library? Or are you planning on retiring?"

"I'm not ready to retire. I like working at the library. But I have lots of vacation time and personal days I've yet to use."

"Fine. But do you really want to spend all of your vacation and personal days at the house? I thought you wanted to travel."

Percy hadn't thought about that.

"What about you?" she asked Lucy. "Wouldn't you like to have a beach house to go to in the summer?"

"I'm not a little kid anymore. I work summers."

"You could go on weekends. Invite your friends. I'm sure they'd love to spend a weekend at a beach house."

"And you'd be okay with that? I know how you are about keeping things clean and tidy. What if we messed things up?"

Percy opened her mouth and then closed it. Maybe she had been too hasty putting in an offer on the house. Could she take it back?

"Look," said Lucy, seeing the expression on her mother's face. "It's a great house, and you could always rent it out for a few years. Then, when you did retire, you could spend as much time there as you wanted."

"I guess," said Percy. It wasn't a bad idea. However, she didn't like the idea of strangers living in her house.

They finished lunch, and Lucy said she wanted to get ice cream.

There was a line out the door of the ice cream shop, but they waited. Finally, it was their turn. Percy got a scoop of strawberry in a cup, and Lucy got a scoop of s'mores on a cone.

"So, what did you think of Ed Mankiewicz?" Percy asked her daughter as they walked around Beauport.

"He seemed like an operator."

"An operator?"

"Like he was trying to make a sale."

"Well, that is his business, selling homes."

"But you already made an offer. He didn't need to suck up to me."

"I didn't think he was sucking up to you. He was just being friendly."

"Mm." She took another bite of her ice cream. "Was Dr. Rob like that?"

"Dr. Rob? Oh no. He was the opposite of Ed, very reserved."

They had stopped to finish their ice creams in a little park when Percy thought she saw Dr. Richardson enter. It was definitely her.

"What's up?" Lucy asked her mother.

"That woman over there," Percy said, indicating Dr. Richardson. "That's Dr. Rob's partner at the Wellness Center."

"What's she doing here?"

"She and her husband have a place here."

"She looks like she's waiting for someone."

As soon as Lucy said it, Percy saw Ed Mankiewicz enter the park and go over to Dr. Richardson.

"Come here," said Percy, pulling Lucy behind a large tree.

"Seriously?" said Lucy.

"Sh!"

"I don't think they can hear us."

Percy watched Ed and Dr. Richardson, peeking out at them from behind the tree. It looked like they were arguing. Then Ed grabbed Dr. Richardson's arm. Dr. Richardson shrugged him off. There was more arguing, then Dr. Richardson said something to Ed, and he left. Percy continued to watch as Dr. Richardson took out her phone and started typing.

"Can we go now?" said Lucy.

"Let's wait until she leaves."

"I doubt she'll notice us. She seems pretty intent on her phone. And we can go out that way," she said, pointing away from where Dr. Richardson was.

"Fine," said Percy. "I just wish I could read lips, so I knew what they had been arguing about."

They were nearly back to Stonebridge when Percy caught her daughter smiling.

"You look happy."

"Jamie just texted me. He apologized for being MIA. Said he was super stressed about his finals and then lost his phone somewhere and just got a new one."

"See," said Percy.

Lucy frowned.

"You don't think he's lying, do you?"

"Why would he lie?"

Lucy looked thoughtful. Then Percy heard Lucy's phone pinging. Lucy immediately focused her attention on her phone again. Percy shook her head. Young people and their phones. Though she knew plenty of people her age, in their forties and older, were also obsessed with their phones. And while she may have been obsessive about some things—okay, a lot of things—her phone wasn't one of them.

"We're here," said Percy, pulling into their driveway. Lucy was still on her phone.

"Hmm?" said Lucy, looking up. "Oh."

"Were you texting with Jamie this whole time?"

Lucy looked sheepish.

"Everything okay?"

"Better than okay. Jamie invited me to come to Boston next weekend."

"Are you going to go?"

"If it's okay with you." Lucy gave her mother a pleading look.

"Fine. Go."

Lucy leaned over and gave her mother a hug.

"You're the best!"

Percy was concerned when she didn't hear back from Ed that afternoon or evening. Had he not heard back from

Sheila? Finally, around eight, she sent him a text.

"Everything okay?" she wrote.

He still hadn't replied by the time she turned off her phone to go to sleep. Well, if he hadn't gotten back to her by nine the following morning, she would call him. Though it was strange for him to go silent when he had been so eager to close the deal.

There was still nothing from Ed when Percy turned on her phone the next morning. Now she was starting to worry. But it was too early to phone him. She would call him when she got back from her run.

She rang Ed's cell phone as soon as she got back, even though it was before nine. But the call went straight to voicemail. That was odd. She was going to call his office, but it was probably closed. Well, she would call at ten if she hadn't heard from him by then.

She had a bowl of cereal and some coffee. Then she went to take a shower.

She was deciding what to wear when she heard a knock at her door, which was ajar.

"May I come in?" said Lucy, poking her head inside.

"Of course," said Percy.

Lucy stepped inside.

"Deciding what to wear on your big date?"

"It's not a date. It's just brunch."

"Whatever. You need help?"

Lucy went over to Percy's closet and started flipping through her clothes.

"Where's he taking you?"

"A place in Northbridge he wanted to try."

"Did you check it out online?"

Percy gave her daughter a look.

"Of course you did. So, is it fancy or casual?"

"I'm thinking casual as it's brunch. It has a pretty outdoor garden where you can sit in warmer weather."

"What about this?" said Lucy, pulling out a sundress that was covered with big red poppies.

"I'm not sure it's warm enough for that."

"You could bring a sweater. Go on, try it on."

Percy reluctantly agreed.

"What do you think?" she said, when she had changed, holding out the skirt and twirling around.

"Very nice. You should definitely wear it. Are you going to wear your hair up or down?"

"I hadn't really thought about it. What do you think?"

"Wear it down. It's sexier."

"I'll put it back."

Lucy rolled her eyes.

"You going to wear makeup?"

"I hadn't gotten that far. Do you think I need to?"

"Maybe a little mascara and some lipstick."

"Fine. Now run along. I need to finish getting ready."

"He still picking you up at noon?"

"He is."

"I can't wait to meet him! And definitely wear heels—unless he's short. Is he short?"

"Shoo!" said Percy.

The doorbell rang at exactly twelve o'clock.

"I'll get it!" called Lucy, running to get the door. "Hi!" she said, opening it. "You must be Hugh."

"And you must be Lucy," Hugh replied, smiling at her.

"Won't you come in? My mother will be right down."

"Hugh," said Percy, descending the stairs.

Lucy saw the way Hugh looked at her mother and smiled.

"You look lovely," he said.

"You don't look so bad yourself," said Percy.

"Shall we?"

Percy turned to her daughter.

"Don't worry about me," said Lucy. "I'm going to go over to Rachel's. They just opened their pool."

"Isn't it a bit chilly for a swim?"

"The pool's heated."

"Well, have fun. Will you be home for dinner?"

"I'll let you know. You guys have fun!"

Percy got into Hugh's SUV. It looked new.

"New car?" she asked.

"No, I just like to keep it clean."

Percy smiled. A man after her own heart.

"Your daughter looks like you," he said.

"Thanks," said Percy. "Though I always thought she looked like Jim."

"She has your chestnut-brown hair and hazel eyes."

"But her features are more like Jim's. What about your daughter? Does she look like you?"

"I'll show you some photos over brunch, and you can decide."

They parked in the lot for the restaurant, and Hugh escorted Percy to the hostess stand.

"We have a reservation for twelve-thirty," Hugh told the hostess. "The last name's Barnes."

"Would you prefer to sit inside or outside?"

Hugh turned to Percy.

"Is the garden buggy?" Percy asked the hostess.

"I don't think so. But if there's a problem, we can move you inside."

"Let's try the garden then. It's such a nice day."

The hostess escorted them to a table surrounded by a bunch of flowering plants.

"This is lovely," said Percy.

"A server will be right with you," said the hostess, placing a couple of menus on the table.

"How did you find out about this place?" Percy asked Hugh after the server left.

"I have my sources. Hopefully, the food is as good as the scenery," he said, looking at her.

CHAPTER 16

"Is everything all right?" Hugh asked Percy after they had ordered drinks. She had been looking down at her phone and frowning.

"Sorry. It's just... I put an offer in on a house in Beauport, and my agent seems to have disappeared."

"Disappeared?"

"I should probably explain."

She was interrupted by the server bringing over their drinks. They thanked him, and Percy went to take a sip, but Hugh stopped her. He was holding out his glass.

Percy stared at it for a few seconds before realizing he wanted to make a toast.

"To new beginnings," he said.

Percy liked that.

"To new beginnings," she said, holding up her glass.

They clinked glasses and then drank.

"You were about to say something about your real estate agent," said Hugh.

"Right," said Percy. "He's Dr. Rob's brother."

"Your real estate agent is Dr. Rob's brother? Did you know he was Dr. Rob's brother when you hired him?"

"I did."

"Did Dr. Rob refer you? I didn't realize you were selling your house in Stonebridge."

"Sorry, I'm not selling the house. I was thinking of

buying one in Beauport, as a summer-slash-weekend place. My late husband and I always dreamed of owning a beach house."

"I see. And Dr. Rob referred you to his brother?"

"Not exactly." Hugh waited as Percy took a sip of her mimosa. "I found Ed on my own."

"And did Dr. Rob know you hired his brother to help you find a house in Beauport?"

"No. I hired Ed after Dr. Rob died." Percy could almost see the thoughts going through Hugh's head. "I thought maybe he could tell me something about his brother."

"Like who might have killed him?"

Percy nodded.

"And you felt he would open up to you if you bought a house from him?"

"Something like that. Though I wasn't planning on buying a house. It just sort of happened. And, technically, I haven't bought it yet. I'm still waiting to hear if my offer was accepted."

"So, did you learn anything from the brother?"

"Not a lot. I don't think Ed liked his brother very much."

"What makes you say that?"

"The way Ed talked about him. He said Dr. Rob thought he was better than everyone."

"He say anything else?"

"That Dr. Rob was a womanizer."

"A womanizer?"

"Ed said that Dr. Rob had a lot of casual affairs, at least when he was younger, and that he broke a lot of hearts. I told you he dated Dr. Richardson back in graduate school and cheated on her."

"You did."

The server came over and asked if they'd like to order. Hugh said they needed a few more minutes.

"We should probably take a look at the menu," he said

to Percy. "Do you know what you're going to have?" he asked her a minute later, seeing her put down her menu.

"The quiche. What about you?"

"I was thinking of getting an omelet or else the salade Niçoise. And how would you feel about sharing a bread basket?"

"Sounds good to me."

Hugh signaled to the server, who came over and took their order. When he left, Hugh asked Percy if she had learned anything else from Ed.

"Actually… I met with Bruce Nathanson. He runs Stonebridge Realty. I wanted to get his advice about the house in Beauport. And he told me that when Ed worked for him, he had this scheme where he would make buyers pay him a fee upfront."

"Is that legal?"

"I'm not sure if it's illegal, but it definitely wasn't kosher. Bruce was going to fire Ed, but Ed told him he was moving to Beauport."

"So Ed worked in Stonebridge."

"Briefly."

"And did Dr. Rob know about his brother's scheme?"

"Bruce told him."

"And how did Dr. Rob react?"

"Bruce said Dr. Rob offered to reimburse any unhappy clients."

"Very nice of him."

Percy nodded.

"You learn anything else about Ed?"

"He met with Dr. Richardson while Lucy and I were there."

"Why was he meeting with Dr. Richardson in Beauport?"

"She has a house there. But as to why they were meeting, I have no idea. I couldn't hear what they were saying, but they didn't look happy."

"Do you think it had something to do with Dr. Rob?"

"Maybe. Or…"

"You think they could be having an affair?"

"The thought crossed my mind, but I can't really imagine it."

"What does Ed look like? Is he attractive?"

"I suppose. But he's not my type. And Dr. Richardson's married."

"Married people have affairs. That's why they're called that."

Percy made a face.

"Well, I would have never cheated on Jim."

"And I would have never cheated on Elizabeth. But we're not typical."

"We aren't?"

"Sadly, no."

Percy took another sip of her mimosa. She didn't like the idea of people cheating on their spouses being a regular thing.

"So, you last saw Ed yesterday afternoon?"

Percy nodded.

"So it hasn't even been twenty-four hours. Give him until tomorrow before you call the cops."

"I wasn't planning on calling the cops. It's just… He was so eager to close the deal. Then, when I finally accept the sellers' counteroffer, poof! He ghosts me.

"Maybe he went somewhere that doesn't have good cell reception."

"Or he skipped town."

Hugh didn't say anything. Then their food arrived.

📖

"So, tell me about your daughter," Percy said to Hugh as they ate. "You said you would show me pictures of her."

Hugh smiled.

"How many do you want to see?"

"Show me as many as you like."

"Just remember, you asked."

He took out his phone and started showing Percy photos.

"And that must be Fluffy with her." Hugh nodded. "She resembles you."

"Are you referring to Fluffy or Madison?"

Percy smiled.

"The cat, of course."

Hugh smiled back at her.

"I think she looks more like Elizabeth. Madison, that is, not the cat."

Percy smiled again.

"Do you have a photo of her, Elizabeth?"

"You really want to see her?"

Percy nodded.

Hugh took back his phone and scrolled down.

"Here," he said, handing the phone back to Percy.

"She's lovely."

"That was taken before she got sick. It's how I like to remember her. And what about Lucy?"

"What about Lucy?"

"What's she like?"

Percy thought.

"Smart. Stubborn. Confident. Knows what she wants. Or thinks she does."

Hugh smiled.

"And she's going to be a junior?"

"Actually, she'll be a senior. She skipped a grade."

"And does she know what she's going to do after college?"

"She claims she wants to be an environmental lawyer."

"You don't believe her?"

"I believe that's what she wants to be now, but who knows? She's still young. Her father was an environmental lawyer, so…"

"Ah."

"So, tell me more about your book, the one about the therapist."

"I'm still fleshing it out."

"You must have an outline."

"Not really. I'm more of what you'd call a pantser."

"You mean, you make it up as you go along?"

"Something like that."

"So is the main character still the therapist?"

"I changed it." Percy waited for him to go on. "In this version, the therapist is murdered."

"Was he shot?"

"I'm still deciding."

"I see. And do Cam and Sophie investigate?" Cam and Sophie were the main characters in Hugh's romantic thriller series.

Hugh gave her a look.

"I thought you hadn't read any of my books."

"I just started the first one."

"I see. Well, to answer your question, I see this book as the first in a new series."

"Will it be a thriller? Who's the new protagonist?"

"It will still be a thriller, but I'm still working out the details."

"Do you know who kills the therapist?"

"Not yet. As I said, I'm still sorting things out."

"Speaking of sorting things out, I was hoping you might be able to provide me with some intel on someone who was either a patient or dated Dr. Rob."

Hugh's eyebrows went up.

"Oh?"

"Her name is Arianna Cardinale. She left a post in the

Facebook group saying that Dr. Rob wasn't a good man. I messaged her about it, but she didn't get back to me. So I wrote to her again. Then she deleted her post. I looked for her online, but it's like she doesn't exist. She has a Facebook page, but it's private."

"Is there a picture of her on her Facebook page?"

"There is. But I don't know if it's recent."

"May I see?"

Percy pulled up Arianna's Facebook profile photo and turned her phone around.

"Hmm," said Hugh, looking at it. "Madison had a friend named Allie Cardinale."

"She had a friend named Allie Cardinale?"

"I believe it's short for Allegra. And I think her mother's name is Arianna."

"You don't know for sure?"

"I only met the woman a couple of times. Elizabeth was the one who usually handled playdates."

Hugh started scrolling on his phone.

"Ah, I was right. It is her. She and Elizabeth were Facebook friends."

Hugh turned his phone around to show Percy.

"I have access to Elizabeth's Facebook account," he explained, seeing the expression on Percy's face.

"So, what do you know about Arianna?"

"Not much. As I said, I only met her a couple of times."

"Is she married? Single?"

"Pretty sure she's single. Divorced, as I recall."

"Do you think she was a patient of Dr. Rob's?"

"I don't know. I don't recall ever seeing her at the Wellness Center, but that doesn't mean anything."

"Could she have dated Dr. Rob?"

"It's possible. She's quite attractive."

Percy frowned, caught herself, and tried to make her expression more neutral.

"Maybe Madison can ask Allie about her mom."

"I don't know. I don't think Madison's that friendly with Allie these days."

"Oh? How come?"

"I don't know for sure."

"Maybe you could ask Madison about her? They could still be friends, just maybe not good ones. And, if they are still friendly, maybe Madison could invite Allie over."

"I don't know."

"Could you just ask Madison about Allie and her mom? I'm worried about Arianna."

"You could always reach out to her."

"I already did. I even suggested we grab a coffee or a drink. But she blew me off."

"I'll think about it."

They finished their meal, and the server asked if they'd like dessert.

"I'm full," said Percy. "But you go ahead."

"I'm pretty full too," said Hugh. "Though, would you mind if I got a coffee?"

"Go ahead."

Hugh ordered a cappuccino, and Percy told the server to make it two.

CHAPTER 17

Hugh asked for the check when they had finished their cappuccinos. Percy went to retrieve her wallet, but Hugh said brunch was on him. After a bit of back-and-forth, Percy gave in, but she insisted that the next time, she would pay.

Hugh smiled.

"So that means there'll be a next time."

"Maybe," she said, but she was smiling too.

They listened to music on the drive home.

"Thanks for brunch," Percy said as they sat parked in her driveway.

"My pleasure," said Hugh. "So, I realize this is a bit forward of me, but are you free for dinner this week?"

Percy didn't speak at first. She was too stunned.

"I… uh…"

"If you're busy or don't want to…"

"Let me check with my daughter and get back to you."

"That's fine. You can send me a text."

"In the meantime, will you ask Madison about Allie and Arianna Cardinale?"

"I will, but I don't expect she'll have much to say."

They sat looking at each other for several seconds. Then Percy said she should go.

She got out of Hugh's SUV and walked to her door. When she got there, she stopped and turned around. Hugh was still there. She smiled at him and waved. He waved back and then slowly backed out.

Percy had noticed that Lucy's car wasn't in the driveway. She must still be at Rachel's. Percy was relieved. She didn't want Lucy grilling her about her date. Of course, that was precisely what Lucy did when she got home later.

"So, did you have fun?" Lucy asked her mother.

"I don't know about *fun*, but we had a nice time. We sat outside in the garden, and the food was very good."

"What did you have?"

Percy told her.

"Are you going to go out with him again?"

"He asked if I was free for dinner this week."

"What did you tell him?"

"That I needed to check with you first."

Lucy rolled her eyes.

"What?"

"You don't need to check with me. Go, have fun. Have dinner with the guy. He seems great."

"You met him for all of thirty seconds, and you could tell that he was a great guy."

"I could."

Percy was skeptical, but she didn't say anything.

"So, you'll tell him you're free?"

"What about us? I've barely seen you the last six months. And you're going to be away in Boston next weekend."

"You'll see plenty of me this summer. Besides, it's just dinner. It's not like he's invited you to go away with him. If you like, you could invite him over here for dinner."

"So you can grill him?"

"I won't grill him. I just want to ask him a few questions."

"What kinds of questions?"

"You know, the usual stuff. Like what he does for a living, what he likes to do when he's not working, what his intentions are regarding my mother."

Percy gave her daughter a stern look.

"I told you, he's an author. And if you want to learn more about him, you can visit his website."

"Not the same. And I want to see his face when I ask him about you."

"Which is why I am not inviting him over for dinner anytime soon."

"Fine. Just promise me you'll go out with him."

"Why do you care so much?"

"I just want you to be happy."

"I am happy. I have you, and Minnie, and Bonnie and Carlo, and a job I enjoy…"

Lucy was making a face.

"What?"

"I just don't want you to be lonely."

"I'm not lonely, Lucy. I just told you…"

"Yeah, yeah, yeah. So, did you hear back from Ed?"

"Not yet." Percy had checked her phone just before Lucy got home. Still no word from him. "And I'm starting to worry."

"He's probably just busy."

"That's what Hugh said."

"Hey, I need to get ready."

"Ready? Where are you going? You just got home."

"I thought I told you. I'm going with some friends to see a movie in Kenwick."

"Will you be home for dinner?"

"Don't count on it."

Percy looked disappointed.

"I can cancel if you want me to. I just thought that since we spent all day together yesterday…"

"No, you should go hang out with your friends. Will you be home for dinner tomorrow?"

"I was planning on it. Unless you want to have dinner with Hugh."

"Let's make it just us tomorrow. I'll go out with Hugh another night. Now go, have fun."

Lucy gave her mother a kiss on the cheek.

"You're the best," she said. Then she ran upstairs.

Percy still hadn't heard from Ed by the time she left for work Monday morning. So she sent him another text. If she hadn't heard from him by lunchtime, she would call him.

"What's with the long face?" Bonnie asked Percy in the staff room. "Is Lucy okay?"

"She's fine. Though I've barely seen her since she got home."

"I thought you two were going to Beauport Saturday."

"We did."

"And? Did she like the house?"

"She did, but she made me realize I'd perhaps been too hasty in putting in an offer."

"Oh?"

"She pointed out that I would probably never use the place, unless I planned on retiring soon, which I don't."

"You could always rent it out."

"That's what Lucy said. But I don't think I'm cut out to be a landlord."

"You could always hire someone to manage the place for you."

"I suppose. In any case, I still haven't heard back from Ed, which is odd. Do you think something could have happened to him?"

"He's probably just busy, or away, or lost his phone. I'm sure you'll hear from him today."

"That's what Hugh said."

"And how is Mr. Darcy?"

"Fine."

"Just fine? You didn't enjoy your brunch with him?"

"Brunch was very nice."

"Where did he take you?"

Percy told her.

"Harry's been wanting to go there. So, you going to go out with him again?"

"He asked if I was free for dinner this week."

"I hope you told him yes."

"I told him I needed to check with Lucy."

Bonnie rolled her eyes.

"What?" said Percy.

"You're a grown woman, Percy. You don't need to check with your daughter when a man asks you out on a date."

"That's what Lucy said."

"Good girl."

"I was just being sensitive. I didn't want Lucy to think I was throwing her over for some guy I just met."

"I doubt she would think that."

"The library is about to open, everyone," Carmen announced.

"I'll catch you later," Bonnie told Percy.

Percy hurried to the staff room when it was time for her lunch break. There was a voicemail from an unfamiliar number. Percy called and listened to the message. It was left by a woman. She said she was calling from Beauport Realty to inform her that Ed was dealing with a personal matter and was unavailable, but he wanted to let Percy know that the sellers had gone with another offer.

Percy felt a combination of relief and annoyance. Why hadn't Ed called or texted her the news himself? But at least she wasn't on the hook for the house. Though... the house had been exactly the type of place that she and Jim had looked for. Would she be able to find another just like it when she was ready to retire?

She sighed and was putting her phone away when she heard Bonnie.

"Did you not hear me?"

"Sorry, I was lost in thought. I just got a strange voicemail, supposedly from Ed Mankiewicz's office. Some woman called to let me know that Ed was dealing with a personal matter and that I didn't get the house."

"You think this woman was scamming you?"

"I don't know."

"You should call Ed, verify that the call was legit."

"Now?"

"Why not?"

Percy looked around. It was just the two of them in the staff room. Percy entered Ed's number, but the call went straight to voicemail, and his mailbox was full. She made a face.

"What's up?"

The call went straight to voicemail, and his mailbox is full.

"Try his office."

Percy entered the number for Beauport Realty and waited as the phone rang. She was expecting the call to go to voicemail when a woman answered.

"Beauport Realty."

The voice sounded familiar.

"Hi there. Is Ed Mankiewicz available?"

"He's not."

"Do you know when he will be?"

"Sorry. Can you hold a minute?"

Before Percy could reply, she was put on hold. She frowned.

"What's going on?" Bonnie loudly whispered.

"I was put on hold."

Percy was about to hang up when the woman came back. "You still there?" she said.

"I am. This is Percy Rollins. I'm a client of Ed's and…"

"Did you get my message about the house?"

That's why her voice sounded familiar. And Percy was pretty sure it was the rude woman who sat at the front desk.

"Is Ed all right?"

"I have no idea. I wasn't here on Sunday, and then he left a message this morning saying he was dealing with a personal matter and wouldn't be in and to let you know that the sellers had taken another offer."

"Do you know where he is? I called his cell phone, but it went to voicemail, and his mailbox is full."

"Sorry. Hey, I need to get this."

Percy was about to say something, but the woman had ended the call.

"Unbelievable!" said Percy.

"What's up?"

"That was Ed's assistant or receptionist or whatever she is. She said Ed's dealing with a personal matter and then hung up on me."

"Well, at least you verified that it wasn't a crank call."

"I guess. But where did Ed go? Doesn't it seem weird that he disappeared right after Lucy and I saw him arguing with Dr. Richardson?"

"Hold up. You saw him arguing with Dr. Richardson?"

"Sorry. I thought I mentioned it. Lucy and I saw them when we were in Beauport."

"And that didn't strike you as odd?"

"A little. But they both have places there and know each other."

"Any idea what they were arguing about?"

"Sadly, no. We were too far away to hear them."

"Did you get back to Hugh about dinner?"

"Not yet."

"Text him."

"I'll text him later."

Bonnie gave her a look.

"What?"

"Text him now."

"I don't want to seem too eager."

Bonnie sighed.

"I doubt he'll think that, especially as he asked you out before your brunch date had ended."

"You just want to make sure I don't wimp out."

"Maybe."

"Fine. If it will make you happy, I'll text him now."

Bonnie waited, and Percy sighed and started typing.

"There," she said, when she had finished.

"Did you really text him, or did you just pretend?"

"Do you want to see my phone?"

Bonnie thought about it for a few seconds.

"Nah, I trust you."

"Gee, thanks. Did you have lunch?"

"I ate something earlier. I promised I'd help the newbie. Catch you later."

Bonnie left, and Percy retrieved her sandwich from the refrigerator. She was checking Facebook when she received a text from Hugh.

Let's have dinner Friday, he had written. (Percy had texted that she was free Tuesday, Thursday, or Friday.)

Friday it is, she wrote back.

Hugh responded with a smiley face. Then she saw that he was typing.

Does 7 work?

Seven is great. Where do you want to go?

You pick.

Percy thought. *Where should they go?*

Any allergies or sensitivities or dislikes? she asked him.

I like pretty much everything. Surprise me.

OK. I'll confirm Friday morning.

Hugh sent her a thumbs-up emoji.

While she was thinking about dinner, she sent Lucy a text.

Do you want me to pick up something for dinner tonight, or do you want to go out?

She didn't hear back from Lucy right away. She was probably hanging out with her friends. Percy returned to Facebook to review the latest batch of comments. There weren't as many as before, most people having moved on. But she still received a few every day.

There was a new comment left by a man named Adam Shapiro. It was a reply to a post asking group members if any of them had heard anything about Dr. Rob.

The police should talk to that woman who came to the Wellness Center looking for him just before he was killed, Adam Shapiro had written. *She was pretty upset.*

What woman? Percy wondered. Could it have been Arianna Cardinale? As the thought crossed her mind, she realized she had never approved the comment that woman had left about Arianna. Should she ask Adam if it could have been Arianna he saw at the Wellness Center?

She went to his Facebook page. He was a local chiropractor. She sent him a message, saying she was the moderator for the Dr. Rob group, and asked if he recognized the woman who had come looking for Dr. Rob at the Wellness Center and knew her name. Though if he had, wouldn't he have mentioned it in his comment? Well, too late now.

She waited a couple of minutes to see if he replied. He didn't. Should she post his comment anyway? She read it again and decided to approve it. Maybe someone else had seen the woman and knew who she was.

CHAPTER 18

Percy checked her phone for messages as soon as her shift ended. Lucy had gotten back to her. She would be making dinner that evening. Percy frowned. It wasn't that Lucy was a bad cook. It was just that Lucy wasn't a very neat cook, using lots of pots and pans and then leaving them for Percy to clean.

Percy wanted to reply that she would cook, or they could go out, but she stopped herself. She got the sense that Lucy wanted to do this as a way of showing her mother that she cared. So she gave Lucy's message a thumbs-up. Then she asked Lucy what she was making.

It's a surprise, Lucy wrote back.

Percy frowned a second time. She didn't like surprises.

But don't worry, Lucy texted. *I know what you like. And I promise to clean up after*, she added with a grinning emoji.

Percy shook her head and chuckled. Then she saw that she had a Facebook notification. She was about to open the app when two assistant librarians came into the staff room. Probably best to wait to check. She would be home soon.

On her way out, Percy saw Bonnie speaking with Carmen.

"Percy!" Carmen called. "Could you come here for a minute?"

Percy went over to the two women.

"I need someone to cover for Grace on Friday. She was

supposed to help Laura with Game Night this month, but something's come up and she can't be there." Laura was the Young Adult librarian who ran Game Night.

"And I'm busy," said Bonnie.

Carmen looked at Percy.

"Sorry, I'd like to help, but I have a date."

"With Mr. Darcy?" said Bonnie.

Percy nodded.

"Mr. Darcy?" said Carmen, looking confused. "You mean Jane Austen's Mr. Darcy? You have a date with a book?"

"Not *that* Mr. Darcy," said Bonnie. "The author, William Darcy, who writes those romantic thrillers."

"Oh!" said Carmen. "I thought he was married. He always dedicates his books to his wife."

"She died two years ago," said Percy.

"Oh," said Carmen. "I didn't realize. So you're going on a date with him? I didn't know that you knew him. Did you meet him through the library? Though it's been ages since he's given a talk here."

"Uh," said Percy.

"They have a mutual acquaintance," said Bonnie.

"Ah. Well, I'm glad to see you putting yourself out there again," said Carmen. "I'll see if Mary Beth is free."

"If she isn't, I could always cancel my date."

"Absolutely not," said her boss. "I'll find someone else."

"Hello?" called Percy.

"In the kitchen!" Lucy called back.

Percy sniffed.

"Mm, something smells good. What are you making?"

"Summer lasagna."

"Summer lasagna?"

"It's lighter than a regular lasagna and made with lots of fresh roasted veggies."

"Sounds great."

Percy looked over at the sink. It was empty.

"I told you I'd clean up," said Lucy. "So, when do you want to eat? The lasagna's ready to go whenever. I just need to stick it in the oven."

It was nearly six o'clock.

"Is seven good?"

"That's fine."

"Okay. I'll see you at seven. I have some stuff I need to do in my office."

"Did you text Hugh about dinner?"

"I did."

"And?"

"I'm seeing him Friday."

Lucy grinned.

Before Lucy could ask her another question, Percy headed upstairs.

The first thing she did was check Facebook. There were a couple of new comments to approve, but no one had replied to Adam Shapiro's comment, and he hadn't gotten back to her. Percy frowned. So was Adam the only one who had witnessed a woman arguing with Dr. Rob at the Wellness Center? What about Carol?

She sent Adam another message, asking if he could describe the woman he had seen at the Wellness Center and when he had seen her there. Percy hoped he would reply. But if he didn't, she knew where he worked and would write to him there.

Percy took a bite of her lasagna and told Lucy it was delicious.

"I'm so glad you like it!" she said.

"Where did you get the recipe?" Percy asked her.

"This cooking blog I follow. It's all about healthy eating. So, where are you and Hugh going for dinner Friday?"

"I don't know. Any suggestions?"

"Hmm. Let me think."

"Not Annie's. I'm having dinner there with Carlo and Bonnie on Wednesday."

"You still doing that?"

"I am."

"Though you see Bonnie at the library."

"I know. But it's not like we have a lot of time to chat at work. And Carlo has his shop. And he's been busy. We're not like you young people who can work anywhere and have unlimited time off. Besides, it gets me out of the house. And that's a good thing, right?"

"You don't have to get all defensive."

"I didn't think I was being defensive."

Lucy gave her mother a look.

"So, how are Bonnie and Carlo?"

"Good. Bonnie's still seeing Harry, and I think it's getting serious."

"You like him?"

"He seems nice enough."

"Now there's a ringing endorsement."

"It doesn't matter what I think. It's what Bonnie thinks of him that matters."

"Uh-huh."

"What does that mean?"

"Don't you care about who your best friend dates?"

"Of course I do. And, as I said, Harry seems perfectly nice. He's clearly smitten with Bonnie. He even took her to meet his daughter."

"How did that go?"

"Well. Bonnie said they got along great."

"So, you think she'll marry him?"

"I don't know about that. She was married to Marv for over twenty years. And I don't think she's in a rush to get married again."

"What about Carlo? Is he seeing anyone?"

"Not that I'm aware of. I think he's been too busy to be in a relationship."

"That's a shame. He's such a nice man."

"He is."

They ate in silence for a couple of minutes, then Percy asked her daughter how things were going with Jamie.

"Good!"

"You still planning on going to Boston this weekend?"

"I am. Why?"

"Just checking."

They were quiet again as they ate more lasagna.

"You done?" Lucy asked her mother, seeing her empty plate.

"I am," said Percy.

Lucy picked up their plates and took them to the sink.

"I can do the washing up," said Percy.

"Nope. I got this. You just sit there."

Percy watched as her daughter rinsed off their plates and utensils and put them in the dishwasher.

"Okay if I put the rest of the lasagna in the fridge? I'll cover it with some foil."

"That's fine."

"And I made dessert."

"Wow. You've been busy."

"It's just oatmeal raisin cookies. They're easy. And I know how you like them."

Now Percy was suspicious. Dinner *and* oatmeal raisin cookies? Lucy definitely wanted something.

"What do you want?"

Lucy stopped what she was doing and looked at her mother.

"What do you mean?"

"You made me dinner *and* oatmeal raisin cookies. And you did the dishes. You must want something."

"Nope. I just felt like cooking."

Percy didn't look convinced.

"Fine. But you promise you won't get mad?"

Now Percy was worried.

"What did you do, Lucy?"

"It's nothing really bad. It's just a little thing, really." Percy waited. "You probably didn't even notice."

"What did you do, Lucy?" Percy asked again.

"I dinged the garage door."

"You dinged the garage door?"

"On the inside. I bet you didn't even notice."

Percy immediately got up and went into the garage. Then she saw it.

"That door opens so slowly, and I guess I wasn't looking, and…"

Percy went over to take a closer look. It didn't look too bad.

"I'll pay to have it fixed," said Lucy. "I'm really sorry."

Percy sighed.

"It's okay, Lucy. These things happen. Just next time, be more careful."

Lucy stared at her mother.

"Who are you, and what have you done with my mother?"

"What do you mean?"

"The old Percy would have been flipping out."

"I've been in therapy. I don't flip out over little things anymore. At least I try not to."

"Wow. That Dr. Rob really was a miracle worker. So, are you going to see this new therapist?"

"I have an appointment to see her this Wednesday."

"Jeremy heard she's hot."

"Who told him that?"

Lucy shrugged.

"Hey, I almost forgot, did you hear anything about the house?"

"I did. I didn't get it."

"Oh. Sorry. I know how much you liked it."

"I did. But you were right about it. I probably wouldn't have used it."

"Shall we go back in and have some oatmeal raisin cookies?"

"Sure."

Lucy went over to the freezer.

"You want some vanilla ice cream to go with?"

"You must have been feeling very guilty," said Percy, smothering a smile.

"I was. So yes or no to the ice cream?"

"Definitely yes, though just a small scoop."

"Coming right up!"

When they were done with their cookies and ice cream, Percy went upstairs to her office. She and Lucy would watch an episode of *Love Island*, the UK version—one of their mother-daughter guilty pleasures—at eight-thirty.

Percy was happy to see that Adam Shapiro had replied to her message. He said he believed the woman's name was Arianna, as that's what Dr. Rob had called her. He didn't know her last name. And he had seen her at the Wellness Center maybe a week or two before Dr. Rob had been killed.

Could the woman be Arianna Cardinale? It had to be. How many Ariannas were there in Stonebridge? Percy thanked him and then asked if he had heard what Arianna had said to Dr. Rob and if he had spoken to the police. She sent the message and sat back. She thought about texting Hugh, to tell him what Adam had said and to see if he had asked Madison about Allie, but she decided to wait.

Instead, she read through the posts and comments in the Dr. Rob group. Several people had wondered if the police were close to arresting anyone. Were they? Percy hadn't heard anything. Should she reach out to Detective Russo and ask him? However, she doubted he would reveal anything to her. Should she tell him about Arianna? But she didn't want to falsely incriminate anyone.

Percy wished she knew someone in the Stonebridge Police Department whom she could ask about the case. She knew lots of people in town, mainly because of the library and Lucy, but she wasn't close friends with anyone outside of the people she worked with and Carlo.

Percy was an introvert by nature, and between Jim and Lucy and work, she hadn't felt the need or had the time to make lots of friends.

She was lost in thought when she heard her daughter calling her.

"Mom? You coming down to watch *Love Island*?"

"I'll be right there!" Percy called back.

CHAPTER 19

Percy's alarm went off at six-thirty. She got out of bed, went to the bathroom, and then put on her running clothes. Then she quietly went downstairs. Minnie appeared in the kitchen just as Percy was about to leave. She meowed at Percy, which was Percy's cue to feed and water her.

Percy thought about making a pot of coffee while Minnie drank from the kitchen faucet, but she decided to wait until she got back from her run. Instead, she did her stretches. Then she was off.

Percy did a longer run as she had a lot on her mind. Lucy was still asleep when she got back. She would let her sleep a little longer. After all, she didn't start work until the following Tuesday.

She set the coffee machine brewing, then checked her phone. Adam hadn't replied to her latest message. And still no one had replied to his comment. In fact, no one had left a comment since last night.

Percy clicked on the Stonebridge group and did a search for *Dr. Rob*. But no one there had mentioned him or the murder for several days. Had people lost interest? She wondered if Hugh had spoken with Madison. She was going to wait to see if he texted her, but she was feeling antsy. So she sent him a text instead, telling him what Adam Shapiro had said.

A few seconds later, her phone rang. It was Hugh.

"Is he sure it was Arianna Cardinale he saw?" he asked her. "And did he hear what they said?"

"He didn't know the woman's last name, but how many Ariannas could there be in Stonebridge? And I asked him if he had heard what Arianna said to Dr. Rob, but he hasn't gotten back to me. What about you? Did you ask Madison about Allie?"

"I did."

"And?"

"She said they're not really friends anymore."

"Did she say why?"

"She said they didn't have any classes together and just kind of drifted apart."

"So no chance of a playdate then, I guess."

"I asked if she wanted to have Allie over sometime, for old times' sake, and she got suspicious."

"Suspicious?"

"She wanted to know why I was suddenly so interested in Allie and if it had something to do with her mom."

"What made her say that?"

"Madison heard some of her friends whispering about Arianna, saying all of the dads wanted to date her."

"What did you tell her?"

"I told her I wasn't interested in dating Allie's mother. I just wanted to ask her some questions for a book I'm working on. But I don't think she believed me."

"So, is Madison not into you dating?" Though he had been on a date when Percy had run into him at the Italian restaurant.

"She's okay with me dating. She just doesn't want me going out with the mother of anyone she knows."

"I can understand that. So, how do we find out what was going on between Dr. Rob and Arianna?"

"Let me think on it."

"Okay. Though… you just said you told Madison you

wanted to speak with Arianna for a book you were working on. You could use that as an excuse to reach out to her."

"I suppose."

"Hey, I need to get ready for work."

"Okay. Oh, by the way, I made an appointment to meet with that new therapist."

"Dr. Yates?"

"Unless they've hired another one."

"When are you meeting with her?"

"Tomorrow at noon."

"I'm seeing her at one."

"We can compare notes over dinner on Friday. You pick a place?"

"Not yet."

Percy thought she heard someone calling Hugh. Probably his daughter.

"I've got to go," he said. "Have a good day."

"You too," said Percy.

Percy kept thinking about Arianna on her walk to work. As she passed the Wellness Center, she decided she would ask Carol about her when she saw her tomorrow. Or maybe she should invite Carol out for a coffee or a drink, so they could talk in private. She could say it was to discuss the books she had recommended.

She entered the library and said good morning to Mary Beth.

"Do you need help setting up for Murder by the Book?" Mary Beth asked her. Miguel had a dentist appointment and wouldn't be in until later.

Percy blinked. She had totally forgotten about the Murder by the Book meeting. That was so unlike her. Fortunately, she had read the book weeks ago and had taken copious notes, which she could print out from the computer in the staff room.

"That would be great," Percy replied.

They headed downstairs and started to arrange the chairs for the book club meeting.

"Bruce said you asked him about Ed Mankiewicz."

"I did," said Percy.

"And that he told you about Ed's side hustle."

"Did you know Ed?" Percy asked her.

"Not well. But I was friendly with his wife, Josie."

"What was she like?"

"Unhappy."

"Unhappy? Unhappy how?"

"I don't know if it had to do with Ed, being a mom to two rambunctious boys, Stonebridge, or some combination of the three, but she was definitely not happy when she lived here. Except when she saw Dr. Rob."

"Was she a patient of his?"

"I don't know if she was a patient, per se."

"What does that mean?"

Mary Beth gave her a look.

"You think she was sleeping with him?"

"I don't know for sure. I just know that she had a big smile on her face whenever she saw him or talked about him."

"What did she say about him?"

"That she wouldn't last here without him. That he always made her feel better about herself."

"So maybe she was seeing him professionally. That sounds like something a patient would say."

"Maybe. But you should have seen the way she looked when she talked about him. They may not have been having an affair, but she definitely had the hots for him. That's probably why Ed had them move to Beauport."

"Did Josie ever come back to Stonebridge after they moved?"

"I saw her here a couple of times."

"Recently?"

Before Mary Beth could answer, Carmen came in.

"You're needed upstairs at the circulation desk, Mary Beth."

"Thanks for your help," Percy said to her. "I can handle the rest of the chairs."

Mary Beth left, and Percy finished setting up the room. Then she went to the staff room to put away her bag and print out her notes. She was reading them over when Victor, one of the volunteers, came in.

"Morning, Percy."

"Morning, Victor. You going to be at book club?"

"Wouldn't miss it."

"What did you think of the book?"

"I enjoyed it. Though I was bothered by the end. The author was a bit sloppy, if you ask me. What did you think?"

"I felt the same way."

"You ever think of writing a murder mystery?"

"Me?" Percy shook her head. "I'm not a writer."

"But you've read plenty of murder mysteries, and you ask good questions. I bet you could write one better than some of the folks we've read."

"There's a big difference between being a reader and a writer."

"I suppose. Anyway, I'll see you at book club."

"See you then."

The Murder by the Book Club met on the third Tuesday of the month at noon. Patrons were allowed to bring food, as long as they cleaned up after themselves. Percy had created the club five years ago. And it had become so popular that people now had to sign up in advance, so they'd know how many seats to put out or if they needed a larger room.

In addition to the dozen or so regulars who showed up at every meeting, there were usually a half dozen or so other people who showed up, depending on the book and the weather. Today was no exception, with Percy seeing several new faces.

Percy greeted everyone and had all of the new people write their names on place cards. (All of the regulars and semi-regulars already had place cards.) When it looked like everyone was there, she closed the door and began the meeting.

"So," she said. "Did everyone read the book?" She always asked this as she knew there were usually one or two people who hadn't but still liked going to book club.

Nearly every hand went up.

"I didn't have time to read the whole thing, so I skipped to the end," said Dolores, one of the regulars. This was not the first time Dolores had skipped to the end of a book.

Percy looked over at the other person who hadn't raised a hand. She was new. According to her place card, her name was Nancy.

"Will you be okay if we discuss the end of the book, Nancy?"

"That's fine," she said. "I wasn't here about the book anyway."

"You do know that this is a book club, yes?"

"So you're not going to discuss that man who got murdered?"

"I, uh…" said Percy, seeing everyone looking at her.

"Weren't you there?" said Sam, another regular.

"I, uh…" said Percy again, feeling all eyes on her.

"Who do you think did it?" asked Agnes, another regular.

"I don't know," said Percy.

"Come on. You must have some idea," said Sam. "Did you see anyone fleeing the scene?"

"I didn't," said Percy.

"I bet it was a patient," said Dolores.

"I bet it was a woman," said Marcia, another regular.

"Have the police arrested anyone?" asked John, another one of the regular attendees. "I haven't heard anything." He turned to another regular, Nate. "Isn't your son a police officer here in town? What's he got to say?"

"Mike doesn't discuss cases with me."

"Did you ask him about it?"

Nate gave John a look that said, *What do you think?*

"And he didn't say anything? They must have some suspects."

Now everyone was looking at Nate.

"All I know," Nate said, "is that they're looking at several people."

"I bet it was a patient," Dolores said again.

"What makes you say that?" Percy asked her.

"Who else would do something crazy like that?"

"Not everyone who sees a therapist is crazy," Percy said. "In fact, most people who seek therapy know that they have a problem and are smart to seek help, which is the opposite of crazy."

Dolores harrumphed.

"Which is why I think it must have been a jilted lover," said Marcia. "That Dr. Rob was a very good-looking man. I bet he broke a lot of hearts."

Percy immediately thought of Arianna Cardinale.

"Are we going to discuss the book?" said Polly, another one of the regulars. "That's supposedly why we're all here."

"Good point," said Percy. "Raise your hand if you enjoyed the book," she asked the group. A little over half of the hands went up. "Okay," said Percy. "Why don't we go around the room, and you can each briefly say why you liked or didn't like this month's book. Then I have some specific questions."

The book club ended at one. Percy said goodbye to everyone and that she hoped to see them again next month. Nearly everyone had left except for one of the newbies, a woman named Vicky, who Percy thought was probably around her age, somewhere in her forties.

"I don't know if you recognize me," said Vicky, who had been quiet during the meeting. "I'm a member of the Dr. Rob Facebook group."

"Oh!" said Percy. "Sorry, I didn't."

"That's all right."

Percy waited for Vicky to go on. When she didn't, Percy asked if she had a question about the book they had just read or the next one.

"It has to do with Dr. Rob," said Vicky.

"What about Dr. Rob?"

"I left a comment in your Facebook group, but I didn't see it. Did you delete it?"

"What was the comment?"

"It was about Arianna Cardinale."

Percy looked at Vicky, and it clicked. Vicky was the one who had left the comment suggesting the police talk to Arianna.

"I wasn't sure if I should post it, and then I forgot about it."

"Oh," said Vicky.

"Why do you think the police should talk to Arianna?"

Vicky hesitated.

"Was she a patient of Dr. Rob's?"

"No, she dated him. And when he dumped her, Arianna went a little crazy."

"Crazy how?"

"She went to his office and confronted him."

So was Arianna the woman Adam Shapiro had seen with Dr. Rob at the Wellness Center?

"And you know this how?"

"She told me she was going to see him."

"Are you friends with her?"

"I am. Or was. She stopped talking to me after I told her she was acting crazy."

"Do you know how long they dated?"

"Not that long. Maybe a few months."

"How did they meet?"

"At some event. Arianna said they were instantly attracted to each other and that the sex was amazing. And then just when she thought things were getting serious, he dumped her."

"And she went to the Wellness Center to confront him?"

Vicky nodded.

"She made an appointment to see him, so he had to see her. I told her she should forget about him. That there were plenty of other guys who would love to date her. But she was stuck on Dr. Rob. Said he'd change his mind when she told him."

"Told him what?"

"I don't know. But she was convinced she could get him back."

"Why are you telling me this?" Percy asked her.

"Because I think she might have killed him."

Percy stared at her.

"You think Arianna shot Dr. Rob?"

"I think she could have. I'd never seen her act this way before about a guy."

"Does she even own a gun?"

"She does."

"Does she know how to use it?"

"She took some course. Arianna doesn't have a great relationship with her ex. It was a nasty divorce, and she was paranoid about him trying to take Allie away from her. She thought a gun would keep them safe."

"Have you spoken to the police, told them about Arianna?"

"No. I didn't want Arianna thinking I snitched on her, even though she dumped me. And I worry about what would happen to Allie if her mom were arrested for murder. I don't think Arianna's ex is a good man."

Yet Vicky had left that comment in the Facebook group, suggesting that the police talk to Arianna. Though it sounded like Vicky now regretted it.

"But if you really believe Arianna shot Dr. Rob…"

Vicky's smartwatch was flashing. She looked down at it and told Percy she needed to go.

"Will I see you in book club next month?" Percy asked her.

"I don't know. Maybe."

Percy watched Vicky leave. Would she tell Detective Russo about Arianna? Percy didn't think so. Should *she* say something to the detective? No. It wasn't her story to tell.

Percy sighed and then looked around the room. She saw a couple of napkins and an empty cup. She picked them up and threw them away. Then she took one more look around the room, turned off the lights, and left.

CHAPTER 20

"So, how was Murder by the Book Club?" Bonnie asked Percy.

"Interesting."

"Interesting how?"

"There was a woman who came, Nancy, who wanted to discuss Dr. Rob's murder, and things kind of spiraled from there."

"Did you learn anything?"

"Sort of. Nate, one of the regulars, has a son, Mike, who works in the police department. Mike wouldn't discuss the case with his dad, but he told him they had several people they were looking at."

"Intriguing," said Bonnie. "I wonder who they're looking at."

"I don't know, but after the book group ended, another newbie, a woman named Vicky who's in the Dr. Rob Facebook group, came up to me. It turns out she's friends with Arianna Cardinale, or was until recently. And according to Vicky, Arianna was obsessed with Dr. Rob."

"Obsessed?"

"She said Arianna had dated Dr. Rob. And when he dumped her, she went a bit crazy."

"Crazy how?"

"She confronted him at the Wellness Center, which jibes with a comment I received about a woman coming to the Wellness Center and attacking Dr. Rob."

"Arianna attacked him?"

"Not physically. At least I don't think so. She confronted him verbally."

"And why was Vicky telling you this?"

"She thinks Arianna might have killed him."

"Has she spoken to the police?"

"Not yet. I think that's why she came to see me. She wanted advice."

"I hope you told her to contact that detective."

"I did, but I'm not sure she will."

"Why not?"

"She's concerned about Arianna's daughter. Apparently, Arianna's ex isn't a nice man. And she didn't want Allie growing up without a mother."

"Mm. Well, for her daughter's sake, I hope Arianna didn't do it. But if she didn't kill him, who did?"

"It's possible Dr. Rob's brother did."

Bonnie stared at her friend.

"You think his brother shot him? I find that hard to believe."

"I know. But hear me out. We know that Ed didn't get along with Dr. Rob, that their relationship was strained."

"My relationship with my brother is strained, too, but I would never shoot him. Though there was that one time…"

Percy made a face.

"As I was saying, it sounds like they didn't get along. And then I heard a rumor that Dr. Rob may have been sleeping with Ed's wife when they lived here."

Bonnie whistled, which caused several patrons and a couple of librarians to look their way.

"Did Ed know?"

"My source seemed to think so—and that that's why they moved to Beauport."

"When did they move?"

"I'm not sure. It was a while ago."

"But if the affair ended a while ago, assuming there was an affair, why would Ed shoot his brother now?"

"Maybe the affair hadn't ended."

"But didn't you say that Ed said that Dr. Rob was the love-'em-and-leave-'em type?"

Bonnie had a point.

"There could be another reason."

"Maybe Dr. Richardson knows something."

Percy looked thoughtful. Dr. Richardson did know both brothers. Maybe she did know something. But would she tell Percy if she did? Doubtful.

"What's going on in that head of yours?" Bonnie asked her.

"I was just thinking about Dr. Richardson. She knew both Dr. Rob and Ed and might know if there was an issue."

"Exactly!" said Bonnie.

"But I doubt she'd say anything to me."

"Can't hurt to ask."

"I suppose. But I'm not going to get my hopes up."

"Well, I'm having dinner with Elyse tonight. I'll pick her brain about Dr. Rob. You know how she collects gossip. And she was a patient of Dr. Rob's. Maybe she knows something."

"Okay. Let me know if she has anything interesting to say."

"Oh, I will. I'll fill you and Carlo in at dinner tomorrow."

Carlo. That reminded Percy: Had Dr. Yates picked up her artwork? Carlo hadn't texted her. She wanted to text him and ask, but she didn't have the time now. Maybe she would stop by his shop after work.

"What were you just thinking about?" asked Bonnie.

"Carlo. He was supposed to text me when Dr. Yates picked up her artwork."

"He's probably just busy."

"Probably."

They heard someone clearing her throat. It was Carmen.

"We were just discussing today's Murder by the Book meeting," said Percy. "Bonnie asked me how it went." *There. That wasn't a lie.*

"How did it go?" asked Carmen.

"Good. We had several new people today. And we had a very good discussion."

"Excellent. By the way, I found someone to cover for Grace on Friday."

"Who did you get?" asked Percy.

"Victor said he'd do it."

"Victor?" said Percy.

"He's a big card player; loves poker, gin, bridge, you name it."

"I think I knew that. I just hope he'll be okay. Game night can get pretty rowdy."

"Laura will be there. So he should be fine."

"Please," said Bonnie. "Have you seen Victor playing gin with his buddies? Talk about rowdy. Those guys could teach basketball players about trash talking."

Carmen and Percy smiled.

At five-thirty, Percy got her things and checked her phone. Adam had written her back. He said that Arianna and Dr. Rob weren't so much arguing as Arianna was shouting at Dr. Rob, saying something like, *You can't treat me like that.*

I forget what Dr. Rob said, he continued. *But I'm pretty sure he told her to calm down, that they could talk about things privately another time. But she was really upset. And I remember her saying something like, "You'll regret this," as he escorted her out of the Wellness Center.*

Percy re-read his message. Maybe Arianna did shoot Dr. Rob. She thought about texting Hugh, but she wanted to get to the frame shop before it closed. So she put her phone away and hurried out of the library.

She arrived at the frame shop a few minutes later and looked in the window. She didn't see Carlo, but Gianna was there. She went inside and said hello to her.

"Hi, Percy. Can I help you?"

"How's your grandmother?" Percy asked her.

"She's doing much better. Thanks."

"That's good. Is Carlo around?"

"He's meeting with a client."

"In his office?"

"No, at their place."

"Must be an important client." Carlo didn't usually make house calls.

"It is."

"Can you tell me who it is?"

"I've been sworn to secrecy."

Now Percy's curiosity was piqued.

"Is it a celebrity?" Percy knew that several famous people lived in Stonebridge.

"My lips are sealed."

"Hmm. Well, speaking of clients, do you happen to know if Miranda Yates picked up her artwork?"

"Why do you ask?"

"Carlo was supposed to tell me if she stopped by, but I didn't hear from him."

"He's been super busy."

"Do you know if she picked up her pieces?"

Gianna hesitated.

"I'm not supposed to discuss clients."

"I just want to know if she picked up her stuff."

Percy could see Gianna struggling with whether or not to say anything.

"She picked up her artwork this weekend."

"Oh," said Percy, clearly disappointed.

"Like I said, we've been super busy. I'm sure Carlo…"

"It's okay, Gianna. Thanks for letting me know."

"Should I tell Carlo you stopped by?"

"Don't bother. I'll see him tomorrow."

"How was dinner with Elyse?" Percy asked Bonnie the next morning.

"Very enlightening."

"Oh? Do tell."

"I'll fill you and Carlo in at dinner."

"Fine," said Percy. Though she wanted to know now.

"You seeing the new therapist later?"

"I am."

"Let me know how it goes. You going to ask her about Dr. Rob?"

"I was thinking about it. I know they went to graduate school together and that Dr. Rob went with her to have her artwork framed."

"Do you think they were shtupping?"

"Shtupping?"

"You know, sleeping together."

"No idea. And I can't exactly ask her that, can I?"

"I would."

Percy shook her head.

"What?"

"I need to go," said Percy, seeing Carmen hovering in the background. "We can talk over dinner."

Percy headed to the Wellness Center a little before one. When she got there, she saw Hugh at the front desk, chatting with Carol. Percy wondered what they were talking about.

She went over to them, but as soon as they saw her, they stopped talking.

"Hi. What were you two chatting about?"

"I was just asking Carol some questions."

"About?" said Percy.

Carol and Hugh exchanged a look, and Hugh said he should be going.

"I'll see you Friday," he told Percy.

Percy watched him leave. Had they been talking about her?

"Dr. Yates is on a call," Carol informed her. "But she shouldn't be long."

"That's okay," said Percy. "Actually, I had a question for you." Carol waited for her to go on. "Do you recall a woman coming here and assaulting Dr. Rob not long before he was killed?"

Percy studied Carol's face as she waited for an answer. Carol looked conflicted.

"I know you're not supposed to talk about patients, but I don't think she was one."

Carol still didn't speak.

"A patient said he saw the whole thing."

Carol sighed.

"That poor woman."

Percy waited to see if Carol would say more.

"She was very upset. Dr. Rob tried to calm her down, but she wasn't having any of it."

"Do you know why she was so upset?"

"No," Carol replied. But Percy had a feeling Carol was lying.

Percy was about to ask her another question, but Dr. Yates had appeared.

"Persephone Rollins?"

"That's me," said Percy. "You must be Dr. Yates."

Dr. Yates smiled at her.

"Shall we go to my office?"

Percy followed her down the hall and was relieved that Dr. Yates wasn't using Dr. Rob's office.

"Please, have a seat," said Dr. Yates.

Percy sat down on a loveseat opposite the therapist.

"Thank you for meeting with me. I'm sure coming here must have been difficult for you after what happened."

Percy didn't know what to say, so she didn't say anything.

"I saw that you'd been a patient of Dr. Rob's for almost two years."

"That's right. I started seeing him after my husband Jim died."

"It was a heart attack, yes?"

Percy nodded.

"He was only forty-eight, and he didn't have a history of heart disease."

"That must have been very hard on you and your daughter."

"It was."

"And your daughter… Lucy, is it?" Percy nodded. "She's in college?"

"She is. She's going to be a senior."

"And you work as a librarian at the Stonebridge Public Library."

"That's right."

Percy didn't understand why Dr. Yates was asking her these questions when the answers were no doubt in Dr. Rob's notes. But she played along.

"Do you enjoy your job?"

"Very much. It's the perfect place for an introvert who loves to read and do research."

Dr. Yates smiled.

"I understand Dr. Rob was also treating you for obsessive-compulsive disorder."

"He was."

"And how was that going?"

"Good. I can't say he cured me, but I don't obsess about stuff as much as I used to."

Percy watched as Dr. Yates took notes.

She looked up when she was done.

"As you may have heard, I specialize in helping people with OCD."

"I read that. So, why did you leave Northwestern University's Feinberg School of Medicine to come here? You'd been there for years, and Stonebridge is a pretty far cry from Chicago."

"I see you've done your research."

"I am a librarian. Research is part of the job."

Dr. Yates smiled again.

"So, why did you leave?"

"I was looking for a change, and this seemed like a good opportunity."

"But to leave a prestigious university like Northwestern with all of those resources, and a city like Chicago, to come to little old Stonebridge to work at the Wellness Center. It seems like a step down."

Percy felt Dr. Yates studying her, deciding what to say.

"To be honest, Persephone…"

Percy cut her off.

"If you don't mind, I prefer to be called Percy."

Dr. Yates nodded and made a note in her little book.

"To be honest, Percy, I was dealing with some personal issues and felt I could use a fresh start. But I don't consider this a step down. I missed working one-on-one with patients. And I went to graduate school here in Connecticut."

"At Yale. With Dr. Rob and Dr. Richardson."

Dr. Yates nodded.

"Were the three of you close in graduate school?"

"Why do you want to know?"

"Just curious."

Dr. Yates looked like she was weighing what to say.

"We were in a study group together."

"Did you and Dr. Rob date?"

"We're not here to discuss my personal life, Percy."

"I heard he dated Dr. Richardson."

"Who told you that?"

"I'd rather not say. Is it true?" Though why would Ed lie?

"Why are you interested in Dr. Rob's personal life? Did you have feelings for him?"

Percy willed herself not to blush.

"He was my therapist."

"It's all right, Percy. Many patients, especially female ones, develop feelings for their therapists, especially if they're good-looking."

"I assure you, I never thought of Dr. Rob that way." Though that wasn't entirely true.

"Okay. Then why do you care about his personal life?"

"To be honest?" Dr. Yates nodded. "I'm trying to find out who killed him."

CHAPTER 21

It took a moment for Dr. Yates to speak after Percy's pronouncement.

"I understand that people react to grief in different ways, Percy. However, finding out who killed Dr. Rob is a matter for the police, not you."

"I understand that. But you can appreciate my need to know since I was here when it happened. Or right after."

The two women eyed each other without speaking for several seconds.

"Have you spoken with Detective Russo?" Dr. Yates asked Percy.

"I did, when he and Officer O'Brien were here. But I haven't heard from him since. And I haven't seen anything in the paper or heard anything."

"And you find that frustrating."

"I do. And while I understand murders aren't solved in a few days in real life, shouldn't we have heard something by now?"

"I understand your frustration, Percy. But as you said, these things take time. I can assure you, the Stonebridge police are doing everything they can to find out who killed him."

"Have you spoken with Detective Russo?"

"I have."

"And what did you think of him?"

"I found him competent."

"Just competent?"

"He knows what he's doing. And contrary to popular belief, we therapists don't analyze everyone we meet."

"Don't you? I would imagine it would be hard not to."

Dr. Yates didn't say anything.

"Did Detective Russo ask you about your relationship with Dr. Rob?"

"He did."

"And what did you tell him?"

"That we were colleagues."

"Nothing more?"

"What is it you want to know, Percy?"

"Were you and Dr. Rob ever in a relationship?"

"As I told you, Percy, we were colleagues."

"So you never dated him?"

"No."

Percy couldn't decide if Dr. Yates was telling the truth, but she decided to give her the benefit of the doubt. For now. Also, she realized she may have sounded a bit obsessed and didn't want Dr. Yates to think she had regressed.

"So there was no issue when he offered you a job at the Wellness Center."

"Dr. Richardson asked me to come here."

"Oh." Percy filed that away.

"But I want to remind you, Percy, we're not here to talk about me. We're here to talk about you. According to Dr. Rob's notes, you were making good progress dealing with your grief and your OCD. However…"

"I'm fine," Percy told her.

"I understand you feel that way, but…"

"Didn't you just say that Dr. Rob wrote that I was making good progress? Did he feel I still needed therapy?"

"He felt that therapy was helping you and assumed you would continue."

"With him. I doubt he knew he'd be shot and replaced with a stranger."

"So am I the issue, Percy?"

"No offense, Dr. Yates, but it took me a while to even try therapy. And it was only because of Dr. Rob that I stuck with it. If I met with you, it would be like starting over again."

"It wouldn't really be starting over. But I understand. Tell you what. You think about things and let me know if you'd like to continue, even on a limited basis. I've worked with many patients with OCD who thought they had it under control and, unfortunately, suffered a relapse. I'd like to work with you to prevent that."

"I appreciate that," said Percy. "As you said, I just need some time to think about things."

"Of course. I'm here if or when you need me."

"Thanks."

Percy realized this might be her last chance to ask Dr. Yates about Dr. Rob's murder. And while she didn't want Dr. Yates to think she was obsessing, she couldn't lose this opportunity.

"Could I ask you one more question?"

"Of course."

"Do you know if any of Dr. Rob's patients ever threatened him?"

Percy studied Dr. Yates's face. Her expression remained neutral.

"I'm afraid I can't share that information with you."

Interesting, thought Percy. *If no one had threatened Dr. Rob, why didn't Dr. Yates just say so? So, who had threatened him?*

Dr. Yates glanced down at her watch.

"I'm afraid our time is up, Ms. Rollins. Phone the office when you're ready to schedule another appointment."

Percy went over to the front desk.

"Would you like to schedule another appointment with Dr. Yates?" Carol asked her.

"Not right now. Though I did have another question for you." Carol waited. "Did you read the books I recommended?"

"I did! Thank you so much for recommending them! I particularly enjoyed *The Briar Club*."

"I'm so glad to hear it. You know, if you'd like to discuss it or the other books, we could meet for a coffee or a drink sometime."

"Really?"

"I wouldn't offer if I didn't mean it."

"That would be great. As I think I mentioned, I don't really have anyone to talk about books with."

"Well, I love talking about books." Which wasn't entirely true. "By any chance, are you free tomorrow after work?"

"Tomorrow?"

"If that's too soon or you're busy…"

"I just need to check with Joanna. That's my daughter. She and the baby are staying with me."

"I understand. Well, you have my number. You can send me a text later or tomorrow."

"I'll do that. Thanks, Percy. So, what did you think of Dr. Yates?"

"She seems nice but…"

"I know what you're going to say: She's not Dr. Rob. But you should give her a chance. Dr. Richardson thinks very highly of her. And she knows her stuff."

A woman hurried in.

"Sorry I'm late, Carol!"

"No worries, Mrs. Fincher. I'll let Dr. Yates know you're here."

Percy glanced over at the woman. She looked to be in her fifties. Was she a member of the Dr. Rob Facebook group? Percy didn't think so.

The woman saw Percy looking at her.

"Can I help you?"

"Sorry," said Percy. Then she quickly left.

"So, what's the new therapist like?" Bonnie asked Percy after they had ordered drinks.

"She's okay, but I don't know if I'll see her."

"Not feeling it?"

"I just don't think I need therapy right now."

Bonnie and Carlo exchanged a look.

"What? You think I do?"

"If you feel you're good…" said Bonnie.

"We left the door open."

"Good. So, did you ask her if she was sleeping with Dr. Rob?"

"I did not. Though I did ask her if they had ever been in a relationship."

"And, what did she say?"

"She said they were colleagues, nothing more."

"You believe her?"

"I'm giving her the benefit of the doubt. Though speaking of Dr. Yates, why didn't you text me when she came to pick up her artwork?" Percy asked Carlo.

"I was busy, Percy. It was crazy this weekend at the gallery. And you were away."

Percy couldn't argue.

"You must be happy to have Gianna back."

"I am, but she's only part-time."

"You could hire her full-time."

"I'm not sure she wants to work for me full-time, and I probably won't have much work for her in another month."

"So, who's this new client who had you going to their house the other day?"

"New client?"

"Gianna said she was sworn to secrecy."

Carlo rolled his eyes.

"Gianna likes drama."

"You have a new mystery client?" said Bonnie.

"Don't start," said Carlo.

"Come on, Carlo. You can tell us. Who is it?"

"I can't say."

"Why can't you?" Bonnie turned to Percy. "It must be someone famous or very wealthy—or both. Though you have to be well off to live in Stonebridge these days."

"That's not true," said Percy. "There are plenty of people here who aren't rich."

"Can we change the subject?" said Carlo. "I don't want to discuss work right now."

The server came over with their drinks, and Carlo took a healthy sip of his.

"Things going that well, eh?" said Bonnie.

"Just busy. I'll be happy when Father's Day and graduation season are over."

"And then what will you do?"

"Take a vacation."

"You, take a vacation?" said Bonnie. Carlo rarely took time off from his gallery.

"Speaking of vacation, what's the latest on the house?" Carlo asked Percy.

"She didn't tell you?" said Bonnie. "She didn't get it."

Carlo looked over at Percy.

"What happened?"

"Someone made a better offer."

"Sorry about that. I know how much you liked it."

"It's probably for the best," said Percy. "I'd probably have never used the place."

They were quiet for a minute.

"So, what did Elyse have to say about Dr. Rob?" Percy asked Bonnie.

"Well," Bonnie began. But they were interrupted by their server, asking if they were ready to order.

"Give us a few minutes," Percy told the young woman. "You were about to say," she said to Bonnie after the server left.

"Well, you know how Elyse loves to gossip. So it was easy to get her going."

"And?" said Percy.

"She knew all about Arianna Cardinale making a scene at the Wellness Center."

"How did she know about that?"

"She wouldn't say. But my money's on Carol. Pretty sure the two of them are friendly."

"Did she have anything else to say?"

Bonnie nodded her head as she took a sip of her drink. Percy waited.

"I asked her if she knew anything about Dr. Rob's brother."

"And?"

"She said she heard he had a gambling problem."

"Did Carol tell her that?"

"She didn't say. But probably. She also said that the brother's wife was seeing Dr. Rob."

"Professionally or…?"

"Not sure. Elyse said she saw her there a couple of times, and the last time she was crying, and Dr. Rob had his arm around her."

"Maybe he was just comforting her," said Percy. "Did Elyse know why Josie was crying?"

"She heard Josie say she couldn't take it anymore."

"Take what anymore?"

"No idea. Maybe her marriage? Elyse didn't get any more because Dr. Rob took Josie back to his office."

"Hmm. And Elyse heard that Ed had a gambling problem?"

"And that he was always asking Dr. Rob for money."

"Interesting. Did you ask her if she thought Ed could have killed him?"

"Not specifically. But I did ask her if she had any suspects."

"And?"

"She mentioned a patient. Some guy named Sean O'Connor."

"Sean O'Connor? I don't think I know him."

"He's a general contractor. Elyse described him as a big guy with a short fuse. He was seeing Dr. Rob for anger management. But I guess it wasn't working. Elyse said O'Connor made a big scene about getting his money back. Said there'd be trouble if he didn't."

"Whoa. When was this?"

"Elyse didn't remember exactly. But she said it wasn't that long ago."

"And did O'Connor get his money back?"

"Elyse had no idea. She just happened to be there when O'Connor flipped his lid, but she didn't see him after that."

"Elyse have anything else to say?"

"That was all the juicy stuff."

"Speaking of juicy stuff," said Carlo. "I need to eat something. I'm famished."

Bonnie picked up her menu, studied it, then put it down.

"You know what you're going to have?" she asked Percy. "No, wait, let me guess: the usual."

"Actually," said Percy. "I was thinking of getting the steak."

"Will wonders never cease!" said Bonnie. "And what about you, Carlo?"

"I was thinking of getting the steak too."

"Huh."

"What?" said Percy.

"I was also thinking about getting the steak."

"Is that a problem?"

"Well, if you two are getting it, I should get something else."

"You don't have to," said Percy. "If that's what you want." Then Percy froze. Dr. Richardson was heading their way, and she was with Dr. Yates.

"Everything all right?" Bonnie asked her.

"Dr. Richardson just came in with Dr. Yates," she said in a low voice, leaning over the table. "And they just took a seat over there. Don't look!"

Of course, Bonnie looked.

"They look awfully chummy," said Bonnie.

"Well, they're colleagues, and probably friends too."

"Hmm."

"What does that mean?"

"Nothing."

Percy saw Carlo peering over at the two women. Dr. Richardson had laid a hand on one of Dr. Yates's. Carlo and Bonnie shared another look.

"Okay, you two, I know what you're thinking, but you're wrong."

"How do you know what we're thinking?" Bonnie asked her.

Percy gave her a look.

"So, are you going to get the steak?"

"I changed my mind. I think I'll have the salmon."

CHAPTER 22

Despite telling Bonnie not to look, Percy couldn't help periodically glancing over at Dr. Richardson and Dr. Yates. She wondered what they were talking about. They seemed to be having a good time, judging by their facial expressions and body language.

"Yoohoo!" It was Bonnie.

"What?" said Percy.

"Stop staring at them."

"I wasn't staring. I was observing."

"Well, stop observing and eat your steak. You've barely touched it."

Percy cut off a piece and shoved it in her mouth.

"Happy now?"

"Don't be snippy."

"Sorry."

They finished their food, and the server asked if they'd like dessert.

"I'm full," said Percy. "But you two can order dessert if you want."

"Carlo?" said Bonnie.

"I need to get back to the gallery."

"You're not working late again, are you? You really need to hire Gianna full-time or get another assistant."

"I don't have the time to train someone else, and in a few weeks it'll be dead."

"Though before you know it, it'll be Christmas."

"I'll start worrying about Christmas in November. For now, I need to make it through June or there won't be a Christmas."

"Do you want a coffee?" Percy asked him. "Or a cappuccino?"

"I'll make myself an espresso at the store."

"Well, if neither of you is getting dessert or coffee, we should just get the check," said Bonnie.

"Are you sure?" Percy asked Bonnie. "If you want dessert or coffee…"

"I'm good," she said. Then she signaled to their server to bring over the check.

As they passed the table belonging to Dr. Richardson and Dr. Yates, Percy hid behind her friends. However, the two women were so engrossed in conversation that they probably wouldn't have noticed her.

"They looked like they were having a nice time," said Bonnie as they approached the door. "Do you think they were discussing patients?"

"Hopefully not as I saw them laughing earlier," said Percy.

They stepped outside, and Percy relaxed.

"Would it have been the worst thing in the world if they saw you?" said Bonnie. "Dr. Richardson must run into patients all the time."

"I suppose, but I wouldn't know what to say."

Bonnie turned to Carlo.

"Are you really going to work?"

"The pictures don't frame themselves."

"I could help," offered Percy. "Lucy's out with her friends, and I've always wanted to learn how to frame stuff."

"Thanks, but I'm good."

"He's worried you won't want to listen to opera or will tell him to turn it down," said Bonnie.

They said goodnight and went their separate ways.

As soon as Percy got home, she checked her phone for messages. There was a text from Hugh, saying he was looking forward to their date on Friday. Percy smiled. Then she remembered: She hadn't told him the latest about Arianna. She started to call him and then stopped. She should text him first.

I'm looking forward to Friday too, she wrote back. *You have a minute to chat? I have some news.*

I'm at the movies with Madison, he replied. *What's up?*

You shouldn't be texting at the movies, Percy typed.

The movie hasn't started yet. They're still showing previews. What did you want to tell me?

I'd rather not text it.

I have some news too. How about we wait until Friday to exchange information?

Percy bit her lip. Could she wait until Friday? Though that was only a couple of days away. And she agreed it would be better to exchange information in person.

Okay, she finally wrote back.

Did you choose a restaurant?

Not yet.

Well, let me know when you have. Gotta go. The movie's about to start.

Percy put her phone in her pocket and went upstairs to her office. She opened the browser on her computer and did a search for restaurants in Stonebridge. She had been to almost all of them. Which one should she go to with Hugh? Or maybe they should eat somewhere else, where they were less likely to run into people they knew.

She went back to the search box and looked for restaurants in Kenwick. She saw a French place that sounded good. Did Hugh like French food? He said he liked everything.

Next, she looked for restaurants in Northbridge. She saw the restaurant Hugh had taken her to. They had a good-sounding dinner menu. But maybe they should try someplace different.

She checked out a half-dozen places and then went back to the list of restaurants in Kenwick. Would Hugh prefer Italian, French, or something more exotic, like Thai or Indian?

Percy could feel herself overthinking. Then she remembered what Dr. Rob had told, or taught, her, about closing her eyes and taking deep breaths when she started to feel this way. She could almost hear his soothing voice as she closed her eyes and took a deep breath, slowly releasing it. She did this a few more times and felt herself start to relax.

"The French place," she said aloud. But just to be on the safe side, she texted Bonnie.

Have you been to the French place in Kenwick, Le Lapin Blanc? she asked her.

Bonnie got back to her right away.

I was just there with Harry. Why?

I was thinking of taking Hugh there on Friday.

Great idea. The place is a bit eclectic, but the food's very good.

Okay, wrote Percy. *Thanks.*

Let me know how the date goes!

It's not a date.

Uh-huh.

Percy made a reservation at Le Lapin Blanc for seven o'clock on Friday and told Hugh she'd meet him there. She received a reply from him as she was getting ready for bed, saying he would pick her up at six forty as it was silly to take two cars.

Fine, she wrote back. Then she texted her daughter, asking when she'd be home.

Lucy replied that she would be home later and not to wait up for her.

Percy sighed. Easier said than done.

As she sat on her bed, her brain started replaying what Bonnie had said over dinner, about Ed and Josie and Dr. Rob. She opened the browser on her phone and typed *Josie Mankiewicz.* There was a link to an Instagram account with her name. Percy clicked on it, hoping the account wasn't private. It wasn't, but Percy thought it probably wasn't the right Josie since the more recent photos showed this Josie with a man who wasn't Ed. Yet the Josie in the photos looked to be the right age, and several of the photos looked to have been taken in Beauport.

Percy scrolled down and found a photo of Josie with two boys, her sons, and a man who looked like Ed. It was a high school graduation photo. So it had to be the right Josie. Percy continued to scroll. There was another older photo with Ed in it, but that was it. *Huh.*

Percy scrolled back up to the more recent photos of Josie looking cozy with the man who wasn't Ed and noticed it was tagged. Percy clicked on the tag and went to the account it linked to. But that Instagram account was private.

Was Josie no longer with Ed?

Percy went back to her search and added *Beauport* after Josie's name. She waited as the screen populated. *Hmm.* Apparently, Josie was big on volunteering. There were also some mentions of her and Ed, but they were older.

Had they separated or gotten divorced? Being a research librarian, Percy knew where to look to find out. But she didn't want to do it on her phone. So she went to her office and got on her computer. *Aha!* They had divorced just over a year ago. She wondered if Dr. Rob had anything to do with it. But Percy hadn't seen any pictures of Dr. Rob in Josie's Instagram feed.

She decided to take another look, just to be sure, and

found a family photo from a few years ago with Dr. Rob and Ed, a woman who looked a bit like Josie, possibly her sister, and an older couple, probably Josie's parents. But that was the only photo Percy saw with Dr. Rob in it.

Percy sat back in her chair. She wondered if Josie knew about Dr. Rob. She must. Did she have any idea who might have killed him? Percy thought about reaching out to her, but what would she say?

As she was mulling it over, Percy remembered Bonnie mentioning an angry patient. What was his name again? Something O'Connor? Percy immediately thought of the actor from *All in the Family*, the one who played Archie Bunker. Then she remembered: the man's name was Sean, Sean O'Connor.

Percy typed his name into the search box. As Bonnie—or Elyse—had said, he was a contractor here in Stonebridge. She looked at his reviews. They were mixed, with some people saying what a great job he had done for them and others complaining about the cost and O'Connor's attitude. There were also a couple of complaints filed with the Better Business Bureau.

Sounded like O'Connor was a bit of a hothead.

Percy continued to scroll. "Ah," she said, finding an article about O'Connor having an altercation with a client and being instructed to get help for anger management. That must be why he was seeing Dr. Rob. But could Sean O'Connor have killed him? Maybe punched him, but shot him?

Percy went to O'Connor's website and clicked on the About page. He was a vet and had served in Afghanistan. *Interesting.* She wondered what he had done there. It didn't take long for Percy to discover he had been a sniper. *Huh.* So he certainly had the skill to have killed Dr. Rob. But how had Dr. Rob been killed exactly? All she knew was that he had been shot. She didn't know if it had been at close range or from far away. Again, she wished she could have seen the crime scene. Maybe Carol would know.

In the meantime, she decided to reach out to Sean O'Connor. He offered a free consultation to new clients, so Percy filled out the contact form. She'd been meaning to update the bathrooms and kitchen for years, but Jim had thought they were fine as is, so Percy hadn't pushed. But now that she wasn't buying a house in Beauport, maybe she should use that money to fix up the Stonebridge house. Not that she would be hiring Sean O'Connor, but it was a good excuse to meet with him.

She finished filling out the form, quickly read over what she had written, and pressed *Submit*. She looked at the time. How had it gotten to be so late? And there was no sign of Lucy.

She went back to her bedroom, got into bed, and picked up Hugh's book. Despite it being a thriller, she found herself falling asleep after just a few minutes.

Lucy was in the kitchen, a mug of coffee in front of her, when Percy returned from her run the next morning.

"You're up early," she said to her daughter.

"Minnie woke me. You forgot to feed her."

Percy looked over at the cat, who was sitting on the counter, a smug look on her face.

"I did not forget to feed her."

Lucy looked over at the cat.

"Did you lie to me, Minnie?"

Minnie proceeded to lick her paw.

"I should go take a shower and get dressed," said Percy. "Did you have breakfast?"

"Not yet."

"If you can wait a few minutes, we can have breakfast together."

"That's fine."

Percy returned a short time later. Lucy hadn't moved.

"What would you like for breakfast?" Percy asked her. "I could make us some eggs or maybe some pancakes?"

"Do you have time to make pancakes? Don't you need to get to the library?"

"They don't take that long."

"I think I'll just have some cereal. I'm not that hungry."

"Suit yourself. I think I'll make myself some scrambled eggs and toast."

Percy went to the refrigerator.

"Well, if you're having scrambled eggs and toast…" said Lucy.

Percy smiled.

"I'll make enough for both of us. So, you have a good time with your friends last night?" Percy asked as she put the bread in the toaster oven and began to whisk the eggs.

"It was all right."

"You looking forward to seeing Jamie this weekend?"

"Mm."

Percy turned around.

"Is everything all right?"

"I'm just tired. I was up late, and Minnie got me up early." She let out a yawn to reinforce the point.

"Okay. Though you know if something's up, you can tell me."

"I know. But really, Mom, everything's fine."

Percy finished scrambling the eggs in the pan and placed half of them on a plate for Lucy, along with two pieces of toast. Then she did the same for herself. When they were done eating, she put the plates and flatware in the dishwasher and quickly washed the pan.

"Will I see you tonight?" she asked Lucy.

"I told you I'd have dinner with you before I left to go to Boston."

"Just checking. You want to order a pizza?" Percy knew how much Lucy liked pizza. "Then we could go out for ice cream after."

"Sounds good. You'd better go. I don't want you to be late."

Percy was in the staff room when she received a text from Carol, saying that, unfortunately, she wasn't free that evening. Percy texted her back, saying she understood and that the offer was good for another time. Then she put her phone in her bag and stored it in her locker.

She retrieved her bag at lunchtime and immediately checked her phone. There was nothing from Sean O'Connor. She put her phone back in her bag and headed out. She was planning on grabbing something, a sandwich or a salad, at the health food store. As she was walking, she thought she saw Hugh in front of Annie's. It was definitely him. She was about to cross the street and say hello when she saw Arianna Cardinale walking towards him. Were they having lunch together? Hugh hadn't said anything. And why were they smiling? She watched as Hugh opened the door for Arianna, and they went inside.

Percy found herself crossing the street to Annie's when a car honked at her.

"Sorry!" she called to the driver, feeling embarrassed. What had she been thinking, not paying attention to traffic? And why hadn't Hugh told her he was having lunch with Arianna?

She stared at the restaurant. Should she go in? No. What would she even say? She stood there, immobilized, for several more seconds, then she continued to the health food store. However, her mind was so preoccupied with Hugh and Arianna that she couldn't decide what to get and wound up getting a protein bar and a vegetable juice drink.

As she headed back to the library, she peered into Annie's. But she couldn't see Hugh and Arianna. What were they talking about? Was it a date?

She forced herself to turn away and return to the library, where she bumped into Bonnie.

"Sorry," said Percy.

"Everything okay?" Bonnie asked her. "You have that look on your face."

"What look?"

"The look you get when you're trying to figure out something but can't."

"I have a look for that?"

Bonnie nodded. Then she looked down at the paper bag Percy was carrying.

"Is that lunch?"

Percy nodded.

"What did you get?"

"A protein bar and a juice."

"Now I know something's wrong. Give."

"Nothing's wrong."

Bonnie gave her a look.

"Fine. As I was walking to the health food store to get lunch, I saw Hugh go into Annie's with Arianna Cardinale."

"I take it you didn't know he was having lunch with her."

"I did not."

"Look, I'm sure it's perfectly innocent. He's probably pumping her for information about Dr. Rob."

"Must you use that word?"

"What word?"

"Pumping."

Bonnie rolled her eyes.

"Do you think I should cancel our date tomorrow?"

"What?! No! Why?"

"Well, if he's dating Arianna Cardinale…"

"Please. As I said, I'm sure there's a perfectly innocent reason they're having lunch."

Percy didn't look convinced.

"Go eat your protein bar. You clearly need food."

Percy headed to the staff room.

"And don't cancel on him!" Bonnie called after her.

CHAPTER 23

Percy still hadn't heard from Sean O'Connor by the end of the day Thursday. Maybe she should call him. No, she would give him one more day, then she would call him. She also hadn't heard from Hugh on Thursday, and she was feeling anxious when she woke up on Friday.

We still good for tonight? she texted him.

He replied with a thumbs-up emoji.

She waited to see if he would write more, but that was it. When she got to the library later, she showed the text to Bonnie.

"What do you think it means?" she asked her friend.

"That he confirmed your date. Why do you ask?"

"Why didn't he say something like, *Can't wait!?*"

"Maybe it was implied."

"Or maybe he doesn't really want to see me. Maybe he'd rather have dinner with Arianna."

Bonnie stared at her friend.

"Don't be ridiculous."

"I'm not being ridiculous. He didn't tell me he was having lunch with her, then I didn't hear from him."

"You're reading too much into it. He's just busy, Percy. You said he was working on a new book. You know how writers get. They lose track of time and don't check their phones."

"Maybe."

"And maybe you should continue therapy if you're going to obsess about Hugh."

"I wasn't obsessing."

Bonnie didn't look convinced.

"So, did you make a reservation at the French place in Kenwick?"

"I did."

"I think you'll like it. What are you planning on wearing?"

"I don't know. What do you think? It's not fancy, right?"

"It's not, but I wouldn't go there in ripped jeans and a t-shirt."

"As if I ever would."

"Wear something sexy."

"I don't know if I own anything sexy."

"What about those skinny jeans and that white lacy top? And you have those spiky sandals."

"I don't know if those jeans still fit me."

"Fine. What about that blue wrap dress? That's sexy."

"I should just cancel. I mean, how can I compare to Arianna? She's gorgeous."

Bonnie groaned.

"Stop comparing yourself to Arianna! You're pretty gorgeous yourself. And I'm sure Hugh has a perfectly good explanation for why he had lunch with her."

"What if he tells me they're seeing each other?"

"Then he's a two-timing weasel and you're better off without him."

"Excuse me, could one of you help me?" It was a patron, a frail-looking woman who looked to be in her seventies or possibly eighties.

"Of course," said Bonnie. "What do you need help with?"

"I'm looking for that book by that chef," said the woman.

"Do you happen to know the chef's name?" Bonnie asked her.

"He's that famous one who died."

"Do you mean Anthony Bourdain?"

"Maybe? He had a TV show where he traveled to different places."

Though lots of chefs had TV shows where they traveled to different places.

"Oh, and it had something to do with kitchens."

"Do you mean *Kitchen Confidential*?" said Percy. "It's Anthony Bourdain's memoir about his years working in restaurants."

"That's it!" said the woman. "My friend Patsy said I should read it. My granddaughter just got a job working as a chef. Do you have it?"

Bonnie got on the computer.

"We have two copies, and they're both checked in."

"I'll take one," said the woman.

"You can find them in the adult nonfiction section." Bonnie gave her the call number. The woman frowned.

"I'll show you where it is," said Percy.

"Thank you, dear," said the woman.

Percy checked her phone at lunchtime. Still nothing from Sean O'Connor. She called the number on his website and got a recorded message. She left her name and number and said she was interested in meeting with him to discuss a bathroom and kitchen renovation project.

Was he busy or away? Or maybe the police had arrested him for Dr. Rob's murder. Though wouldn't she have heard if there had been an arrest? She opened Facebook and checked the Dr. Rob group. As she thought, there was nothing about an arrest. Then she checked the Stonebridge group. Nothing there either.

She thought about putting up a post, asking if anyone had heard anything. But surely if the police had arrested anyone, someone would have posted something in the group or on the Stonebridge page, or the local paper would have reported it.

Percy sighed and put her phone away.

Normally, Percy wouldn't have checked her phone again until it was time to leave. But she was feeling anxious. So around three-thirty, she slipped into the staff room to check it.

There was still nothing from Sean O'Connor. But she had a notification from Facebook. Someone had just left a comment saying he heard that the police were about to make an arrest. Percy immediately approved the comment and asked the man who had left it if he knew who the police were going to arrest.

"Everything all right?" It was Mary Beth.

Percy jumped. She hadn't heard or seen Mary Beth enter the staff room.

"Sorry. Is everything okay? You were staring intently at your phone."

"I just read that the police were close to arresting someone in the Dr. Rob murder."

"Oh? I didn't see anything in the police blotter." Mary Beth checked the police blotter daily to see what, if any, crimes had been committed in Stonebridge and the surrounding area. "You should ask Nate. His son works in the police department."

"I know. But Nate said his son doesn't discuss active cases with him."

"Oh well. Well, I'm sure as soon as there's been an arrest, we'll hear about it."

"I suppose," said Percy. "Well, if I don't see you, have a good weekend."

"You too."

Percy was staring at her clothes and muttering.

"Wear something sexy."

She wished Lucy were there to help her, but she was in Boston. Percy took out her skinny jeans and put them on. She hadn't worn them in a while, and they felt tight. She looked at herself in the full-length mirror, moving from side to side. Were the jeans *too* tight? Though as she moved, they seemed to stretch and loosen a bit.

What to wear with them… She pulled out the lacy white top Bonnie had mentioned. She had bought it on a trip to Mexico with Jim years ago. She put it on and looked at herself in the mirror again. She didn't know about sexy, but she thought she looked nice, and the top brought back good memories. Though if she wore it, would she be thinking of Jim the whole evening? She debated with herself for a couple of minutes, finally deciding to leave it on.

She went into the bathroom, pulled her hair into a ponytail, and applied some makeup. When she was done, she regarded herself in the mirror. Should she wear her hair up or down? Again, she heard Bonnie telling her to look sexy. She removed the ponytail holder and shook her hair. Then she pulled her hair back again. She was about to remove the ponytail holder a second time when she heard the doorbell. That must be Hugh. She looked at her watch. He was early.

She took one last look at herself in the mirror and removed the ponytail holder. Then she went downstairs and opened the door. Hugh was also in jeans and was wearing a white button-down shirt.

"Great minds," he said, smiling at Percy. "Are you ready?"

"I just need to grab my bag and put on a pair of shoes. You want to come in for a second?"

"Is Lucy here?"

"No, she's in Boston with her boyfriend."

"Right. I think you told me she was away this weekend."

Minnie appeared and sat down in front of Hugh.

"Hello, Minnie," Hugh said, peering down at the cat.

Minnie continued to look up at him.

"I think she's checking me out. Is it okay to pet her?"

"You can try. Let her sniff you first."

Hugh bent his knees and held out his hand. Minnie sniffed his hand and then rubbed her head against it. Hugh scratched her chin, and Minnie began to purr.

"She likes you," said Percy.

Hugh scratched Minnie's back.

"Keep that up and you're going to need a lint roller."

Hugh stood up and rubbed his hands, sending fur to the floor. Percy stopped herself from going to get a Dustbuster and vacuuming it up.

"Let's go," she said. She would vacuum later.

"You're awfully quiet," said Hugh as they drove to Kenwick. "Is everything all right?"

Percy thought about saying that everything was fine. But everything wasn't fine. And she was tired of obsessing about what Hugh had been doing with Arianna Cardinale.

"I saw you go into Annie's with Arianna Cardinale yesterday."

"Ah," said Hugh. "I was going to tell you about that, but then I figured I should wait."

"I thought Madison forbade you from going out with her."

"Madison didn't forbid me. And even if she had, I don't

take orders from my daughter. Well, at least not about some things.”

Percy didn't say anything.

“And it wasn't a date. I took your advice and told her I was working on a book and could use her help.”

“I see. And she agreed to meet you for lunch?” Though obviously, she had. “What did she have to say? Did you ask her about Dr. Rob?”

“We're almost at the restaurant. I'll tell you over dinner.”

“So, tell me about your lunch with Arianna,” Percy said, after Hugh had ordered a bottle of wine. “Do you think she shot him?”

“She claims she didn't.”

“You asked her?” Percy was surprised.

“I did. Though not right away. We talked about other things first. Apparently, she's read all of my books and is a big fan.”

“Of course she is. So, what was the deal with her and Dr. Rob?”

The waiter came over with their bottle of wine and poured some into Hugh's glass. Hugh tasted it and nodded, and the waiter poured some into Percy's glass before filling Hugh's.

“Go on,” said Percy, after the waiter had left.

“You're not going to have a sip of your wine?”

“Just tell me about Arianna and Dr. Rob. How did they meet?” Arianna's friend Vicky had said they had met at some event, but Percy wanted to know what Arianna had told Hugh.

Hugh took a sip of his wine before speaking.

“She said the two of them met at a gallery opening in Northbridge. They got to talking about art, went out for a drink after the opening, and then wound up at Dr. Rob's place."

"I see. And they started dating right after?"

Hugh nodded.

"Arianna said she was smitten right away. And she thought Dr. Rob was too."

"I sense there's a but coming."

"Arianna said that after the first few dates, she started to feel like he was only interested in her for the sex."

"So she was his booty call?"

"Sounded that way."

"Did she say something?"

"No. She said the sex was amazing, and she thought he was just preoccupied with work, and that things would get better."

"I have a feeling they didn't though."

"No."

"So how long did this go on for?"

"Two, maybe three, months?"

"And then he dumped her?"

Hugh nodded as he took another sip of wine.

"Did he give a reason?"

"No. He just stopped calling and texting her and wouldn't return her calls or texts."

"So she has no idea why he ghosted her?"

"Actually…" Percy waited. "Arianna thinks it's because she told Dr. Rob she was late."

"Late as in her period was late?"

Another nod.

"Was she pregnant?"

"She thought she might be."

"And she thought Dr. Rob was the father?"

"Arianna said she hadn't slept with anyone else."

"Do you believe her?"

"That she thought she was pregnant and that Dr. Rob was the father?"

Percy nodded.

"I do."

"Didn't they use protection?"

"Even if you use protection, you can still get pregnant."

"So, what did Dr. Rob say when she told him she was late?"

"He said it was probably just stress and that he had an appointment and had to go."

"Ouch. And that was it?"

"That was it."

"And she didn't hear from him again?"

"Nope."

"Wow." Percy couldn't believe it. "So, was Arianna pregnant?"

"She said she was."

"Is that why she went to the Wellness Center, to confront him? I heard from a patient that she caused quite a scene."

"She had gone to speak with him at his place first, but he wouldn't let her in."

"Why not?"

"There was a woman there."

"She saw a woman at Dr. Rob's?"

Hugh nodded.

"A very young, very pretty, and very pregnant woman."

"And Dr. Rob wouldn't let Arianna in?"

"He told her now wasn't a good time and closed the door."

Percy took a sip of her wine. This sounded like something from a soap opera or an episode of *The Real Housewives*.

"Could the woman have been a patient or maybe a relative? How young was she?"

"Arianna thought she was in her early or mid-twenties. And she doubted the woman was a patient or a relative."

"And Arianna didn't know who the woman was."

"No. But she said that if she saw her again, she would recognize her."

"And Arianna told you that she went to the Wellness Center to have it out with him."

"She did. She's quite embarrassed about it. She didn't mean to make a scene. She claims it was hormones."

"Did she tell you that she threatened Dr. Rob?"

"She threatened him? How do you know that?"

"A patient saw the whole thing and told me about it."

"I know what you're thinking, Percy, but she didn't shoot him."

"How do you know that?"

"She has an alibi."

"Where was she?"

"At work."

"Where does she work?"

"At that big pharmaceutical company here in Stonebridge."

"So? It's not far from there to downtown. She could have easily snuck out during lunch, gone to the Wellness Center, shot him, and been back at work before you knew it."

"True, but I don't think she did it."

"She has a gun."

"Which she keeps locked in a safe at home."

Percy wondered how Hugh knew that but didn't ask.

"Has she talked to the police?"

"She said she spoke with Detective Russo."

Percy wondered if she really had.

"So, what happened to the baby?"

"What do you mean?"

"You said that Arianna thought she was pregnant with Dr. Rob's baby. But when I saw her at Annie's, she didn't look pregnant."

"She said she lost it."

"She lost it?"

"She miscarried."

"When?"

"Right after Dr. Rob was shot. She thinks it was the shock."

"Uh-huh. Doesn't that seem awfully convenient? Maybe she just made up the pregnancy."

"Why would she do that?"

"To trap him. Her friend Vicky said that Arianna was obsessed with Dr. Rob and was desperate when he dumped her."

"I think you're being unfair, Percy."

"And I think you want to believe her because you find her attractive."

Hugh sighed.

"I'm not interested in Arianna. She's not my type."

"And what is your type?"

"Librarians," he said with a smile.

The waiter came over to see if they were ready to order, and Hugh told him they needed a few minutes.

CHAPTER 24

"So, how was your meeting with Dr. Yates?" Percy asked Hugh after they had ordered.

"It was fine."

"Are you going to see her again?"

"I don't think so. I had planned on stopping therapy before Dr. Rob died. And I still feel that way."

"What about your book? Maybe Dr. Yates could provide you with some insights."

"I got what I needed from Dr. Rob."

"Did you ask her about Dr. Rob?"

"I did."

"And what did she have to say?"

"Nothing that I didn't already know."

"Do you think they were involved?"

"Involved?"

"Romantically."

"I don't think so."

"What about in the past?"

"It's possible, but I don't think so."

"Why not? She's an attractive woman, he's an attractive man, and he dated Dr. Richardson."

"Call it writer's intuition."

"I see. And has this writer's intuition of yours ever been wrong?"

"Rarely."

"And what did your writer's intuition say about me?"

"That you were someone I should get to know."

"Oh? How come?"

"I found you intriguing."

"I don't think anyone's ever used that word to describe me. Usually, people describe me as being an overthinker and/or a perfectionist."

"You don't strike me as either."

"That's because you don't know me that well."

"But I'd like to."

Percy felt her face grow warm. Time to change the subject.

"I finished reading *Love on the Run*."

"Did you enjoy it? Wait. Don't answer."

Percy smiled.

"I did enjoy it. I liked the banter between Cam and Sophie. Did you model the characters on yourself and Elizabeth? The dialogue felt very realistic. Well, except for all the spy talk. Though, for all I know, you could be a spy, and this author thing is your cover."

Hugh smiled.

"I'm not a spy."

"Just what a spy would say."

"Speaking of spying, you said you had information to share."

Percy told him about Bonnie's dinner with Elyse and what Elyse had told Bonnie about Josie Mankiewicz and Sean O'Connor. And that she hoped to meet with the contractor, if he ever got back to her.

"Interesting. However, do you think it's wise to meet with Sean O'Connor alone? He could be a killer."

"I'll be fine. I doubt he'll bring a gun to the appointment. And it's not like I'm going to accuse him of murdering Dr. Rob. I just want to ask him a few questions."

"What kinds of questions?"

"What he did in the military, why he was upset with Dr. Rob, if he got his money back."

"Mm. I still don't like the idea of you meeting with him alone. If you tell me when he's coming over, I could join you."

"I appreciate your concern, but as I said, I'll be fine."

"Just do me a favor and let me know when you're meeting with him, and then text me after to let me know you're okay."

"If it will make you happy."

"Thank you."

Their food arrived, and they took a break from discussing Dr. Rob's murder.

"So, how's the new book coming?" Percy asked him as they ate.

"Good, I think."

"Can you tell me about it?"

"I'd rather not. I typically don't discuss my work until I'm done with the first or second draft. I'm still working on the plot, and it's already changed once."

"Well, I'd love to read it when you're ready."

They finished their entrees and decided to share a piece of key lime pie for dessert.

"I just thought of something," Percy said as she sipped her decaf cappuccino. Hugh waited for her to go on. "Did Dr. Rob have a will? And, if so, who benefited? Elyse said Ed had a gambling problem. Do you think Dr. Rob planned on leaving him money to pay off his gambling debts? And if so, did Ed know and then kill Dr. Rob to get the money?"

"I would think murder would negate his claim to any inheritance."

"True."

Percy looked thoughtful as she took another sip of her cappuccino.

"If he did leave a will, it would need to be probated. And

once it goes to probate court, it becomes public record, and anyone can request to view it. Unless it's confidential."

"And you know this how?"

"I'm a research librarian, Hugh. People ask us that sort of thing all the time. Well, maybe not so much now that there's the internet. But librarians still need to know these things."

"So I could visit the local probate court and see if Dr. Rob had a will?"

"If it's been probated."

"Maybe I'll just do that."

"I'll do it," said Percy. "I know someone who used to be a judge over there. I'm sure he can find out for me."

"Very good. Let me know what you find out."

They finished up, and Hugh asked for the check. The waiter brought it over, but as Hugh reached for it, Percy grabbed it.

"Dinner's on me," she said.

"You don't," he began. But Percy stopped him.

"I told you that the next time I would pay."

"I know, but…"

"No buts."

"Fine," said Hugh.

Percy smiled. She liked that he didn't insist. She handed the waiter her credit card, and a few minutes later, they left the restaurant.

"Good choice," said Hugh.

"I'm glad you enjoyed it. Bonnie said it was a good place."

"How about next time I cook?"

"So, you think there'll be a next time?" said Percy, trying not to grin.

"I'd like to think so."

They got in Hugh's SUV and headed back to Stonebridge.

"So, what do you like to eat? Or maybe I should ask, what don't you like?"

"I'll send you a list."

"You have a list?"

"I do. But I haven't updated it in a while."

Hugh shook his head.

"What?" said Percy.

"Do you have a list for everything?"

"Not everything, just for groceries, things I need to do, books I've read…"

"Stop," said Hugh. "I was kidding."

"Oh."

Neither spoke for a couple of minutes.

"So, dinner next week? I'd invite you over this weekend, but Madison and I are going to be in the city," by which he meant New York City.

"Oh? What are you two doing there?"

"We're going to a concert at Madison Square Garden tomorrow night and then staying over."

"Who are you seeing?"

"Dua Lipa."

"Nice."

"You like her?"

"I do."

"Huh."

"What? You didn't think I would like Dua Lipa? I love good dance music."

"Maybe you should go with Madison."

"You're not a fan of Dua Lipa?"

"She's all right. I'm more of a jazz and blues kind of guy."

"Duly noted."

They arrived back at Percy's place.

"Would it be all right if I gave you a kiss goodnight?" Hugh asked her.

Percy smiled.

"I think that would be acceptable."

Hugh leaned over, and Percy closed her eyes. The kiss was gentle at first, then it grew more passionate, and Percy could feel herself sigh. It had been a long time since she had been kissed, and Hugh's kiss awakened something in her.

Hugh slowly pulled back and raised his hand to touch Percy's cheek. They sat there, silently looking at each other for several seconds. Then Hugh said goodnight.

"Goodnight," Percy repeated. Neither moved.

Finally, Percy turned and got out.

"I'll text you this weekend," he called out the window as Percy walked to her door.

"Send me pictures from the concert!" Percy called back.

Hugh waited until Percy was inside, then he slowly backed out of her driveway.

Percy woke up in a good mood the next morning and went for a long run. When she got back, she found a message from Hugh, saying what a great time he had. That made her smile.

She made herself some coffee and then went to take a shower. She was sitting down to eat breakfast when her phone rang. It was the Wellness Center.

"Hello?" she said.

"Percy? It's Carol."

"Is everything okay?" Percy asked her.

"Everything's fine. I just wanted to know if that offer to talk about those books is still good."

"Of course! Just let me know when."

"Actually, are you free for lunch later? I'm working until one, but I'm free after. We could meet somewhere in town."

"I have a better idea. Why don't you come here, and I'll make us something?"

"I don't want you to go to any trouble. I know this is very last-minute."

"No trouble. Would you be okay having a frittata and a salad?"

"That sounds delicious. Can I bring anything?"

"Just yourself. Shoot me a text when you're leaving the Wellness Center, in case you're running late."

"I'll do that. And thank you."

"No need to thank me. This'll be fun."

They ended the call, and Percy went to look in her fridge. She was pretty sure she had everything she needed to make a frittata and a salad, but if she didn't, she could run over to the health food store or the supermarket.

CHAPTER 25

Carol showed up a little after one with a bottle of prosecco. Percy led her to the kitchen and told her to have a seat. Lunch was almost ready.

"Mm, smells good. Did you bake bread?"

"No, I'm just warming up a loaf I got in the oven, to go with the frittata and salad."

"You didn't have to go to so much trouble."

"It was no trouble," said Percy. "Shall I make us some mimosas? I'm pretty sure I have orange juice."

"Please."

Percy opened the bottle of prosecco and poured some into two glasses. Then she added orange juice to each. She handed one of the glasses to Carol, who immediately took a sip. Percy thought she seemed a bit nervous.

A timer went off, and Percy removed the frittata and loaf of bread from the oven. She cut up both and put a piece of each on a plate, handing one to Carol.

"And help yourself to salad."

"Mm!" said Carol, swallowing a bite of the frittata. "This is delicious!"

"I'm glad you like it."

Percy noticed that Carol had nearly finished her mimosa. That was fast.

"Is everything all right?" Percy asked her.

She waited as Carol finished chewing.

"Sorry, the baby had a bad night, and things have been hectic at the Wellness Center the last couple of weeks, as you can imagine. And that detective isn't helping things."

"He's been back? Did he get a search warrant?"

"He's been to the Wellness Center a few times, and he did. I hated to do it, but I had to give him all of the files he requested."

"Patient files?" Carol nodded. "So he thinks one of Dr. Rob's patients killed him?"

"Seems that way. But I just can't picture any of them shooting him."

"Though," said Percy. "I heard that one of his patients, Sean O'Connor, had been a military sniper, had a problem with Dr. Rob, and made a big scene at the Wellness Center."

"How do you know about that?"

"It's a small town. Word gets around."

Carol went to take a sip of her mimosa, then realized her glass was empty.

"Would you like some more?" Percy asked her.

"If you wouldn't mind."

Percy fixed her a second glass. Carol thanked her and took a sip.

"Did you tell the police about Mr. O'Connor?" Percy asked her.

"I did. Though I'm only telling you this because you said you knew about him. Dr. Rob did his best to help that man, but Mr. O'Connor was a tough one. Always angry about something. Still, I can't believe he would shoot Dr. Rob. But I suppose if anyone could have done it…" She took another sip of her drink.

"You mentioned the police asked for several files. Who else's file did the detective request?"

"I can't tell you."

"Did Detective Russo ask about me?"

Carol hesitated, then nodded.

"What did you tell him?"

"I told him that you would never harm Dr. Rob, that you were one of his best patients. Dr. Rob was very proud of you, you know."

Percy didn't know what to say.

"Did the detective ask about Hugh—I mean, Mr. Barnes?"

Carol smiled.

"He likes you."

"How do you know that?"

"He told me."

"Did Detective Russo ask you about him?" Percy asked a second time. "After all, Hugh was supposed to have been at the Wellness Center when Dr. Rob was shot, and he had canceled his appointment last minute."

What was she saying or suggesting? She didn't really think Hugh could have killed Dr. Rob, did she?

Carol looked like she was debating with herself.

"He did ask about Mr. Barnes, but I told him Mr. Barnes wouldn't hurt anyone. He just killed off people in his books."

Percy wasn't so sure that was the right thing to say, but she didn't comment. Instead, she asked Carol if she'd like more frittata or salad.

"Thank you, but I'm full," Carol replied.

Percy was about to remove their plates but stopped herself. She had a few more questions she wanted to ask Carol.

"Do you know Dr. Rob's sister-in-law, Josie?"

"Why do you ask?"

"Was she a patient of Dr. Rob's?"

"I… Not officially. Though she was always seeking Dr. Rob's advice."

"Do you know what about?"

Carol didn't say anything.

"I heard she wasn't happy here and that Ed had a gambling problem."

"How do you know about...?" She trailed off and sighed. "I guess it wasn't a secret."

"Did Ed ever ask his brother for money?"

"Dr. Rob loved his brother, but I overheard him saying to Dr. Richardson that Ed was never going to get any better if he kept helping him. But Ed kept showing up at the Wellness Center, saying Dr. Rob had to help him, that he was desperate."

"So did Dr. Rob give him money?"

"Dr. Rob told him he wasn't going to give him another dime until Ed got help."

"How did Ed take that?"

"Not well. He said such nasty things to Dr. Rob the last time he saw him, and that he would regret not helping him."

"When was this?"

"Maybe a week before Dr. Rob was shot? I don't remember exactly."

"Do you think Ed could have shot his brother?"

"I hate to think so, but if you had seen the look on his face that day..."

"Did you tell the police about Ed?"

"I felt I had to. And about Dr. Richardson, too, though I didn't want to."

"The detective asked about Dr. Richardson?"

Carol nodded as she finished off her second mimosa.

"But Dr. Richardson wasn't there when Dr. Rob was shot. Was there something that made the detective ask about her?"

Carol glanced around, as though she was afraid someone would overhear them.

"She and Dr. Rob had a big argument before he died."

"What was the argument about?"

"I don't know exactly. But I'm pretty sure it had to do

with the Wellness Center. Then afterwards, I heard Dr. Richardson talking on the phone. I'm not one to eavesdrop, but I was passing by her office, and she had her door open, and I heard her tell someone she had to get rid of him for the sake of the business."

"And you think she was talking about Dr. Rob?"

"Who else could she have meant?"

"And she said she had to get rid of him? Those were her exact words?"

"I…" Carol looked down at her watch. "I need to go. I promised Joanna I'd be home to take care of Ella by three."

"Ella is your granddaughter?"

Carol nodded.

"Do you have a picture of her?"

"I have many," she said with a smile.

"Could I see one?"

Carol retrieved her phone from her bag and showed Percy several photos.

"She's adorable. And I assume that's your daughter with her."

Carol nodded again.

"She's very pretty."

"Thank you. She takes after Alf, my late husband."

Percy vaguely remembered that Carol was a widow.

"When did he die?"

"Almost ten years ago now."

"I'm sorry."

"It wasn't your fault he got killed. It was the creep who shot him."

"He was shot? How awful. Did they catch the guy?"

"Alf's partner got him."

Percy looked confused.

"His partner?"

"Sorry, Alf was a cop, a good one too. He was chasing this guy who'd been dealing drugs to minors in Kenwick when the guy turned, pulled out a gun, and fired at him."

"How horrible."

"It was. Joanna was devastated. She adored her father. And you know how impressionable teenage girls can be."

Percy looked again at the picture of Joanna and Ella.

"How old is Joanna now?"

"Twenty-four."

"And how old is Ella?"

"Almost two months."

Percy handed the phone back to Carol.

"Is Ella sleeping through the night yet?"

"Not yet, which is why I have these bags under my eyes. I've been taking turns with Joanna, trying to get Ella back to sleep."

"Where's Ella's father?"

"I really should be going. Though, can I help you clean up?"

"I can do it. But we have a little time if you want to discuss those books."

"I have to run an errand. Another time."

"Okay," said Percy, wondering if something she had said had set Carol off. "Are you okay to drive?"

"Why wouldn't I be?"

Percy glanced over at the empty mimosa glass.

"I'm fine, Percy. But thank you for your concern."

Percy walked Carol to the front door.

"I've been wondering," Percy said as they stood by the door. "Do you know if Dr. Rob had a will or if the Wellness Center had insurance for him?"

"I don't know about a will. But I'm pretty sure he and Dr. Richardson had an agreement that if anything happened to one of them, the other would get that person's share of the business."

That made sense, thought Percy. Could it also be a motive?

She opened the door for Carol, but Carol hesitated.

"Please don't post anything I told you in your Facebook group. I probably shouldn't have said anything about Mr. O'Connor, or Dr. Rob's brother, or the investigation."

"Of course," said Percy. "I promise, I won't post anything you told me on Facebook." Though Percy planned on sharing the information with Bonnie and Carlo, and possibly Hugh.

"Thank you. I know Dr. Richardson wouldn't be happy to hear I've been talking about patients."

"Well, she won't hear it from me."

"Thank you. And will you let me know if the police contact you?"

"I will. But I already told them everything I know."

"Okay. Well, thanks again for lunch. I'll see you around."

Percy watched as Carol got in her car and slowly backed out of the driveway. Carol had given her a lot to think about, including several possible suspects.

The rest of the weekend passed quietly. Hugh sent Percy photos from the Dua Lipa concert at Madison Square Garden, including a selfie of him and Madison, which made Percy smile.

A little before six on Sunday, Lucy got home.

"You have a good time with Jamie?" Percy asked her.

"I did."

"What did you do?"

"Stuff."

"Could you be a bit more specific?"

"Can I tell you over dinner? I'm exhausted. There was a ton of traffic, and I didn't get a lot of sleep last night."

"Of course," said Percy. "I was thinking I would grill some burgers since it's nice out and maybe make some sweet potato fries to go with."

"Sounds good."

"What time do you want to eat?"

"Seven? I need to chill for a bit. Give me a shout when dinner's ready."

Percy said that she would, and Lucy headed upstairs.

Over dinner, Lucy told Percy about her weekend. It sounded like she had had a good time with Jamie. Then they watched an episode of *Love Island*. When it was over, Lucy said she was going to bed.

Percy gave her a kiss goodnight and waited until she heard Lucy's door close. Then she got her phone and texted Hugh.

You home?

I am, he replied.

You have a good time in NYC?

Very good.

You have a minute to talk?

I have a minute now if you want to call.

Percy pressed the call button, and Hugh immediately picked up.

"What's up?" he said.

"I saw Carol yesterday. She came over for lunch, and she told me that Detective Russo was asking about you."

"So?"

"Is there something I should know?"

"Like what?"

Like, did you kill Dr. Rob? Percy silently asked.

"I was at the vet's when Dr. Rob was shot."

"With Fluffy."

"Yes."

"And you were there the whole time."

She heard Hugh sigh.

"You don't believe me?"

She wanted to. But why had Detective Russo asked Carol about him and requested his file?

Percy didn't say anything.

"I didn't kill Dr. Rob, Percy. I can show you the bill from the vet. Do you want me to email it to you?"

A part of her wanted to say *yes*, but she told him that wasn't necessary.

"I know you have no reason to believe me, Percy, but I would never lie to you."

Percy wanted to believe him, but…

"I need to go," Hugh said. "Are we good?"

"Yeah."

"So, you'll have dinner with me this week?"

"Let's talk this week."

CHAPTER 26

Percy spent a quiet Memorial Day with Lucy, the library being closed. She hadn't heard from Sean O'Connor over the weekend and planned on calling him one last time on Tuesday. However, Tuesday morning, as she was finishing breakfast, she received a call from O'Connor Construction.

"Hello?" said Percy.

"Is this Percy Rollins?" said a male voice.

"It is," said Percy. "And who am I speaking with?"

"This is Sean O'Connor of O'Connor Construction, returning your call. You said you needed help with a bathroom and kitchen renovation."

"That's right. Do you have time this week to come over and take a look?"

"What's the address?"

Percy told him.

"I have another project not far from you. Could I stop by around five-thirty?"

"Five-thirty today?"

"If that doesn't work…"

"No, today at five-thirty would be great. I work at the Stonebridge Library and should be home by then. Could you send me a text letting me know when you're heading over or if you're running late?"

"No problem. See you this afternoon."

Percy was grinning.

"You seem happy," said Lucy. "Who was that?"

"A contractor I'm thinking of hiring."

"To do what?"

"Update the bathrooms and kitchen."

"Do they need updating?"

Percy gave her daughter a look.

"Won't that be noisy and messy?"

"Probably."

"And you're sure you want to do it now? I mean, it's not like I'm going to be living here, or you do a lot of entertaining. And the bathrooms and kitchen seem fine."

"You sound like your father."

"Well, he was a sensible man."

Percy smiled.

"Yes, he was. But he didn't do the cooking, and those bathrooms could use a refresh."

Lucy shrugged.

"It's your money."

"You heading off to your internship?"

"In a few. I figured I should eat something first."

"Good girl. I hope you have a good first day. Will you be home for dinner?"

"I was planning on it."

"Would you be okay doing takeout or going out? The contractor is going to be here at five-thirty, so I won't have time to go to the supermarket and get food."

"Takeout's fine. Or maybe I'll pick up something on my way home from work and cook."

"If you'd like to."

"So, how was your weekend?" Bonnie asked Percy as they were putting away their bags.

"Interesting."

"Interesting in what way? Did you see Hugh?"

"No, he was in New York with his daughter. They went to see Dua Lipa."

"Fun. So, what made your weekend so interesting?"

"Carol came over for lunch on Saturday."

"I don't remember you saying she was coming over."

"It was a last-minute thing. She phoned me Saturday morning, asking if I was free for lunch."

"Why was she asking you out for lunch?"

"I had recommended some books to her, and I told her I would be happy to discuss them with her when she had time."

"Isn't that what book clubs are for?"

"She's not in a book club, and she said most of her friends aren't readers."

"I don't understand how people can be against reading. So, what books did you recommend?"

Percy told her.

"And what did she think of them?"

"We didn't actually get around to discussing them."

"So, what did you discuss? Wait. Let me guess: Dr. Rob."

"Correct."

"And... What did Carol have to say?"

"She said that the police had been around, asking a lot of questions, and had requested several patient files."

"Did she say whose files they requested?"

"No, as that would be against healthcare privacy rules. But, I did manage to get her to admit that the detective had asked about me and Hugh and that contractor Elyse mentioned, Sean O'Connor."

"Well done, you!"

"She also disclosed that Dr. Rob's brother Ed had asked Dr. Rob for money, which Dr. Rob refused to give him, and that Dr. Richardson had had a big argument with Dr. Rob not long before he was killed."

"Sounds like you had a very productive lunch. Good sleuthing. So, who's your prime suspect?"

"I'm leaning towards Sean O'Connor. He had anger management issues, was mad at Dr. Rob, and he's a former military sniper."

"He's a former military sniper?"

Percy nodded.

"He fought in Afghanistan."

"Huh. So he could have easily shot Dr. Rob. I wonder why the police haven't arrested him."

"Maybe they don't have enough evidence yet. In any case, I'm meeting with him this afternoon at my place."

"Excuse me? You're planning on meeting with Dr. Rob's killer after work at your home? Are you crazy?"

"We don't know for sure that he's the killer. And I've been wanting to redo the kitchen and bathrooms for ages. Two birds, one stone."

"You left out an important word in that saying: *kill*. Which is why you shouldn't meet with him alone."

"I'll be fine, Bonnie. It's not like I plan on asking him if he killed Dr. Rob."

"Uh-huh."

"Okay, maybe I thought about asking him, but I'm not that stupid."

"What time are you meeting with him?"

"Five-thirty. Why?"

"I'm coming with you."

"No."

"What do you mean, no?"

"I mean, I don't want you there."

"Why not?"

"It would look weird. And…"

"And what?"

"Fine. I want to ask him about Dr. Rob. And he might not talk if you're there."

"I knew it!"

"But I wasn't going to ask if he shot him. Anyway, we should go. The library's about to open."

Over lunch, Bonnie had tried to convince Percy to let her be there when she met with Sean O'Connor, but Percy refused.

"What about Hugh?" said Bonnie.

"What about him?"

"Why don't you ask him to join you? This O'Connor guy won't jerk you around if there's another guy there."

"What makes you think he'll jerk me around?"

"He's a contractor!"

"Not all contractors are looking to rip people off, Bonnie. And besides, Hugh already suggested he be there when O'Connor stopped by, and I told him it wasn't necessary."

"What if he has a gun?"

"Do you really think he'd bring a gun to a consultation?"

"You never know."

Percy shook her head.

"Look, I promise to text you right after O'Connor leaves."

"What if he shoots you and you can't text me? If you insist on meeting with him alone, I'm going to call you at six. And if you don't answer, I'm coming over."

"We may not be done by six. Besides, Lucy should be home by then. So I won't be alone."

"Like Lucy could tackle some six-foot-two sniper."

"How do you know how tall he is?"

"I looked him up. And trust me, you do not want to get into it with this guy."

Percy sighed.

"I'll be fine, Bonnie."

"Yeah, well, I'm still calling you at six."

Lucy had texted Percy later that afternoon, asking if it was okay if she went out with some of the people from the office after work, and Percy told her that was fine. She wouldn't count on her for dinner. She thought about what Bonnie had said about being alone with Sean O'Connor and started to second-guess herself.

She sent a text to Hugh, asking if he was free for dinner that evening, hoping he was paying attention to his phone. As luck would have it, he was. However, instead of going to her place, he suggested that Percy come to his and have dinner with him and Madison.

Percy wasn't sure she was ready for that, but Hugh insisted it was no big deal. He had told Madison about Percy.

What exactly did you tell her about me? Percy wrote.

Just come over, he replied. *We're making pizzas. It'll be fun.*

Percy thought.

Fine. What time? O'Connor's supposed to come by at 5:30, so I could be there at 6:30.

6:30 is perfect. See you then. And call me if O'Connor hassles you. I won't let him. So, can I bring something?

Just yourself.

Percy arrived home a few minutes before Sean O'Connor said he would be there. Minnie was in a mood, claiming she was starving, though there was still a little dry food in her bowl. Percy quickly fed her and then ran the kitchen faucet for her. As the water was running, the doorbell rang. It must be Sean O'Connor.

Percy looked at her watch. He was right on time. Must be the military training.

She hurried to the door to let him in.

"Mr. O'Connor?" He was a big man, over six feet and stocky.

"That's me. And you must be Ms. Rollins."

"Please, call me Percy."

"And you can call me Sean. May I come in?"

"Please," said Percy, ushering him inside.

"Would you like me to take off my shoes?" he said, seeing the neat rows of shoes by the door.

"If you don't mind."

As he removed his shoes, Minnie came over to check him out.

"Hey, Kitty," he said, holding out a hand for Minnie to sniff. She must have liked how he smelled because she started to rub up against him and purr.

Percy smiled.

"She likes you."

"I have two kitties at home," he said, stroking Minnie.

"Any dogs?" He seemed like the kind of person who would have a big dog.

"I'm out too much. Cats are fine being left alone; dogs, not so much." He got up, much to Minnie's disappointment. "You want to show me the kitchen and bathrooms?"

"This way," said Percy, taking him to the kitchen first.

"So, how did you hear about me?" he asked as he looked around the kitchen.

"Through the Wellness Center."

He stopped what he was doing and looked at her.

"The Wellness Center?"

Percy suddenly felt nervous.

"I'm pretty sure that's where it was. I think I heard a patient mention you, saying what a great job you did. I'm a patient there myself, or was."

Percy knew she was rambling, which she did when she was nervous.

"Mm," said O'Connor. "Was it Laura Hastings? I did a bunch of work for her."

"Laura Hastings? Yes, that's probably who it was." Though Percy didn't know a Laura Hastings.

"So, what do you want to do here?" O'Connor asked her.

"Replace the appliances and the countertops for starters," which were some kind of laminate that was popular 40 or 50 years ago. "And either paint or replace the cabinets."

"Mm," said O'Connor. "What's your budget?"

"I haven't decided. Why don't I show you the bathrooms, and then we can discuss?"

Percy showed him the bathrooms and answered his questions about what she was hoping to do with them. Then they went back downstairs to the kitchen.

"I think I have a pretty good idea of what you want," he said. "I'll work up some designs and send them to you along with an estimate."

"That would be great. Though I'm a bit worried about the price. I'd really like to keep it under a hundred thousand if humanly possible."

"From what you said you wanted, I don't think there's a lot of construction involved. No moving walls or plumbing around. It's mostly cosmetic work. Though I'll still probably need to pull a permit. But I think it's doable within your budget."

"Good to know. Thanks."

Percy hadn't gotten up the nerve to ask O'Connor about Dr. Rob. It was now or never.

"Can I ask you a personal question?"

He seemed amused.

"Shoot."

"I heard you were also a patient of Dr. Rob's, but that you weren't happy with him and wanted the Wellness Center to refund you. Can I ask why?"

She watched his face, but he didn't seem angry. In fact, the whole time he was there, he was friendly and polite, not at all like she had pictured him or how Carol had described him.

"You heard about what happened?"

Percy nodded.

"Not one of my finest moments. But I'm a changed man. And it's in part thanks to Dr. Rob."

"Oh?"

"I was feeling pretty frustrated. I felt I wasn't getting anywhere. And I kind of blew my top, blamed Dr. Rob when it was really my fault. Then I talked to a friend. He told me I had unrealistic expectations and that it was unfair of me to lash out at Dr. Rob and his staff. He told me I should apologize and give therapy another shot."

"And did you apologize?"

"I did. And I spoke with Dr. Rob. He suggested I meet with a colleague of his, a psychiatrist who dealt with PTSD cases like mine. He thought what I needed was medication, not just talk therapy. And I said I was willing to try. The anger, it was eating me up."

"Did you meet with the psychiatrist Dr. Rob referred you to?"

"I did. He's a vet, just like me. We talked about things, and he gave me something to help with the anger and PTSD."

"I take it it worked," said Percy, as O'Connor seemed quite relaxed.

He nodded.

"I only wish I had gotten the meds sooner. Anyway, I should get going. I'll send you my thoughts in a few days."

"Great," said Percy.

Minnie appeared and was staring up at Sean O'Connor.

"You come to say goodbye, Kitty Cat?" He bent down and scratched her chin. Minnie closed her eyes and purred.

"She's a sweetie," he said, straightening up.

"She can be," said Percy. "Well, thanks again for stopping by."

She let O'Connor out and then went to grab her phone. It was six fifteen, and she saw that Bonnie had called and texted her. Percy called her back.

"You're alive! I was about to head over there."

"I told you you had nothing to worry about."

"So, it went okay? Did you ask him about Dr. Rob?"

"I did. And he admitted to being angry with him, but he said that Dr. Rob actually helped him."

"Helped him how?"

"He referred him to a psychiatrist who was able to prescribe something for his PTSD and anger management issues. Anyway, I can't talk. I need to get to Hugh's."

"You having dinner with him?"

"I am. He invited me to make pizza with him and Madison."

"Oho! The plot thickens! He must really like you if he invited you over to hang out with his kid."

Hearing Bonnie say that made Percy nervous again.

"It's just pizza, Bonnie."

"Uh-huh. Well, I'll let you go. Call me when you get home? Or were you planning on staying over?"

"Bonnie!"

"What? You're both adults. And when's the last time you got some?"

"That's none of your business."

"As I thought. Go, have fun. I'll check in later."

Percy ended the call, checked herself in the mirror, and then grabbed her bag and her car keys and left.

CHAPTER 27

"Welcome!" said Hugh, ushering Percy into his home.

Percy glanced around.

"Where's Madison?"

"Up in her room."

"And you're sure she's okay with me being here for pizza night?"

"Totally fine. She finds it amusing that I'm seeing a librarian. I think she pictures you as some old lady with glasses."

"Though she must have seen me at the library."

"No offense, but I doubt she noticed you."

Percy understood. Nowadays, especially with self-checkout, patrons didn't interact with librarians as much as they used to.

"Would you like the tour?"

"Sure."

Hugh took her into the open living room, and Percy couldn't help noticing all of the bookshelves filled with books.

"That's quite a collection you've got there."

"That's only a part of it. I have more in my study and in the bedroom. And Madison has her own collection."

"A family of readers. I like that."

He showed her the kitchen, the guest bedroom, the powder room, and his study, which, as he had said, was filled with books, including a shelf of his. Then he took her upstairs.

"That's Madison's room," he said, pointing to a door with a sign that said, *Remember to Knock*. Percy smiled at that. "And this is my room," he said, opening a door.

Percy stepped inside. It was a big room with bookcases lining one of the walls. She glanced at the titles. She guessed that many of the books had belonged to Elizabeth.

"Was Elizabeth a big reader too?"

Hugh nodded.

"She was. She taught English over in Kenwick."

Percy couldn't help noticing the king-sized bed. Was it the same bed that he had shared with his late wife?

"I thought about getting something smaller after Lizzy died," he said, seeing Percy look at the bed. "But Madison would often come in and insist on staying, saying she missed her mom. And well…"

"No need to explain," said Percy. "I understand. I still have the bed that Jim and I slept in, though it's a queen, not a king."

"Let me show you the bathroom. It was Lizzy's favorite room."

The bathroom had a big walk-in shower, a clawfoot bathtub with a window that looked onto a garden, a double vanity, a separate little room for the toilet, and next door was a large walk-in closet.

"I can see why she liked it in here," said Percy.

Hugh smiled.

"Shall we go downstairs and make some pizzas?"

"Lead the way!"

They walked by Madison's room. Hugh knocked, but there was no response.

"Is she okay?" asked Percy.

"She's probably listening to music with her headphones on. I'll just text her."

Hugh pulled out his phone and quickly typed.

"She said she'd be down in a minute."

That reminded Percy: she hadn't heard from Lucy. She went to retrieve her phone from her bag when they went downstairs.

Lucy had replied to Percy's text saying that she had gone to dinner at Hugh's and wouldn't be back late.

Have fun and don't hurry home! Lucy had written her back.

"Everything okay?" Hugh asked her.

"Everything's fine. I was just checking in with my daughter. Today was the first day of her internship, and she went out with some people from the office after work."

"That's nice. Where's she interning?"

"At a law firm over in Kenwick."

"Ah. I think you told me that she wanted to be a lawyer."

"Good memory."

Percy heard someone coming down the stairs. It was Madison. She stopped when she saw Percy.

"*You're* Percy?" She seemed surprised.

"I am," said Percy.

"And you're a librarian?"

Percy smiled.

"I am."

"Huh."

"Who wants to make some pizzas?" said Hugh.

"Me!" said Madison.

Percy had enjoyed making her Margherita pizza. And it had tasted good too. She saw Madison glancing at her as they ate. Percy wondered what exactly Hugh had told his daughter about her.

"So, how was the Dua Lipa concert?" Percy asked her. It seemed a safe topic.

"You know who she is?" said Madison.

"Of course!" said Percy. "I love her music. I put her on when I'm cleaning. Makes it go faster."

Percy hummed a few bars of "Levitating" and mimed cleaning, which made Madison giggle.

She stopped and then asked Madison what other artists she liked.

She rattled off a bunch of names, some of which Percy knew, mainly from Lucy.

"My daughter likes them too," said Percy, in response to one of the bands Madison named.

"Cool. How old is your daughter? Is she my age?"

"No, she just turned twenty. She's going to be a senior in college."

"Isn't that young to be a senior?"

"She skipped a grade. And I hear you're starting high school in the fall."

Madison nodded.

"You excited?"

"She's a little nervous," said Hugh.

"Dad!"

"But I told her she had nothing to worry about."

"I just don't like change," said Madison.

"I don't either."

They finished their pizzas, and Madison asked to be excused.

"You don't want ice cream?"

"I'm good," said Madison. "Can I go?"

"After you put your plate in the dishwasher."

Madison got up, quickly rinsed her plate, and put it in the dishwasher.

"Okay?" she said.

Hugh nodded, and Madison hurried up the stairs.

"Is she all right?"

"She's fine. Probably wants to chat with her friends. Would you like some ice cream?"

"I'm full from the pizza and salad, but you go ahead."

"That's all right. What about coffee?"

"I'd take some decaf if you have it."

"You fancy a decaf cappuccino? I have an espresso machine and can whip one up."

"An espresso machine, eh?"

"I know it's a bit of an extravagance, but I use it all the time. Italy ruined me. Now I can't start or end my day without a cappuccino or an espresso."

Talk of Italy reminded Percy.

"Have you heard from Arianna Cardinale since your lunch?"

"No. Why?"

"Just curious."

She watched as Hugh began making the cappuccino.

"I told you, I'm not interested in Arianna."

"And you still think she didn't shoot Dr. Rob."

"I do. So, how was your meeting with Sean O'Connor?"

"Good! He was very polite, and Minnie adored him."

"Is she a good judge of character?"

"I'd like to think so. Though she definitely prefers men to women, at least when it comes to strangers. Speaking of cats, where's Fluffy? I haven't seen him all evening. Is he all right, or is he at the vet's again?"

"He's probably in Madison's room. He's Madison's emotional support animal."

"Does Madison still need an emotional support animal?" She seemed fine to Percy, but what did Percy know?

"Sometimes. Mostly, though, I think he just likes sleeping on Madison's bed. And Madison likes having him around."

Percy smiled.

"So Fluffy's all better now?"

"Yup. Back to his old diva self."

"Who's your vet?"

"We use Stonebridge Veterinary Clinic."

"That's who we use too."

Hugh steamed a small container of milk and then gently poured it into the cups of decaf espresso.

"Here you go," he said, handing Percy a cup. "Would you like some sugar?"

"Let me take a sip first." She took a sip. "Maybe just a little."

"I know, it's a bit strong."

He handed her a glass bowl filled with sugar along with a spoon. Percy scooped a little sugar into her cappuccino, stirred, and took another sip.

"Mm."

"Good?"

"Good."

"Shall we go sit in the living room? It's more comfortable."

"Sure."

Percy followed Hugh into the living room and took a seat next to him on a couch.

"So, how's the book coming?"

"Good! I know it's wrong to say this, but Dr. Rob's murder inspired me."

"Oh?"

"It's taken the book in a whole new direction, but I think my agent's going to love it."

"And you still won't tell me about it?"

"Not until I'm done with the first draft."

"I heard that the police were close to making an arrest."

"Oh? Detective Russo didn't say anything."

"When did you speak with him?"

"This morning. I was hoping he might throw me a bone. Apparently, he's a fan of my work."

Of course, thought Percy.

"And?"

"He said he couldn't discuss an active investigation."

"Bummer."

"It was. But I'm not giving up. So, how was your visit with Sean O'Connor?"

"Good."

"Did you ask him about Dr. Rob?"

"I did."

"And was he angry that you asked about him?"

"Not at all. He was actually quite forthcoming."

"Oh?"

"He admitted to being angry with Dr. Rob and demanding his money back. Said it wasn't his finest moment. But he said he went back to the Wellness Center a few days later and apologized to everyone. Then he started seeing a psychiatrist who put him on meds, and he said he's doing much better."

"Huh. So, you don't think he shot him?"

"I do not."

"Then who do you think could have killed him?"

"Well, you believe Arianna is innocent, so that pretty much leaves Ed, Dr. Rob's brother. Or possibly Dr. Richardson." *Or you*, Percy silently thought. But she really didn't want the killer to be Hugh and tried to banish the thought.

"Wait. Dr. Richardson is a suspect? Wasn't she in Beauport at the time?"

"Supposedly. But Carol said that she and Dr. Rob had had a big argument just before he died, and then Carol overheard Dr. Richardson saying that she needed to get rid of him. And Dr. Richardson gets Dr. Rob's share of the business now that he's gone. Or so Carol said. So…"

"I suppose that's a motive, but I can't see her shooting him. My money's on the brother. From what you've said, Ed was clearly envious of Dr. Rob. Plus, Dr. Rob wouldn't give him money. And then the guy disappears. Sounds guilty to me."

Percy couldn't deny that Hugh had a point. Ed was the obvious suspect. But would he really shoot his brother? Percy didn't have any siblings, but she'd like to think that if she did, she would never harm them, even if they annoyed her.

"Or it could be someone we don't know about," she said. "Didn't Arianna say that she saw a young woman at Dr. Rob's?"

"She did."

"Maybe she's the killer."

Hugh looked thoughtful.

"What was her motive?"

"Who knows? Though Arianna said the young woman was pregnant. Maybe Dr. Rob was the baby daddy, but he didn't want the baby. Isn't that why Arianna believes Dr. Rob dumped her?"

"Do you honestly believe Dr. Rob was running around town impregnating women and then abandoning them?"

An image of Dr. Rob surrounded by a bunch of pregnant women popped into Percy's head, but she shook it off.

"I don't like to think so, but…"

"She was probably a patient of his."

"Did he see patients at home?"

"I don't know. Maybe."

"You don't think the young woman could have been his…?" Percy didn't know what word to use. *Paramour? Lover? Girlfriend?* They all seemed wrong.

"Arianna said the woman looked to be in her early twenties. Dr. Rob was old enough to be her father."

"Please. As if an older man never dated a much younger woman."

Hugh's expression turned sour.

"Look, we both liked Dr. Rob and wanted to think of him as perfect."

"I never thought he was perfect."

"The point is, he admitted he was flawed. And maybe his flaw was needing to sleep with women."

"He didn't say *he* was flawed. He said therapists in general were often flawed."

Percy gave him a look.

"Whatever. The point is, we don't really know that much about Dr. Rob or the people in his life. And it's possible this young woman or someone else we don't know about killed him."

"I think the brother did it."

"Is that what your writer's intuition is telling you?"

"Sometimes the most obvious solution is the right one."

"Not in mysteries."

"Those are books, Percy. They're not real. The real world doesn't operate like one of your mystery novels, which you'd realize if you got out more."

Percy stared at Hugh. Had he really just said that?

"I need to go," she said, getting up.

"I've upset you," said Hugh.

"You haven't upset me," Percy said, trying to keep her voice even and not letting Hugh know how his patronizing tone and dismissiveness had hurt her. "I'm just tired. It's been a long day, and I want to hear how Lucy's first day of work was."

"If you're sure it wasn't something I said."

"What do you want me to do with the cappuccino cup?"

"Leave it. I'll take care of it."

"Are you sure?"

"It's fine."

He walked Percy to the door.

"Thank you for the pizza," she said. "I enjoyed meeting Madison."

"You're welcome anytime."

They lingered at the door for several seconds. Then Percy turned and opened it.

She unlocked her car and opened the door. She sensed that Hugh was watching her, but she refused to turn around.

CHAPTER 28

"So, how was dinner with Hugh?" Lucy asked her mother.

"It was fine."

"Just fine? Is he not a good cook? What did he make you?"

"We made pizzas, and I met his daughter, Madison."

"Was she cool with you seeing her dad?"

"She seemed okay, though I don't know what exactly Hugh told her."

"So, why are you home so early?"

"It's not that early." Lucy gave her mother a look. "I just wanted to see you, find out how your first day was."

"You could have asked me about it in the morning. Unless you didn't get home until after I left for work," Lucy added with a grin.

"Lucy!"

"Oh, come on, Mom. I'm not a little kid. So, did Hugh say or do something to piss you off?"

Percy sighed.

"We disagreed about who killed Dr. Rob. And I found his attitude towards my theories patronizing."

"You need to let go of this need to figure out who killed Dr. Rob. It's wrecking your relationship."

"Hugh and I aren't in a relationship. And if he's going to patronize me, I'm not sure I want to be in one with him."

"What did he say exactly?"

"He insinuated that I spent too much time reading mysteries and needed to get out more."

Lucy gave her mother a look.

"What? You agree with him?"

"You do spend a lot of time reading mysteries."

Percy looked annoyed. Not everyone was cut out to be a social butterfly. And what was wrong with reading?

"Just give the guy another chance. I'm sure whatever he said, he didn't really mean it."

"I wouldn't be so sure about that."

"Remember what you always tell me, about giving guys a second chance?" Percy made a face. "He clearly likes you. Otherwise, he wouldn't have invited you over to make pizzas with his daughter. And shouldn't you let the police find Dr. Rob's killer?"

"I suppose you're right, but… I feel like I'm so close to finding out who killed him. Like the solution's right in front of me, but I just can't see it. And now there's this new twist."

"I know I'm going to regret asking this, but… What's the new twist?"

"Dr. Rob may have been seeing someone."

"So?"

"The woman in question is much younger than he is. And she was very pregnant when she was spotted with Dr. Rob."

"And you think Dr. Rob could be the baby daddy?"

"It's possible."

"And you think she could have something to do with Dr. Rob's death?"

"I do. But Hugh disagrees with me."

"So, who does he think killed Dr. Rob?"

"He thinks it was Ed. Word is Ed had money troubles, and Dr. Rob refused to help him."

"But you don't think Ed did it?"

"I don't know. All of the information we have points to him, but…"

"But?"

"I can't see him killing his brother, even if Ed didn't like Dr. Rob." Percy sighed. "Maybe Hugh's right, and I have read too many mysteries. In any case, the police are probably going to make an arrest soon, and then we'll know."

"You seem bummed."

"I was just hoping to figure it out before the police did. I know that's silly, but…"

"It's not silly. I get it. But you need to try to let it go. I know: Easier said than done. Anyway, I'm going upstairs."

"Wait. You didn't tell me: How was your first day?"

"It was good. Everyone there seems nice. And we went out for a drink afterwards."

"They know you're underage, yes?"

"Yes, Mom. I had a Coke."

"Well, have a good night. I'll see you in the morning."

That night, Percy had the same dream, or nightmare, over and over again. She was in Dr. Rob's office, invisible, watching as each of the suspects, including Hugh and a faceless pregnant young woman, walked in and shot Dr. Rob.

She woke up around four, sweating, and couldn't fall back to sleep. Finally, around five-thirty, she got up and went for a long run.

As she ran, she decided she would pay a visit to the vet, to see if Hugh had actually been there when he claimed he had. Though she wasn't entirely sure how she would find that out. As to how to find out about the young woman… Maybe Dr. Richardson knew something. She would make an appointment to see her. Though what would be her excuse? She would figure out something. That decided, she headed home.

Percy was having her coffee in the kitchen when Lucy came in.

"Morning," she said to her daughter. "Coffee?"

"Please."

Percy poured her a mug, adding sugar and milk.

"Thanks," said Lucy, taking a sip. "You were up early."

"You heard me?"

Lucy nodded.

"Sorry."

"It's okay. I went back to sleep. Why were you up?"

"I couldn't sleep. Say, is your friend Daphne working at Stonebridge Veterinary again this summer?"

"She is. Why?"

"I have a favor to ask."

"If you need someone to watch Minnie, so you and Hugh can go away for a weekend, I can do it."

"Whoa. Slow down. That's not what I wanted to ask her."

"Oh. What did you want?"

"It's about Hugh's cat, Fluffy."

"Hugh has a cat named Fluffy?" Lucy seemed amused.

"His daughter named him. He's a big Maine Coon, though I didn't see him."

"What do you want to know?"

"I want to know if Hugh brought Fluffy in a few weeks ago, and, if so, what time his appointment was, and if he waited or left."

Lucy looked at her mother suspiciously.

"And why do you want to know that? This has to do with Dr. Rob, doesn't it? You don't think Hugh killed him, do you? Last night, you said you thought it was some young woman or Ed."

"I know. I don't really think Hugh did it. But I heard the police were asking about him. Hugh was supposed to meet with Dr. Rob at noon that day, but he canceled that morning."

"I can't imagine Hugh killing Dr. Rob. What motive did he have?"

"Maybe Dr. Rob didn't want Hugh writing a book about him."

"Hugh was writing a book about Dr. Rob?"

"He claimed it wasn't about Dr. Rob personally. It was about a therapist like Dr. Rob."

"And what? Dr. Rob told him to stop, and Hugh killed him?"

When Lucy said it like that, it did sound far-fetched.

Percy sighed.

"I just need to know that Hugh didn't lie to me. So can you just confirm with Daphne that he was at the vet's when Dr. Rob was shot?"

"Fine. If it gets Hugh off your suspect list, I'll ask her."

"Thank you." Percy looked over at the clock. "I need to brush my teeth and then get to the library."

"So early?"

"I have some things I need to do. Have a good second day, and remember to eat something."

"Yes, Mom."

Bonnie went over to Percy as soon as she got to the library and insisted that Percy tell her all about her dinner with Hugh. Percy repeated what she had told Lucy.

"Hmm," said Bonnie. "I don't like that he discounted your theories, but he does have a point. Ed is the obvious choice."

"I know. But something tells me he didn't do it."

"Librarian's intuition?"

"Something like that. I just need to find out who the mystery woman was, assuming she really exists."

"You think Arianna made her up?"

"It's possible."

"But why would she do that?"

"Maybe she wanted to throw suspicion off of herself. Anyway, I'm going to make an appointment to see Dr. Richardson. Maybe she knows who the mystery woman is."

"Even if she does, I doubt she would tell you if the woman was a patient."

"I realize that. But I have to at least try. And she'll know if Dr. Rob had a will and what happens to the Wellness Center."

"Okay. Good luck. And let me know what Dr. Richardson says."

"I will."

At lunchtime, Percy called the Wellness Center to make an appointment with Dr. Richardson.

"You don't want to see Dr. Yates?" Carol asked her.

"I was hoping to see Dr. Richardson. Can she squeeze me in this week?"

"Let me see," said Carol. "Can you hold for a sec?"

Percy said she could and waited.

"Are you still there?" said Carol a couple of minutes later.

"I am."

"Sorry for the delay. As it happens, Dr. Richardson's four-thirty appointment canceled. I know you're probably working then, but the next lunchtime or evening appointment isn't until next week."

"Four-thirty today?" said Percy.

"That's right."

"I'll take it!"

"Okay! I'll put you in. Gotta go. I'll see you later."

Percy grinned. Maybe she would have the answers she needed by this evening.

She went to find Carmen, to tell her she had a doctor's

appointment and needed to leave a little early. Hopefully, Carmen would be okay with that.

"Everything okay?" Carmen asked her.

"I just need to get something checked."

Carmen said she hoped nothing was wrong and that it wasn't a problem. Percy thanked her and said she would make it up. But Carmen told her not to worry about it.

Percy sat in the Wellness Center's waiting room, her right leg jiggling. Dr. Richardson was running late, and Percy was feeling anxious. Finally, Dr. Richardson came out.

"Hi, Percy. Would you like to come back?"

Percy nodded and followed Dr. Richardson to her office.

"Sorry to be late," said Dr. Richardson, taking a seat. "I had to take a call. So, why did you want to meet with me? I thought you had a good session with Dr. Yates."

Percy wondered what Dr. Yates had told her.

"It was all right. There was just something I thought only you could help me with."

Dr. Richardson waited for Percy to go on.

"It's about Dr. Rob." *Did Dr. Richardson look annoyed?* "Though really, it's about the Wellness Center," Percy quickly added.

"Go on."

"Did Dr. Rob have a will?"

"A will?"

Percy nodded.

"Why do you want to know if he had a will?"

"I wanted to know what happens to the Wellness Center now that he's gone. Do you have to sell it?"

Dr. Richardson seemed to relax. She even smiled.

"Dr. Rob left his shares of the business to me. And I have no plans to sell it."

"Phew!" said Percy, trying to sound relieved. "So he didn't leave the business to his brother?"

Dr. Richardson looked confused.

"Why would he leave the business to his brother?"

"Isn't he Dr. Rob's next of kin? Or is there someone else? Did he mention anyone in his will?"

Dr. Richardson was giving Percy a funny look.

"Is there some other reason you want to know if Dr. Rob had a will, Percy?"

Percy hesitated.

"Can't you just tell me if he had a will?"

They regarded each other for several seconds.

"If I tell you, will you tell me why you want to know?"

Percy nodded.

"He left a will, but it's in probate."

"Thank you." If the will was being probated, she could request a copy.

"Now it's your turn. Why did you really want to know if Dr. Rob had a will?"

"I was concerned about the Wellness Center." Dr. Richardson wasn't buying it. "And I wanted to know if he mentioned a woman."

"A woman?"

"I heard he was seeing someone, romantically." Dr. Richardson's eyebrows went up. "And I wondered if he mentioned her in his will."

"Did you have romantic feelings for Dr. Rob, Percy?"

"What?! Me?! No! I just wanted to know if Dr. Rob was leaving someone behind, someone who was special to him, say a young woman in her twenties?" *Who may be having or just had his baby*, Percy silently added.

Judging by the expression on Dr. Richardson's face, Percy knew she had botched it. Dr. Richardson was never going to tell her if Dr. Rob was seeing someone or who that someone was.

"You need to let Dr. Rob go, Percy. I know it's hard. But you need to try. And if you can't, I highly recommend you meet with Dr. Yates again. She specializes in patients dealing with obsessive thoughts. And I really think she could help you."

"I'm not obsessing. I just need to know who killed him and why."

Dr. Richardson gave her a sympathetic look.

"We all want to know that, Percy. As do the police."

"But they haven't arrested anyone. And it's been three weeks."

"These things take time. Now, if you don't have any more questions?"

"Actually… Did you know that Hugh Barnes was working on a book with Dr. Rob?"

"I did."

"What did you think about that?"

"I found it odd. Dr. Rob is—or was—a very private person."

"But Dr. Rob was okay with Hugh writing a book based on him."

Dr. Richardson frowned.

"The book wasn't based on him. Dr. Rob would have never allowed that."

So, had Dr. Rob told Hugh to stop?

"Speaking of Mr. Barnes," said Dr. Richardson, "I heard the two of you were seeing each other."

"Who told you that?"

Dr. Richardson didn't answer.

"We're just friends."

Dr. Richardson looked like she didn't believe that.

"Just be careful."

"Be careful?" *Did Dr. Richardson know something about Hugh?*

"I don't think he's over his late wife. They were quite

close. He dedicated all of his books to her, you know."

"Oh," Percy said, somewhat relieved that was what Dr. Richardson was warning her about. "I know about his wife and the books. And, as I said, we're just friends."

"Okay." Dr. Richardson looked down at her watch. "I'm afraid our time is up. I hope you'll consider giving Dr. Yates another try."

"I'll think about it."

Percy saw a young woman at the front desk, speaking to Carol. She had a baby with her. Percy thought the young woman looked familiar, but she couldn't place her. Was she a patient?

"Percy!" said Carol, seeing Percy waiting a few feet away. "Come meet my daughter. Joanna, this is Percy. She's the one who recommended those books. She works at the Stonebridge Library."

Joanna smiled.

"Nice to meet you, Percy. And this is Ella," she said, turning the baby towards Percy. She was an adorable baby with a thatch of dark brown hair and big blue eyes like her mother.

"Hi, Ella!" said Percy, smiling at the baby. "She's a cutie."

"Thanks. Though she can be a little demon when she wants to be."

"Your mother said she wasn't sleeping through the night yet."

"Joanna insists on nursing her," said Carol.

"I understand," said Percy. "I nursed Lucy until she was nearly twelve months. Though I pumped."

"I'll probably have to do that too when I go back to school and to work."

"You're in school?" She didn't seem that young.

"Graduate school."

"Joanna's getting her MSW," which stood for Master of Social Work, "at Western Connecticut," said Carol.

"Good for you!" said Percy. "So, do you want to be a social worker?"

"Or a therapist," said Joanna.

"Joanna used to help me out here during the summer when she was in college."

"I don't remember seeing you here," Percy said to Joanna.

"This was before you started coming here," said Carol. "Percy's husband died two years ago," she told her daughter.

"I'm so sorry to hear that," said Joanna.

"Thank you. I still miss him."

Percy noticed that Joanna wasn't wearing a wedding ring and wondered about the baby's father. She vaguely recalled Carol saying he wasn't around. Was he in the military or had he abandoned them?

Ella started to fuss.

"I should go check her diaper," said Joanna.

"It was nice meeting the two of you," said Percy.

"Nice meeting you too."

Ella let out a wail, and Joanna hurried to the bathroom.

"Ella is adorable," Percy said to Carol.

"I think so, but I'm biased."

"You didn't tell me your daughter wanted to be a therapist. Did it have something to do with you working here?"

"Not really. Jo had some issues when she was younger. We took her to see a therapist, and she felt it really helped her."

"I see."

"Then, when she was in college and deciding what to major in, and was thinking about majoring in psychology, I suggested she speak with Dr. Richardson. I was working here at the time, and Dr. Richardson said Joanna could spend the summer here."

"That was very nice of her."

"It was. And she and Joanna hit it off."

"And I take it Joanna decided to major in psychology as a result."

"She did. And she spent the next summer here as well."

A patient had come in while Percy had been talking to Carol.

"Sorry," Percy said to the man.

"No worries," the man replied. "I'm early."

Percy turned back to Carol.

"Let me know if you still want to discuss those books or if you'd like more recommendations."

Carol said she'd let her know, and Percy left.

CHAPTER 29

Carlo had asked Bonnie and Percy if they could move their dinner to Thursday, just this one time, and they had agreed. So Percy was having dinner with Lucy that evening. As they ate, Percy asked Lucy if she had spoken with Daphne.

"I texted her, but she said she was super busy."

"Did she ask you why you wanted to know about Fluffy?"

"She did."

"And what did you tell her?"

"The truth."

Percy stared at her daughter.

"What?" said Lucy.

"You told her the truth? What exactly did you tell her?"

"I told her that my mom was trying to solve Dr. Rob's murder and needed to know if Hugh Barnes was there with his cat Fluffy at the time."

"You weren't supposed to tell her that, Lucy! What if she tells Hugh I was checking up on him?"

"I doubt she'd do that. She seemed amused. I think she dug the idea of you playing amateur detective. She's into murder mysteries."

Percy looked annoyed.

"Well, what's done is done. So, do you think she'll be able to find out if he was there?"

"I'm sure she will. She just has to find a time when no

one's around to check the computer or else ask one of the assistants."

"Please tell her to be discreet."

"You can count on Daphne. She won't rat you out."

Percy wasn't so sure about that.

"So, how was day two?"

"Good, though boring. There's not a whole lot for me to do. I've mostly been fetching and filing."

"At least the people are nice and you're getting paid."

"I know. And I'm sure they'll give me more stuff to do once I prove myself."

They finished dinner, and Percy asked Lucy if she wanted to watch something. But Lucy said she was going to FaceTime with Jamie. Maybe later.

As she cleaned the kitchen, Percy realized she hadn't heard from Hugh. Was he angry with her for leaving? Percy told herself she didn't care. But she did.

As she was staring out the window, her phone started buzzing. Could it be Hugh, calling to apologize? But no, it was Bonnie.

"How did things go with Dr. Richardson? Did you learn anything?"

"Not really. As I suspected, she's now in charge of the Wellness Center."

"Sounds like a motive to me."

"I suppose. But I just can't picture her shooting him. She'd be more subtle."

"Mm. So, Dr. Rob had a will?"

"He did, but it's in probate. I was thinking I'd call Marty Lefkowitz."

"Who?"

"He's a retired probate judge. He and Jim played pickleball."

"Good idea. Anything else?"

"I met Carol's daughter, Joanna, and her little girl, Ella.

Cute little thing. Joanna's getting her MSW."

"You think she'll join the practice?"

"Maybe. Carol said Joanna used to help out at the Wellness Center during the summer when she was in college."

"Did she shadow Dr. Rob?"

"I don't know. Carol only mentioned Dr. Richardson."

"Does Joanna want to work with adolescents?"

"I didn't ask. Though Carol said Joanna had some issues when she was an adolescent and that therapy really helped her. So maybe Joanna wants to pay it forward."

"Nice. So, have you heard from Hugh?"

"No. I think he may be upset with me."

"He's probably just busy. You know how writers get."

"I suppose."

"You could always text him."

"I thought about it."

"I sense a but."

"But I'm still kind of annoyed with him. He didn't have to be so patronizing. Just because he's a famous author of thrillers doesn't mean my theories aren't valid."

"Of course not. But give him a chance to apologize. Hey, Harry's here, but I wanted to check in. I'll see you tomorrow at the library."

"See you tomorrow."

As soon as the call ended, Percy checked her contacts for Marty Lefkowitz's phone number. Percy didn't know him that well. He had been Jim's friend. But she and Jim had had dinner with Marty and his wife, Ruth, a few times, and she had liked them. And Marty had helped her after Jim died.

Percy looked at the clock. It was a little after eight. Maybe she should wait until tomorrow to call. Though she would be at the library most of the day. She could always call him before she left for work. But maybe Marty wasn't an early riser.

A little voice in her head said, *Just call him already!*

His phone rang four times. Percy was preparing to leave a voicemail message or hang up when he answered.

"Hello?"

"Is this Marty?"

"Speaking. Who is this?"

"It's Percy Rollins, Jim's wife."

"Percy! How are you? You know, I still miss my weekly pickleball game with your husband."

"I miss him too."

"I'm sure you do. So, to what do I owe the pleasure of this call?"

"Actually, I have a favor to ask you."

"Ask away."

"It's about a will. It's in probate, and I wanted to know if you could help me get a copy or let me know what it says."

"You can request a copy yourself if it's in probate. Unless it's confidential."

"That's why I'm reaching out to you. Could you check for me? I just want to know who the beneficiaries are."

"Whose will are we talking about?"

"Robert Mankiewicz's."

"Ah, Dr. Rob."

"Did you know him?"

"I met him a couple of times, but I didn't know him well. Why do you want to know about his will?"

"I was a patient of his. And I was there, at the Wellness Center, right after he was shot."

"That must have been quite traumatic."

"It was a bit traumatic."

"And why are you interested in his will?" he asked again.

"It could reveal who shot him."

Marty didn't say anything.

"Are you still there?"

"Jim always said you had an inquisitive mind. I suppose you need one to be a librarian. But Percy, Dr. Rob's murder is a matter for the police."

"I know. But... I feel as though I have a vested interest. Please, Marty. Will you help me? I just want to know who benefits from his death."

She heard him sigh.

"Very well. I'll see what I can do."

"Thank you."

"You really think one of his beneficiaries killed him?"

"It's possible. Money is often a motive for murder."

"I need to go. I hear Ruth calling me."

"Please give her my best."

"I will. How's your daughter? Did she graduate?" Percy could hear a woman's voice in the background, but Marty was ignoring it. "I know she was in college when Jim died."

"She's going to be a senior. And she's doing well. She wants to be a lawyer, like her dad."

"He was one of the good ones. Still can't believe he's not with us."

"I know. Neither can I."

"Well, gotta go. I'll be in touch when I have news."

"Thanks, Marty. Have a good night."

The next morning, Lucy promised her mother that she would follow up with Daphne that afternoon if she hadn't heard from her. Then Percy headed to the library. All morning, she kept thinking about what Daphne and Marty would have to say.

"You okay?" said Mary Beth. They were working the circulation desk together.

"Hmm?" said Percy.

"You seem preoccupied."

"Sorry. I just have a lot going on."

"Oh?"

A patron came over before Percy could answer. Percy smiled at the woman, who was picking up a book on hold, and got the book for her. She was followed by several more patrons, wanting to pick up or check out books, or who had questions.

Finally, it was time for Percy's lunch break. She immediately went to get her bag and retrieve her phone. There was nothing from Lucy or Marty. Though she didn't really expect either of them to have messaged her. It was too soon.

"Everything okay?" It was Bonnie. "You're making that face."

"What face?"

"The face you make when you're frustrated."

"I didn't realize I had a specific face for that." Percy made a mental note to work on schooling her face, so she didn't show what she was feeling.

"So, what's frustrating you?"

"I'm waiting for some people to get back to me. And you know how much I love waiting."

"Who are you waiting to get back to you?"

"Lucy and Marty Lefkowitz."

"You spoke with him?"

"I did."

"And?"

"He said he'd see what he could find out."

"Let me know if he finds out anything juicy. And what's up with Lucy?"

"I asked her to speak with her friend Daphne, who works at Stockbridge Veterinary."

"Is Minnie okay?"

"Minnie's fine. I wanted to know if Hugh really brought his cat in on the day Dr. Rob was shot. And, if he did, if he was there the whole time."

"You don't believe him?"

"I want to but…"

"You don't really think Hugh could have shot Dr. Rob, do you? Does he even own a gun?"

"I don't know. But why would the police have asked Carol about him if he was innocent?"

"Didn't you say they asked Carol about you too?"

Percy made another face.

"Well, for your sake, and Hugh's, I hope Lucy's friend gets back to her soon and tells her that Hugh was at the vet's the whole time."

"I hope so too."

"Well, I should get back to work. We can talk more at dinner. Maybe by then you'll have heard something from Lucy and Marty."

"Mom? You home?" called Lucy.

"I'm upstairs!" Percy called back.

Lucy went up to Percy's office.

"How was work?" Percy asked her.

"Good."

"They give you something to do other than filing?"

"Today I got to photocopy. Woohoo!" Percy gave her a sympathetic look. "It's fine. The other intern's in the same boat."

"Who's the other intern?"

"Some guy from Kenwick who's studying political science at Yale."

"He nice?"

"He's okay. Anyway, I wanted to tell you, I heard back from Daphne." Percy waited for Lucy to go on. "She confirmed that Fluffy had an appointment that day at noon and that Hugh dropped her off."

"He dropped her off? He didn't stay?"

"According to Daphne, he told Sharise, who was at the

front desk that day, that he had to go do something, but he'd be back within half an hour."

"And was he?"

"Daphne said Sharise wasn't sure what time Hugh got back. They were pretty busy."

Percy frowned.

"You okay, Mom?"

"Sorry. I'm fine. Thanks for asking Daphne about Hugh."

"No problem." She looked down at her mother. "Don't you need to get ready for dinner?"

Percy was wearing the outfit she had worn to work, a striped button-down shirt and a skirt.

"We're just going to Annie's."

Lucy didn't say anything.

"What?"

"Nothing."

"You don't like what I'm wearing?"

"It's fine. It's just, didn't you wear that to work?"

"So?"

"Don't you want to change?"

"I'm good. So, what are you doing about dinner?"

"I'm meeting up with Cassie and some of the gang at Pizzata."

"Have fun."

CHAPTER 30

Percy sat with Bonnie and Carlo at their usual table.

"How are things at the gallery this week?" she asked Carlo. "Any better?"

"Still busy."

"What about getting a college student to help out?"

"I told you, by the end of June, it'll be like a tomb, what with people going away for the summer."

"You going to take a vacation?" Bonnie asked him. "You deserve one."

"My friend Barney invited me to go to his place in Provincetown in July."

"Barney? Do we know Barney?"

"I've mentioned him before."

Bonnie looked at Percy.

"Do you recall Carlo mentioning a Barney before?"

"The only Barneys I know are a purple dinosaur and Rubble," said Percy.

Carlo didn't look amused.

"I'm sure I've mentioned him. We used to work together."

"Where?" said Bonnie.

"At *Fashionable Living*. He was the fashion editor."

"Oh, I remember Barney now!" said Percy. "He came here to visit you a few years ago. He was very..." Percy searched for the right word. The Barney she had met had been rather flamboyant, dressing in bright colors and different patterns and pontificating on everything.

"Barney is a bit extra," said Carlo. "But he's been a good friend."

"So, are you going to visit him in Provincetown?" asked Bonnie.

"I'm thinking about it. I just need to make sure Gianna can cover for me."

"Or you could close the store for a week. You said yourself it would probably be dead here."

Their drinks arrived, and they paused their conversation to sip them.

"So, you hear back from Marty Lefkowitz?" Bonnie asked Percy.

"Not yet. But I knew it could take a couple of days."

"Who's Marty Lefkowitz?" asked Carlo.

"He's a retired probate judge," Percy explained. "He and Jim played pickleball together."

"Percy wants to know about Dr. Rob's will, and she thought Old Marty could help."

"You think someone knew they were going to get a lot of money and killed Dr. Rob to get it?" Carlo asked Percy.

"Possibly," she said. "Though we don't know if Dr. Rob was well off. For all we know, he could have been in debt."

"Wasn't the Wellness Center successful?" asked Bonnie.

"They seemed to have a lot of patients, but that doesn't mean they were making a lot of money."

"Do you think the business will be sold now that Dr. Rob's no longer there?" asked Carlo.

"I asked Dr. Richardson that, and she said she had no plans to sell."

"So, she's in charge now?" Bonnie asked her.

"That's what she said. Apparently, she and Dr. Rob had an agreement. Should anything happen to one of them, the other got their shares."

"Hmm. Sounds like a motive to me. And you said she wanted to get rid of him."

"You two don't really think Dr. Richardson could have shot Dr. Rob, do you?" said Carlo.

"Not really," said Percy. "At least I don't. But we can't count her out just yet. And I just found out Hugh's alibi isn't as airtight as we thought, so…"

"Hold up," said Bonnie. "Did you find out something about Hugh?"

Percy nodded.

"Lucy has a friend who works for the vet. She said Hugh dropped Fluffy off at noon, but then he left to take care of something and was gone for a while."

"Do you know where he went?"

"I don't."

"Are you going to ask him?"

"I want to, but…"

"You don't seriously think Hugh murdered Dr. Rob, do you?" Carlo asked her.

"I don't want to, but Dr. Richardson told me that she didn't think Dr. Rob was happy about Hugh writing that book."

"You need to talk to him, Percy."

"And say what? He already told me he didn't murder Dr. Rob."

"You asked him?" said Bonnie.

Percy didn't answer.

Bonnie sighed, and none of them spoke for several seconds.

"Do you know what you're going to have?" she asked Carlo.

"I was thinking of getting the rotisserie chicken."

Bonnie stared at him.

"Really?"

"Is there something wrong with that?"

"No, it's just… You never get the rotisserie chicken."

"Well, there's always a first time. What are you going to get?"

"I was thinking of getting the salmon."

She turned to Percy.

"What are you going to get?"

"I was thinking of getting the ribs."

Bonnie stared at her.

"What is this, Freaky Thursday? You never get the ribs. You always get the chicken."

"I thought I'd switch it up."

Bonnie shook her head.

They signaled to the server and placed their order.

"So, you and Harry have plans for the weekend?" Percy asked Bonnie.

"I don't want to talk about Harry."

"Did something happen?"

"Everything's fine," Bonnie snapped. "I just don't want to talk about him."

Clearly, everything wasn't fine, but Percy didn't push.

"How's the summer reading challenge going?" Carlo asked them. "Who do you think will read more books this summer, children or adults?"

"My money's on the kids," said Percy. "They get stickers for every book they read. And there's a prize for the child who reads the most books."

"Ah," said Carlo. "Nothing like a little incentive."

"Speaking of books," said Percy. "I can't remember the last time I saw you at the library."

"I've been listening to audiobooks lately," he replied. "I haven't had time to read. But I can listen while I frame."

"And here I thought you just listened to opera," said Bonnie.

"What have you been listening to?" Percy asked him.

The conversation then turned to books, which was fine by Percy.

After they had finished their main course, Percy excused herself to go to the bathroom. As she headed there, she thought she saw Hugh seated at the bar. And was that Arianna with him? Percy thought of going over there, but the bar was crowded, and she really needed to pee.

She looked over at the bar when she was done. It was doing a brisk business, and she couldn't tell if the couple she had seen were Hugh and Arianna. She started to head over and nearly collided with a waiter. She apologized, turned, and headed back to her table. She was being paranoid.

As they headed out of the restaurant a little later, Percy glanced over at the bar. The couple she had seen earlier wasn't there.

"Looking for someone?" asked Bonnie.

"I thought I saw someone I knew there earlier," said Percy. "But I must have been mistaken."

Bonnie gave her a funny look but didn't say anything.

They were nearly to the door when Bonnie said she needed to use the bathroom.

"I'll wait for you," said Percy.

"That's all right," said Bonnie.

"Well, I need to get to the gallery. I'll see you ladies next week."

They said goodnight, and Carlo and Percy stepped outside.

As soon as Carlo left, Percy got out her phone and checked for messages.

"Anything interesting?"

Percy startled. She hadn't seen Bonnie come over.

"Sorry, I didn't mean to surprise you. Hugh text you?"

"No."

"You should text him. Or, better yet, call him."

"And say what?"

"That you know he wasn't at the vet's when he said he was."

"He'll just get defensive."

"Maybe, or maybe he'll have a perfectly good explanation for why he left."

"Maybe."

"Look, Percy. I know you. You're going to obsess about this. Just ask him where he was."

"He already told me he was at the vet's. Even offered to send me the invoice. And he said he'd never lie to me."

"And yet he did. You need to have a talk with him."

"I'll think about it."

"Fine. I should head home."

"Before you go, are things not okay with you and Harry? You snapped at me at the restaurant when I asked about him."

Bonnie sighed.

"We just had an argument. That's all."

"About?"

"I'd rather not discuss it right now. Let's just say, I have a lot to think about."

"Okay. But if you ever want to talk, about Harry or anything, you know I'm here for you."

Bonnie smiled.

"I know."

Percy thought about calling or texting Hugh as she walked home. Finally, as she stood outside her front door, she sent him a text.

We need to talk.

He replied instantly.

I was just about to text you.

You were?

I agree. We need to talk. I have something I need to tell you.

Percy wondered what it was. Could he be about to confess to killing Dr. Rob? *Don't be silly*, that little voice in her head said.

Do you want to call me?

I'd rather talk in person. You free for breakfast tomorrow?

As it happened, Percy was working the second shift the next day. (She preferred to work the first shift, which meant she'd be home by six at the latest, but she occasionally had to work the second shift, which was from noon until eight or eight-thirty, depending on whether she had to close.)

What time and where? I don't have to be at the library until noon.

The Over Easy Café at 9? I know you like to get a run in first thing.

That's fine, wrote Percy. *See you then.*

Percy found it hard to fall asleep that night. She kept wondering what Hugh had to say to her—and worrying how he'd react when she told him she knew he hadn't been at the vet's the whole time.

She was up at five-thirty the next morning and went for a run, being as quiet as possible as she went down the stairs so as not to wake Lucy. She fed Minnie and let her drink from the faucet. Then she did a few stretches and was out the door.

She was showered and dressed by the time Lucy appeared in the kitchen at eight.

"You look nice," said Lucy. "I thought you didn't have to be at work until noon today. Why are you so dressed up?"

"I'm not dressed up. It's just supposed to be a nice day, and I thought I'd wear a dress."

"Uh-huh. You meeting someone?"

"Just Hugh. He invited me to breakfast."

Lucy grinned.

"That explains the dress and the makeup."

Percy made a face.

"Well, have fun. I need to get to work."

"You're not going to have breakfast?"

"No time. I need to be there by eight-thirty. And they have stuff to eat at the office."

"Nothing healthy, I'm guessing. Take a protein bar."

"Fine. Gotta run! Have fun with Hugh!"

Lucy gave her mother a quick kiss on the cheek. Then she was gone.

Percy looked at the clock. It was only ten after eight. She didn't need to head to Over Easy for another thirty-five minutes. She looked over at the coffee pot. She had already had a cup of coffee, which had done nothing to help her nerves. Probably best not to have another one.

Minnie was rubbing herself against Percy's legs. Percy checked her phone again. Still nothing from Marty. Could there be something in the will that was confidential? Even if there was, surely Marty, as a former probate judge, could find out what it said.

She looked at the clock again. It was as though time was standing still. She needed a distraction. She checked the Dr. Rob Facebook group, but people had pretty much stopped posting there. Then she checked the Stonebridge Facebook group. There were just the usual posts: Pictures taken from around Stonebridge, people looking for some kind of help, and reminders about upcoming meetings and events.

She pulled up the local paper and went to the police blotter. Nothing much there either.

She looked at the time. She still had fifteen minutes until it was time to go. She should have arranged to meet Hugh earlier. She managed to occupy herself for another ten minutes. Then she decided to just leave. Better to get there early than to sit around the house making herself nuts.

CHAPTER 31

Percy arrived at the café a few minutes early. Hugh was already there. Did he look nervous? He was fidgeting. She went over to him, putting a smile on her face.

"Hello," she said. "You beat me here."

He smiled back at her.

"I know you don't like it when people are late. Please, have a seat."

Percy took the seat opposite him.

"So, what did you want to see me about?"

Before she could answer, a server came over, asking Percy if she'd like coffee.

"Please," she said, even though her nerves were jangling. "Actually, do you have any herbal tea?"

"What kind would you like?"

"What kind do you have?" Percy rarely ordered herbal tea, even though she knew it was good for you.

The server rattled off several names of teas.

"I'll have a cup of chamomile," she said. "Thanks."

The server went away.

"So?" she said, looking at Hugh.

"Are you angry with me?"

"Angry with you?"

"You left in a hurry Monday, and I wondered… Was it something I said?"

Percy sighed.

"I wasn't angry." Hugh's look said he didn't believe her. "Okay, maybe a little annoyed."

"It was because I discounted your theory, wasn't it?"

"Maybe."

"I'm sorry if I was being patronizing. It's a bad habit of mine, one Elizabeth was always chastising me about. But she hasn't been around to nudge me when I act that way."

The server brought over Percy's herbal tea. Percy thanked her and remembered what Dr. Richardson said about Hugh maybe not being over his late wife.

"Thank you for apologizing."

"You're welcome. And, for what it's worth, I thought about what you said after you left, and I reached out to Arianna."

Wait. What?

"Why did you reach out to her?"

"I wanted to know more about the young woman she saw at Dr. Rob's. Maybe she had remembered something, something that could help us identify her."

"And?"

"And it turns out she saw her again."

"Arianna saw the young woman she had seen at Dr. Rob's again?" Hugh nodded. "Where?"

"At the Wellness Center."

"At the Wellness Center? Was the young woman a patient? And what was Arianna doing at the Wellness Center?"

"She's been seeing Dr. Yates."

"She has?"

Hugh nodded.

"Was the young woman a patient of Dr. Yates's?"

"No."

"Who is she? Does Arianna know?"

"She does."

Percy was feeling exasperated.

"Who is she, Hugh?"

"She's Carol Fielding's daughter."

"What?!" Percy wasn't expecting that. "Arianna must be mistaken."

"Arianna's sure the young woman she saw at the Wellness Center is the same woman she saw at Dr. Rob's."

"How can she be so sure?"

"She saw the baby."

"Baby?" Percy felt her heart sink.

Hugh nodded again.

"Arianna said she was a cute little thing, around two months old, about how old she thought the woman's baby would be now."

Percy felt sick. Joanna couldn't be the killer, could she? She wanted to help people, not hurt them.

"Are you okay? You look a bit pale."

"I'm just…" Percy didn't know what she felt. "Arianna's positive it was Joanna she saw at Dr. Rob's?"

"She is."

"Do you think Dr. Rob could be the baby's father?"

"It's a possibility."

"Though maybe Joanna had just gone to see Dr. Rob for help. She knew him from the Wellness Center. And Carol said the baby's father wasn't around."

"Did you ask Carol about the baby's father before or after Dr. Rob died?"

Percy had that sinking feeling again.

"After. But you discounted my theory about the young woman."

"That was before I knew who she was."

"And you think she could have killed Dr. Rob?"

"I don't know."

"Do you think Carol knew who the baby's father was?"

"I don't know. Maybe not. Do you think she could have continued to work for Dr. Rob if she knew he had gotten her daughter pregnant?"

"Probably not. So, did Arianna say something to Joanna?"

"No. Besides, what would she have said to her?"

Hugh had a point.

As Percy digested Hugh's news, she continued to feel heartsick. Would Dr. Rob really have slept with the daughter of his office manager, who was young enough to be his daughter? She knew Joanna had lost her father at an impressionable age. Had she seen Dr. Rob as a father figure and developed a crush on him while working at the Wellness Center? Even if she had, Dr. Rob knew better.

"I can see that brain of yours working. What are you thinking?"

"I just don't want to believe that Dr. Rob would allow himself to get involved with Joanna."

"Maybe she came on to him. He's a good-looking older man, a person in a position of authority…"

Percy frowned.

"Even if she did flirt with him, he knew better."

"These things happen, unfortunately. And didn't you tell me that Dr. Rob's brother said that Dr. Rob couldn't resist a pretty woman? And per Arianna, Joanna's quite attractive."

Percy continued to frown.

"Maybe Arianna's lying. Maybe she made the whole thing up."

"Why would she do that?"

"To rationalize why Dr. Rob dumped her."

"I don't think that's the case, Percy."

"Because you know her so well?"

Just then, the server came over, asking if they were ready to order. However, Percy had lost her appetite.

"Do you know what you want?" Hugh asked her.

"I'm not hungry."

"You should eat something."

Percy was going to say something snappish, but she stopped herself.

"I'll have a short stack of blueberry pancakes," she told the server.

"And I'll have the French toast with a side of bacon," said Hugh.

The server wrote down their order and went away.

"You're upset," said Hugh.

"I'm not upset," Percy replied. Though she was. "I just don't know what to think. The idea of Dr. Rob seducing that young woman…"

"She may have come onto him."

"It doesn't matter. He knew better. And then to get her pregnant…" Suddenly, Percy had a vision of Joanna holding a gun and pointing it at Dr. Rob.

"What?" said Hugh.

"I just had an image of Joanna pointing a gun at Dr. Rob. But I just can't picture her actually killing him."

"What if he refused to acknowledge the baby, wouldn't help Joanna take of it? After all, he dumped Arianna as soon as she told him she might be pregnant."

Percy frowned.

"But why wait until now to shoot him?"

"I don't know. Maybe she was biding her time, formulating a plan."

"But why shoot him at the Wellness Center and not at his place? Surely, his place would be more private. People are constantly going in and out of the building that houses the Wellness Center."

"I don't know. Though there was no one at the Wellness Center when he was shot."

"Speaking of which, where were you when Dr. Rob was shot?"

"I told you, I was at the vet with Fluffy."

"You weren't there the whole time."

"What do you mean? I told you, I have the invoice."

"I know what you told me. But I also know that you

dropped Fluffy off and then returned a half-hour later."

"How do you know that?"

"I cannot reveal my sources. Is it true, Hugh? Did you leave?"

Hugh ran a hand through his hair. Then he sighed.

"It's true. But I promise you, I didn't go to the Wellness Center and shoot Dr. Rob."

"Where were you?"

"I went home and then went to the post office. I needed to mail something, but I realized I had forgotten the package when I got to the vet."

Percy wanted to believe him, but…

"I can show you the receipt from the post office if you don't believe me. I showed it to Detective Russo, along with the one from the vet."

Percy was about to say something, but just then the server appeared with their food.

"Here you go!" she said, a smile on her face. "One order of blueberry pancakes and one French toast with a side of bacon!"

Hugh thanked her.

Percy still wasn't hungry and picked at her pancakes.

"What can I say to make things better between us?" Hugh asked her.

"I don't know. I just need some time to think." She moved a bit of blueberry pancake around on her plate. "Do you really think Dr. Rob could be the father of Joanna's baby and that she could have killed him? Though, did Joanna even have a gun?" Then she remembered: Joanna's father had been a cop. Maybe Carol had kept his gun. Or Joanna could have purchased one somewhere.

Hugh sighed.

"I think Dr. Rob may well be the father of Joanna's baby. But, for what it's worth, I still think the killer is Dr. Rob's brother. I did a bit of digging, and Ed owed a lot of money."

"And we know that Dr. Rob refused to help him. You could be right."

Percy continued to pick at her food.

"You find out about his will?" Hugh asked her.

"Not yet. I asked a friend who's a recently retired probate judge to look into it, figuring he'd be able to access it faster than I could, but I haven't heard from him. At this point, I just want the police to arrest someone already."

"Does this mean you're giving up on trying to solve the case?"

"I've discovered that it's a lot harder to solve a murder in real life than in books."

Hugh smiled.

"What?"

"It's good that you realized that."

Percy didn't say anything.

They finished breakfast. Or, rather, Hugh finished his breakfast and Percy finished picking at hers. Hugh signaled to the server for a check.

"Do you want to take that home?" the server asked Percy.

Percy looked down at her mostly uneaten pancakes.

"Sure."

"I'll be right back with a container."

She brought over a container for Percy's pancakes, and Hugh reached for the check. Percy didn't bother to argue with him this time.

"Thanks for breakfast," she said to Hugh as they stood outside.

"My pleasure," he said. "Are you around this weekend?"

"I wasn't planning on going anywhere."

"Would you like to come over for dinner one night?"

"Don't you need to check with Madison?"

"She's leaving for the Cape with a friend after school and won't be home until late on Sunday."

"That's nice."

"So, can I make you dinner?"

Percy still wasn't sure how she felt about Hugh. She no longer believed he had shot Dr. Rob. Not that she ever really did. But she couldn't stop thinking about what Dr. Richardson had said, about Hugh not being over his late wife.

"Let me see what Lucy's up to and get back to you."

"Of course. You know how to reach me."

They said goodbye, and Percy headed home. However, she turned around after a block and headed to the Wellness Center instead.

CHAPTER 32

Percy stood outside the building that housed the Wellness Center, wondering if she should go in and ask Carol about Joanna and Dr. Rob. No. She needed to think things through. And maybe the Wellness Center wasn't the best place to speak with her. Instead, she walked around downtown Stonebridge, gazing absent-mindedly at the store windows and then winding up at the little park where they held concerts on summer Tuesdays or Thursdays.

She sat on a bench for a little while, watching some children play on the playground. Then she decided to go to the library. She wasn't due there for another hour, but surely no one would object to her being there early.

"You're early," said Bonnie. "You miss me that much?"

"Something like that," Percy said with a smile.

"How was your breakfast with Hugh?"

Percy had texted Bonnie that morning, before she left, letting her know she was having breakfast with him.

She sighed.

"That doesn't sound good. What happened? Did you tell him you knew he hadn't been at the vet's the whole time?"

"I did."

"And?"

"He confessed."

"He confessed to murdering Dr. Rob?"

"No, he confessed to leaving Fluffy there, at the vet's,

going home to get a package, and then taking it to the post office."

"Do you believe him?"

"I do. He said he had receipts to prove it and had shown them to Detective Russo."

"So why don't you look happy? That means you can cross him off the suspect list."

"We have a new suspect."

"Who?"

"Carol's daughter, Joanna."

"Excuse me? Why would Carol's daughter shoot Dr. Rob?"

"She may have been having an affair with him."

Bonnie stared at her.

"Dr. Rob had an affair with the office manager's daughter? How old is she?"

"Twenty-four. But that's not all. She just had a baby, and Dr. Rob is likely the baby's father."

"Whoa."

"Yeah."

"And Hugh told you all of this?" Percy nodded. "How did he find out?"

"He talked to Arianna Cardinale again. You remember that she said that she saw a young woman—a young, very pretty, very pregnant woman—with Dr. Rob when she went to his place to confront him a couple of months ago?"

"I remember. But didn't you say she didn't know who the chick was?"

"I did."

"And now suddenly Arianna's convinced that the young woman she saw with Dr. Rob is Carol's daughter, Joanna?" Bonnie sounded skeptical.

"Arianna only realized it was her when she saw her again."

"Where did she see her?"

"At the Wellness Center."

"What was Arianna doing at the Wellness Center?"

"Apparently, she's been seeing Dr. Yates."

"Huh. Well, good for her. And Carol's daughter was there?"

"With the baby. Arianna told Hugh that as soon as she saw them, she knew it was her, the young woman she had seen at Dr. Rob's."

"And she's sure about that."

"Hugh said she was."

"She could be lying."

"Why would she lie?"

"To throw suspicion off herself."

"I thought the same thing at first, but I think she's telling the truth."

"Do you think Arianna told the police about Joanna?"

"I don't know. Maybe."

"And you really think Joanna could have killed Dr. Rob?"

"I don't want to think so, but I can't completely rule her out. She may have been angry at Dr. Rob for not being there for her and the baby."

"Well, if she shot him, he definitely wouldn't be."

"You know what I mean. But I just can't see her doing it. If you saw her with little Ella, Bonnie... And she's studying to become a therapist. She wants to help people, not hurt them."

"You don't think a therapist could kill someone? If I had to listen to people moan and groan all day, I'd want to kill someone."

"Good thing you're not a therapist."

"Probably."

"Also, how would Joanna know that Dr. Rob was alone?"

"Uh, hello? Her mother works there. Carol could have

told Joanna she was going to run errands because Dr. Rob's noon appointment had canceled and there was no one there."

"And what, she drove there with the baby from Kenwick, which is a good twenty minutes away, and shot him?"

"She probably left the baby at home in one of those super safe playpens."

"No mother would leave her newborn alone." Bonnie gave her a look. "Okay, let's say she did leave Ella, which I doubt. It still would have taken her at least twenty minutes to get to the office, and Carol said she had been gone less than half an hour. Surely, she would have seen Joanna."

"Maybe, maybe not."

Percy frowned. Then she saw Carmen coming towards them.

"Oh, good, you're here," she said to Percy. "I could use your help."

"I'll catch you later," Bonnie said to Percy.

The whole Joanna–Dr. Rob thing nagged at Percy all afternoon. She wanted to text Carol to arrange a time to see her, to ask about Joanna, but she kept putting it off. And Marty still hadn't gotten back to her. She would follow up with him over the weekend or on Monday. Maybe she would stop by the Wellness Center then, too, on her way into work.

The house was empty when Percy got home that evening. Well, empty except for Minnie. Lucy was out with friends again. Percy was glad her daughter had an active social life, but she had been hoping to spend more time with her. Soon, Lucy would be going back to college and then getting a job somewhere, probably far from Stonebridge. Or maybe she would go straight to law school.

Percy had asked Lucy about that the other night, and

Lucy had said she was still thinking about what she wanted to do after she graduated. Maybe she would take a year off from school to travel and do volunteer work. Unlike many of her friends, she hadn't gone abroad during her junior year and was hoping to see some of the world before she started graduate school or a job.

Percy made herself a vegetable omelet and some toast and took her plate into the living room. She had been too much in her head all day and needed a distraction. She turned on the TV, opened Netflix, and clicked on *Somebody Feed Phil*. He was in Montreal this episode.

"I should go to Montreal," she said to Minnie, who had been eyeing Percy's plate, even though she hadn't eaten the piece of omelet Percy had offered her. "I could drive there. Do you think Lucy would go with me?" Minnie stared at her with a look that said, *What do I know? I'm a cat.* "Maybe I'll ask her. I haven't taken a vacation in forever."

Percy finished her omelet and toast and brought her empty plate back to the kitchen when *Somebody Feed Phil* was over. As she was tidying up, Lucy came home.

"You have fun with your friends?" Percy asked her.

"I did."

"What did you do?"

"We hung out at Rachel's pool and barbecued."

"That sounds nice. So, I was thinking. Why don't we go to Montreal for a long weekend before you go back to school?"

"What made you think of Montreal?"

"Phil just went there."

"Phil?"

"You know, Phil Rosenthal, of *Somebody Feed Phil*."

"Right. I'd love to go, but I'm not sure that I can. I have to be back at school by the end of August, and I'm working pretty much up until then. And I want to go see Jamie again."

"He could always come here."

"You'd be okay with that? I know how you feel about guests. And he's not the neatest person in the world."

"I think I can handle him for one weekend."

"If you're sure."

"Go ahead and invite him down."

"Okay."

"Just check with me before you finalize anything."

"Will do. I'm going upstairs. See you in the morning."

Percy sat on the edge of her bed, her phone in her hands. She had been trying to compose a text to Carol, but she couldn't think what to say.

Just say you have a question you want to ask her in private, and ask if she can meet you after work tomorrow. You don't need to get specific, said the little voice in her head.

"Fine," Percy said aloud.

She opened her texting app and asked Carol if she was free for lunch tomorrow. Then she waited. But after ten minutes, she gave up and turned off her phone.

The next morning, as soon as she got up, Percy turned on her phone. Carol hadn't replied to her text. However, there was a text from Hugh, asking if she had spoken to Lucy about this weekend. Percy had not. And she wasn't sure she wanted to have dinner with him, even though she no longer believed he was Dr. Rob's killer.

She thought about texting him back, saying she was busy. But she hated to lie. She would go for a run and then decide what to tell him.

She checked her phone again when she got home. There

was still nothing from Carol. Then again, it was still early. But she still hadn't heard from her by nine, and she was starting to worry. Carol didn't seem like the sort of person who would blow off a lunch invitation. Had something happened to little Ella?

"Everything all right, Mom?"

"Everything's fine. Why?"

"You have that look on your face."

"What look?"

"The look you get when you're worried about something."

Percy really needed to do a better job of hiding what she was thinking. Good thing she wasn't a professional poker player.

"I messaged a friend last night, and she hasn't gotten back to me. And I'm a bit worried."

"She's probably just busy."

"You're probably right. I'll follow up with her later if I haven't heard from her by noon."

"You have plans for today?" Percy asked her daughter as they ate breakfast.

"I'm going to the beach with Jeremy and some friends."

"What about this evening?"

"Sorry."

"Tomorrow?"

"Nothing as of now."

"Could we do something?"

"Sure. What did you have in mind?"

"Was there something you wanted to do? Something maybe your friends aren't interested in doing?"

"Hmm. Let me think about that."

"We could go to the sculpture garden in Woodbury and then have brunch, or have brunch and then go."

"Maybe."

They finished breakfast, and Lucy got up and brought her plate to the sink.

"You should ask Hugh if he's free later."

"Um."

"What?"

"He actually asked me if I was around."

"And?"

"I told him I needed to check with you."

Lucy rolled her eyes.

"I told you: You don't need to check with me, Mom. Get your phone and tell him you're free."

Percy made a face, which produced another eye roll from her daughter.

"I'm not moving until you text him."

They had a brief staring contest, then Percy sighed and went to get her phone.

CHAPTER 33

Percy told Hugh that she was free that evening if he was and still wanted to get together. He wrote her back a few minutes later. He had something going on that evening, but would she be interested in going to Block Island tomorrow?

Tomorrow? She texted him back. *Isn't the ferry sold out?*

I checked. There are a few spots left.

Percy hesitated and looked over at Lucy.

"He has plans tonight, but he wants to know if I can go to Block Island with him tomorrow."

"Go!" said Lucy.

"Are you sure?"

"Yes. I'm going upstairs. No backing out while I'm gone."

What time were you thinking? Percy wrote back.

I was thinking we could catch the 10 a.m. ferry from New London and come back on the 4:55, getting dinner on the way back to Stonebridge. Does that work? We'd need to leave around 7:30.

Percy hadn't been to Block Island in years, and she always enjoyed being there.

Okay, she replied.

Excellent! Do you want to bring a bike, or should we rent ones there? I'm fine either way.

Percy had a bike, but she hadn't ridden it in ages.

We should probably rent ones there. Or I can rent one if you have one you want to bring.

OK, wrote Hugh. *I'll sort it out. So, pick you up at 7:30 tomorrow?*

See you then.

Percy had just put down her phone when it started to ring. It was Ed Mankiewicz. She stared at her phone for several seconds before answering.

"Ed?"

She wasn't expecting to hear from him and was still miffed that he hadn't personally let her know about the house, even though a part of her was relieved she didn't get it.

"Percy! Sorry for not being in touch. Had some personal business I needed to take care of. But I'm back now, and I had some news I thought might interest you."

"Yes?"

"The people who made the winning offer on the house you wanted just backed out, and the sellers wanted to know if you were still interested."

Percy didn't know what to say.

"Why did they back out? Did they find something wrong with the house?"

"No, nothing like that. They weren't able to secure a mortgage."

"I see."

"Anyway, the place hasn't officially gone back on the market, so if you still want it…"

A part of Percy felt like it was fate telling her to get the house, but the rational part of her brain reminded her that she would probably never use it. Still, here was an opportunity to ask Ed some questions, like whether his brother left him money and if he knew about Ella.

"Could I come down tomorrow and take another look at the place?"

"Tomorrow's fine. What time were you thinking?"

"Actually, can I call you back in a few? I need to check something."

"Of course. Call me back when you can. Just be aware, the sellers plan on relisting the house this week. So don't take too long."

"I won't."

Percy ended the call with Ed and immediately called Hugh.

"Did you buy the ferry tickets?" she asked him as soon as he answered.

"I was about to. Why?"

"Can we go to Block Island another day and just have dinner tomorrow?"

"Is something wrong?"

"I need to go to Beauport tomorrow."

"Why do you need to go to Beauport?"

"Ed Mankiewicz just phoned me. The house I was interested in there just came back on the market."

"I thought you had decided not to get a place there. Did you change your mind?"

"No, but this is an opportunity to ask Ed some questions."

"I don't know if that's a good idea, Percy. I heard the police have been talking to him."

"Where'd you hear that?"

"I'm not at liberty to say. I just know that he's a person of interest."

"Are they planning on arresting him?"

"I don't know."

"Well, I promise to be careful. So, dinner tomorrow?"

"Or I could go with you to Beauport."

Percy thought about that for a few seconds. It might be nice to spend the day in Beauport with Hugh. But would Ed spill to her if Hugh was there?

"That's very nice of you, but I'm not sure Ed will talk if you're around."

"You never know. I'm pretty good at getting information out of people."

"Fine. You can come with me. I'll give Ed a call back and see what time he's free."

"Great. Let me know."

Percy called Ed back and made an appointment to meet him at eleven-thirty the next day. He could show Hugh the house, and then she and Hugh could have lunch in Beauport and take a walk on the beach.

She still hadn't heard from Carol, so she decided to walk to the Wellness Center and see if she was there. But it was Joanna who greeted her at the front desk.

"Is Carol here?" Percy asked Joanna.

"No, she's at home with Ella."

"Is Ella okay?"

"She has a cold."

"And you didn't want to be with her?" Percy regretted the words as soon as they were out of her mouth.

"My mother's with her," she cooly replied. "And I didn't want to miss work."

Percy was confused.

"Are you working at the Wellness Center?"

"You didn't get the email?"

Percy shook her head.

"Huh," said Joanna.

"Maybe it's because I'm not currently a patient?"

"You still should have received it."

"What did the email say?"

"That I would be working at the Wellness Center, helping Carol."

"Is Carol okay?"

"She's fine. She just wanted to be able to spend time with Ella, and I'll get credit for school as well as some money."

"And Dr. Richardson's okay with this?"

"She was the one who suggested it."

Percy glanced around the waiting room. There was no one there. Should she ask Joanna about Dr. Rob?

"Is there something I can help you with, Ms. Rollins?"

Percy turned back to look at Joanna.

"I just stopped by to see Carol. I had a question I wanted to ask her."

"I'd be happy to pass it along."

"Actually, it's about you."

"About me?" said Joanna.

"Well, technically about Ella."

"What about Ella?"

Just spit it out, said the little voice inside Percy's head.

"Is Dr. Rob her father?"

Percy saw the look on Joanna's face. Was it fear? Anger? Some combination of the two?

"I think you should go," Joanna told her.

"Did he deny the baby was his?"

"Please leave, Ms. Rollins."

Just then, Dr. Yates came out. She saw the looks on Joanna's and Percy's faces and asked if everything was all right.

"Ms. Rollins just stopped by to see Carol. I told her Carol was at home with Ella, and she was just leaving." Joanna gave Percy a pointed look.

Percy could feel her face growing warm. She glanced at Dr. Yates, thanked Joanna, and left the Wellness Center. She stood outside, feeling her heart thumping inside her chest. The look on Joanna's face when Percy asked her about Dr. Rob… She was reminded of the expression, if looks could kill. Maybe she had been wrong about Joanna not shooting him.

Percy returned home and found a voicemail from Marty Lefkowitz, saying to call him. She immediately called him back.

"Percy!" he said.

"I got your message. What did you find out? Did you see the will?"

"I did. It's pretty straightforward."

"Who are the main beneficiaries?"

"He left his share of the business to Dr. Richardson."

"Okay."

"And he left cash bequests to his two nephews; his brother Edward; Carol Fielding, his office manager…"

"How much did he leave to his brother and his nephews?"

"He left twenty-five thousand dollars to his brother…"

Not bad, thought Percy. *But not the kind of money you would kill for. Unless Ed was really desperate. Though maybe Ed thought his brother would leave him more.*

"And his nephews were each to receive a hundred thousand dollars in trust, to be used for education, housing, or their general welfare."

"Very nice of him. Who was in charge of the trust?"

"Dr. Rob's accountant, George Bass, and the boys' mother, Josephine Mankiewicz."

So Ed couldn't get his hands on it.

"And how much did he leave to Carol Fielding?"

"Twenty-five thousand."

"Interesting. He left her the same amount as his brother. He make any other bequests?"

"I was about to tell you."

"Sorry. Please go on."

He rattled off the names of a few people Percy had never heard of.

"What about the remainder of his estate?"

"He instructed that a trust be created for one Ella Fielding, which was to be funded with the balance of his estate once all taxes and fees were paid, and bequests had been made."

"Do you know how much his estate is worth?"

"I do not. You'd have to ask his attorney or financial advisor."

"Do you know who his trusts and estate attorney is?"

"Craig Mancuso."

"Craig did our wills. Do you know when Dr. Rob's will was drafted?"

"He signed it shortly before he died."

Percy wondered who knew about the will.

"Anything else interesting?"

"Not really. As I said, the will was pretty straightforward. Though I'm curious to know who Ella Fielding is. Is she related to Carol Fielding, his office manager?"

"She's Carol's granddaughter. And I'm pretty sure she's Dr. Rob's daughter."

There was silence on the other end of the line.

"Did the will say anything about a Joanna Fielding? She's Ella's mother."

"She was to be a trustee on the trust created for Ella, along with George Bass."

"Okay. Thank you for your help, Marty. I really appreciate you looking into Dr. Rob's will for me."

"No problem. So, do you think one of them might have killed him?"

"I don't know."

As soon as they ended the call, Percy sent Craig Mancuso an email. Even though it was a Saturday, she knew Craig checked his email regularly. However, she immediately received an automated reply, saying that Craig was out of the office and wouldn't be back until June 9th. Percy frowned.

She wondered who Dr. Rob's financial advisor was. Then again, even if she knew, she doubted he or she would tell her Dr. Rob's net worth. Though she could always ask Ed.

As she was sitting there, she decided to text Carol. But would Carol talk to her? If Joanna had told her what Percy had said, probably not. Well, there was only one way to find out.

Hi, Carol, Percy typed. *Just following up.* She wrote that she had a question she wanted to ask her and then deleted it. Best to wait until she saw Carol to ask about Joanna. Instead, she wrote, *Would love to get together to discuss books with you. Let me know when you are free.*

She pressed *Send* and then waited.

CHAPTER 34

Lucy had left. Carol hadn't replied to her text. And Percy was feeling restless. So she decided to go to the library, even though she wasn't scheduled to work that day. Bonnie was seated at the circulation desk, looking at something on the computer.

"Hey," said Percy.

Bonnie looked up.

"What are you doing here?"

"You free for lunch?" It was a little after noon.

"I didn't make any plans."

"What time were you planning on taking a break?"

"Go ahead," said Victor, who was seated nearby. "I can handle the desk."

"Are you sure?" Bonnie asked him.

"Go," he said.

"I'll be back by one."

"Take your time. I've a feeling it's going to be slow."

Bonnie grabbed her bag, and she and Percy headed out of the library.

"What's up?" she asked Percy as soon as they stepped outside. "Everything okay?"

"I'm just feeling a bit restless."

"Where's Lucy?"

"Off with her friends again."

"Where do you want to eat?"

"You pick."

"Oh no. It's much better if you pick."

"Fine," said Percy. "You want to just go to Annie's?"

"Fine."

They headed to the restaurant, got a table, and ordered.

"So, what's up? Why are you feeling restless?"

Percy told her about the house in Beauport, and Joanna, and the will.

"Wow," said Bonnie when Percy was done. "That's a lot."

"I know."

"Do you think she could have killed him?" She being Joanna.

"I don't know what to think. This case just keeps getting more complicated."

"And I thought you had decided against getting a place in Beauport."

"I did, but I figured it was an opportunity to ask Ed some more questions. Hugh heard that the police talked to him. Apparently, Ed's a person of interest."

"I knew it was him!"

"We don't know that for sure. The police haven't arrested him."

"It's just a matter of time." She paused. "Are you sure it's wise to question him? He could be dangerous."

"I doubt he'll do anything to me with Hugh there."

"Hugh's going with you? I thought you were still annoyed with him."

"Lucy told me to give him another chance."

"Good girl. So, when are you two going?"

"We have an appointment to see Ed at eleven-thirty tomorrow. Figured we'd make a day out of it."

"Nice. Just please don't do anything rash."

"Have you ever known me to be rash?"

"No, but you've never tried to solve an actual murder before."

"So, what are you up to the rest of this weekend? You patch things up with Harry?"

"Yeah. We had a long talk, and I told him I wasn't ready for us to live together."

"You didn't tell me he wanted the two of you to live together!"

"Because I'm not ready to even think about it. I really like him, but it hasn't even been six months."

"So, what did you tell him?"

"I told him I wasn't against the idea in principle, but I needed a bit longer."

"And was he okay with that?"

"He said he was. It was kind of sweet, actually. He said he wanted us to live together because he misses me so much when we're not together."

"Aw. That's sweet."

"I guess. I just worry he could be one of those guys who hate to be alone. And you know how I feel about clingy people."

"I do. So, are you going to see him this weekend?"

"Yeah. We're going to hang out on his friend's boat up on Candlewood Lake tomorrow."

"Nice."

They finished eating, and Bonnie said she needed to get back to the library. Percy walked with her.

"You need to get a hobby, Percy. Something other than trying to solve murders."

"I run, and I read. And I tried gardening. But I don't have a green thumb."

"Maybe volunteer somewhere. I know the historical society is always looking for help."

"I've thought about it. But wouldn't it be similar to working at the library, just answering people's questions?"

"I suppose. But you know so much about Stonebridge's history."

"Not that much."

"Or maybe do something creative. What about taking an art class?"

"Maybe. Anyway, have fun with Harry tomorrow."

"And have fun with Hugh. Just be careful!"

"I will."

"So what's the plan?" Hugh asked Percy as they drove to Beauport the next day.

"I don't really have one. I just want to ask Ed about Dr. Rob's will, and if he knew about Ella and Joanna."

Percy had told Hugh about her conversation with Marty Lefkowitz.

"I'm also curious to know what the police asked him. How did you find out he was a person of interest?"

"I can't tell you."

Percy frowned.

"Sorry. But I need to protect my sources."

"You sound like a spy."

Hugh didn't say anything.

Percy looked out the window. It was a sunny day with temperatures in the low seventies. Then she turned back to Hugh.

"And your source didn't tell you if the police planned to arrest him?"

"They're doing their due diligence, dotting their i's and crossing their t's. But I got the sense they were close to arresting someone."

"Did Arianna tell them about Joanna?"

"I don't know. But based on what you said about the will, I'm sure they've talked to her."

"You mean Joanna."

Hugh nodded.

"Do you still think Ed killed his brother?"

"The fact that the police let him go makes me think he didn't. Or that they don't think he did it."

"Or maybe they're just dotting their i's and crossing their t's before they arrest him."

Hugh smiled.

"So, if he didn't do it, who did?"

"Based on what we now know, I'd say it was Joanna."

"But Dr. Rob acknowledged that Ella was his daughter in the will."

"Did he specifically refer to her as his daughter?"

Percy thought. Marty had asked her who Ella Fielding was. So maybe Dr. Rob hadn't acknowledged her as his daughter.

"No, but he left her the bulk of his estate and named Joanna as a co-trustee. Why would he do that unless he believed her to be his daughter?"

"I don't know. We also don't know if Joanna knew about the will. Didn't you say that the will was signed just a few days before he died?"

"That's what Marty said. But even if Joanna was angry with him for not acknowledging Ella, I can't picture her shooting him." Though there was that moment at the Wellness Center.

"Take it from me, being a new mom can make you say and do crazy things."

"Oh?" said Percy sarcastically. "Are you speaking from experience?"

Hugh didn't seem to notice Percy's gibe.

"After Elizabeth had Madison, she had serious mood swings."

"How serious?"

"One evening, when she was making dinner, she threatened me with a big chef's knife, just because I asked her when dinner would be ready."

"Wow. Pretty sure I never threatened Jim with a chef's knife after I had Lucy. Though I became super obsessive about cleaning. You could have operated on our kitchen table, it was so clean."

Hugh chuckled.

They arrived in Beauport a short time later and found a spot in the municipal lot.

"You sure about this?" Hugh asked her.

"I'm sure."

They entered Beauport Realty, and Percy saw the same woman she had seen the last time she was there. The woman was looking at her computer. Hugh cleared his throat to get her attention.

"May I help you?" she said.

Hugh smiled at her.

"My friend and I have an appointment with Mr. Mankiewicz."

"He's in his office. Your name?"

"Tell him Percy Rollins is here," said Percy.

The woman continued to look at Hugh.

"Could you please let him know that Ms. Rollins is here?" he asked her nicely.

The woman got up and went to the back, Percy assumed to get Ed.

"Percy!" said Ed, appearing a minute later. "So nice to see you! And who is this you've brought with you?"

"This is my friend, Hugh Barnes."

Ed was studying him.

"Have we met before? You look familiar."

Hugh smiled.

"Maybe you attended one of my book talks or read one of my books."

"You're an author?"

"His pen name is William Darcy," said Percy.

"No! Really? I'm a huge fan, Mr. Darcy. I've read all of your books."

Percy mentally rolled her eyes as Hugh smiled at Ed.

"Always nice to meet a fan."

"If I had known you would be coming, I'd have brought some of my books for you to sign."

"Another time, perhaps."

"I was so sad to read about your wife."

"Thank you."

"So, are you really done with writing?"

"As a matter of fact, I've been working on a new novel."

"Oh? Can you tell me what it's about? Or is it hush-hush?"

"Could we show Hugh the house?" Percy said, interrupting Ed's fanboying.

"Of course, of course. I just can't believe William Darcy is here in my office! Shall we take my car? It's just in back. Unless you'd rather walk. It's only about a mile from here."

"Your car's fine," said Hugh.

"Excellent. This way."

Ed insisted that Hugh sit up front, forcing Percy to sit in the back. Percy was thankful the house wasn't far, so she didn't have to hear Ed continue to gush over Hugh for long.

"And this is the place!" said Ed, getting out.

"Looks nice," said Hugh.

"Just wait until you see the inside! The sellers just moved, so it's empty. But the views!"

Hugh and Percy exchanged a look, then they followed Ed inside.

Ed gave them the tour, addressing all of his comments to Hugh. Maybe Hugh had been right that Ed would open up to him. Of course, it helped that Ed was a huge fan.

"So, what do you think?" Ed asked Hugh when they were done.

"It's a great place," he told Ed. "I can see why you wanted to buy it," he said to Percy.

"You still can," said Ed. "The sellers are very motivated."

"I need to think about it," said Percy.

"What about you?" Ed said, turning to Hugh. "This would be a great place to work on your next novel."

"True," said Hugh.

"Could you give me a little hint regarding what it's about?"

"It involves a therapist who gets murdered."

Ed stared at Hugh.

"Are you serious?"

"Deadly."

Was it Percy's imagination, or did Ed look a little pale?

"Your brother was helping Hugh with it," she said, interested to see how Ed would react.

"Rob knew about your book and that he'd be murdered? That's a bit macabre."

"The book isn't actually about your brother," said Hugh. "He was just giving me some insights."

"Hugh was originally planning on making the therapist the amateur sleuth," Percy said, hoping Hugh wouldn't mind her interjecting.

"Oh. What made you change it?"

"I'd say that's rather obvious," Percy mumbled.

"And you say Rob was helping you?" Ed asked Hugh.

"He was. He told me all sorts of interesting things."

Percy wondered if Hugh was baiting Ed, as she thought Hugh had said that Dr. Rob hadn't revealed any personal information.

"Like what?"

"I understand you had some money troubles and that you asked your brother for help, but he refused to bail you out until you got help."

"Rob told you that?" Ed looked surprised. "But surely, he must have also told you that I was getting help for my gambling addiction."

Before Hugh could answer, Percy jumped in.

"Did you know he planned on leaving you money in his will?"

"I had no idea until his lawyer contacted me after Rob died."

"Were you upset he didn't leave you more?"

"Frankly, I was surprised he left me anything."

"Even though he knew you were getting help for your addiction."

"I don't think he trusted me to stay on the wagon, so to speak. That's why he left money to the boys separately and made sure I couldn't touch it."

"But he did leave you something."

"Twenty-five thousand. Not a lot, considering how much he had."

"Was Dr. Rob rich?" asked Percy.

"He wasn't poor."

"Did you know about his daughter, Ella?"

Ed hesitated.

"Did he tell you about her?" he asked Hugh.

"Not specifically," Hugh replied. "He just told me that therapists weren't saints. That they had flaws like the rest of us, including him."

Ed snorted.

"He got that right."

"He also said that he made some mistakes, mistakes he regretted. Though he was trying to fix some of them."

Again, Percy wondered if Dr. Rob had really said that to Hugh or if Hugh was ad-libbing.

"So like Rob to consider a little girl a mistake."

"So you knew about Ella," said Percy.

Ed sighed.

"He didn't want to believe her at first. He thought he had been careful."

"By *her*, you mean Joanna Fielding?" said Hugh.

Ed nodded.

"She had a massive crush on him. Had since she was a teenager and spent a summer there. He thought she had a father fixation, her father having died when she was young."

"When did he start sleeping with her?" Percy asked. "Was it when she interned at the Wellness Center?"

"No. Rob may have been stupid when it came to women, but he wasn't that stupid. Joanna was practically a child when she started there."

"So when did they start sleeping together?"

"I don't know for sure. I think it was around a year ago, after Joanna had graduated from college. And it didn't last long. I think he only slept with her once." Hugh gave him a look. "Or maybe twice. But Rob knew he had made a mistake right away and told Joanna they needed to break it off. You ask me, I think he was afraid of what Carol would do to him if she found out."

"Carol didn't know about her daughter and Dr. Rob?"

"Rob didn't think so. And he certainly wasn't going to tell her. And no way was Joanna going to tell her mother she was sleeping with her boss."

"Why not?" asked Percy.

Ed gave her a look.

"Would you want your mother to know you were sleeping with her boss?"

He had a point.

"Also, Rob told me that Carol had told him to stay away from Joanna back when she had interned there."

"And when Joanna got pregnant, you don't think she told her mother then, about Dr. Rob being the baby's father?" Percy asked Ed.

"I don't think so. Rob didn't even know Joanna was pregnant until she went to see him."

"When was that?"

"She was pretty far along, maybe eight months? I think she was scared."

Percy and Hugh exchanged a look. That must have been when Arianna stopped by Dr. Rob's place.

"And she told Dr. Rob that the baby was his."

Ed nodded.

"Did he believe her?"

"He didn't want to. Like I said, he claimed he'd been careful. That's probably why she went and got that paternity test."

"She ordered a paternity test?" said Percy. "When was this?"

"I don't know for sure."

"And she told your brother when she got the result?" said Hugh.

Ed nodded.

"Do you know when she told him?" Percy asked him.

"I don't."

"How do you know about it?"

"Rob told me."

"When?"

"Maybe a few days before he died? I don't remember exactly."

"What about Dr. Richardson? Did she know about the baby and that it was Dr. Rob's?"

"Not at first. But she must have overheard Rob talking to me or Joanna."

"Did she say something to Dr. Rob?"

"Oh yeah. Farrah let him have it."

"That could be why she said she wanted to get rid of him," Percy said to Hugh. "She saw him as a liability."

"What are you talking about?" said Ed.

"Carol told me she overheard Dr. Richardson telling someone she wanted to get rid of your brother. Do you think she could have killed him?"

Ed stared at her.

"You think Farrah killed Rob?"

"If word got out he was impregnating women and then ghosting them, I imagine it wouldn't look good for the business."

"But Farrah was here in Beauport when Rob was shot. As was I," he added.

"You know that for sure?"

"I do."

"Are the two of you having an affair?"

Ed looked at Percy as though she were crazy.

"Farrah's happily married."

"So? Lots of married people have affairs."

"I never cheated on Elizabeth," said Hugh.

Percy shot him a look. Then she turned back to Ed.

"So, where were you that day?"

"I was having lunch with a friend here in town."

"Can you prove it?"

"Look, I already spoke with the police."

"What about Farrah, I mean, Dr. Richardson? Where was she?"

Ed ran a hand over his face.

"We were having lunch together. But we're not having an affair!"

Percy looked like she didn't believe him.

"And what were you and Dr. Richardson arguing about that day when I came to see you?"

Ed looked confused.

"Lucy and I saw you two in the park, after lunch that day. Dr. Richardson looked angry."

"It was a private matter."

"But you're not having an affair."

Ed didn't say anything.

"Did it have to do with Dr. Rob?" Hugh asked him.

Ed looked down at his smartwatch, which was flashing.

"I need to get back to the office. I have another appointment. Did you want to take one last look around?" he asked Hugh.

"I'm good," Hugh replied.

"If you two want to wait outside. I just need to lock up. Then I'll drive you back."

"We can walk," said Percy.

"Are you sure?" Ed asked them.

"We're sure."

Ed looked disappointed. Clearly, he wanted to chat some more with Hugh.

"Well, good luck with the book," he said to Hugh. "And if you change your mind about the house…"

"I'll let you know," Hugh said.

CHAPTER 35

"What are you thinking about?" Hugh asked Percy as they walked back to town. He could tell she was preoccupied.

"Dr. Rob."

"What about him?"

"If neither Ed nor Dr. Richardson killed him, who did?"

"Assuming it wasn't a random killing, someone walking in off the street, which I think is highly unlikely, that leaves Joanna or Carol."

"Carol? Why would she shoot him?"

Hugh gave her a look.

"How would you feel if you found out your boss got Lucy pregnant and then disavowed her and the baby?"

"I'd be very surprised as my boss is a woman." Hugh gave her another look. "But I know what you mean. I'd be furious. But did Carol know about Joanna and Dr. Rob? Ed didn't think so."

"Maybe she found out."

"Let's say that she did. Do you really think she would shoot him? We're talking about Carol."

It was hard for Percy to imagine Carol, who always had a smile and a kind word for everyone, shooting anyone, but...

"Her late husband was a cop. Maybe she had his gun. Or she could have picked one up somewhere."

"I suppose. Do you know if the police found the gun that killed him?"

"I don't."

"Your source didn't know or wouldn't tell you?"

Hugh didn't say anything.

"Did he or she mention Carol?"

"No."

"Or the killer could be Joanna. She had as much motive to kill him as Carol, if not more. Do you think she knew about the will?"

"It's possible. Though if Dr. Rob was planning on leaving Ella money, maybe he also planned on providing for her now."

"But did Joanna know that? And if she did, why kill him?"

"I wonder if Carol knew about the will."

"She claimed not to."

They walked in silence for a block.

"Maybe she didn't mean to kill him," said Hugh.

"Who didn't mean to?"

"Either of them. Maybe Joanna—or Carol—went to confront Dr. Rob, to persuade him to do right by Ella, and…"

"With a gun?" said Percy, interrupting.

"Let me finish. Maybe Carol or Joanna went to confront him, but she was nervous, on edge, and the gun went off accidentally."

"I don't know. I guess it's possible, but… Why bring a gun?"

"To show Dr. Rob that she meant business, to give herself the upper hand. But she wasn't actually planning on using it."

Neither said anything until they reached the edge of town.

"So, where's a good place to have lunch here?" Hugh asked Percy.

Percy stopped and stared at him.

"How can you even think about food right now?"

"I only had coffee for breakfast. I'm hungry."

Percy shook her head.

"What do you feel like having?"

"I'd be good with a sandwich, or maybe fish and chips, or a lobster roll? Is there a good seafood place around here?"

Percy sighed.

"Come on."

"Where are you taking me?"

"To the Shanty Shack."

"The Shanty Shack?"

"They have the best lobster rolls, fried oysters, and clams in Beauport. Just be prepared to wait."

There was a line at the Shanty Shack, but Percy assured Hugh that it was worth the wait.

Finally, it was their turn. Hugh ordered the Connecticut-style lobster roll, which was served warm on a toasted bun with melted butter. Percy got the fried oyster po boy. And they shared an order of homemade kettle chips.

They sat outside on the deck overlooking Long Island Sound.

"Maybe I should buy that house," said Hugh. "I could get used to this."

"Would you actually use it?"

He thought for a minute.

"If I bought it, I would use it. It's not like I have an office I have to go to. And I think Madison would like it here."

Percy quietly ate her po boy.

"And you could visit us. Unless you were reconsidering and wanted it for yourself."

"No. Lucy was right. I doubt I would use it. If you like it and think you'll use it, you should put in an offer. I'm sure your new BFF Ed could get you a good deal."

"He's not my BFF."

"But he'd like to be," said Percy, smiling at him.

They finished lunch, and Percy asked Hugh if he'd like some ice cream.

"Twist my arm," he said with a smile. "Though maybe let's go for a walk first."

"You good taking a walk on the beach?"

"Lead the way."

Percy texted Bonnie on the way back to Stonebridge, letting her know she was alive and had lots to tell her. Bonnie wanted Percy to tell her what she had found out NOW, but Percy said she would fill her in later.

Hugh had convinced Percy to let him cook her dinner at his place. But she needed to check on Minnie first, as she doubted Lucy was home. They pulled up in front of Percy's place a little after five, and Hugh followed Percy inside.

Minnie was there to greet them at the front door, looking cross. Percy went to check her bowl and saw that it was empty. She filled it with dry food, and Minnie went over to sniff before taking a tentative bite.

"She does this every time," Percy informed Hugh.

As Minnie ate, Percy emptied and refilled Minnie's water bowl.

"Though she prefers to drink from a tap," she told Hugh. "You want some fresh water, Minnie?" she asked the cat when she was done eating.

Percy turned on the kitchen faucet, and Minnie jumped up on the counter, watching the water.

"You thinking or drinking?" Percy asked her. Minnie continued to stare at the water. "I'm going to count to five, then the water goes off. One... two... three... four..."

As she was about to say five, Minnie moved her head and started licking the water. Hugh seemed amused.

"I know," said Percy. She waited until Minnie was done.

Then she turned off the water. "We can go now," she told Hugh.

"Are you sure? What if Minnie wants more water?"

"She can drink from her bowl."

"How hungry are you?" Hugh asked Percy when they got to his place.

"I could eat. How long will it take to grill the steak and corn?"

"Not long. I can start them now if you like."

He went to turn on the grill. Then he seasoned the steak and wrapped the corn in aluminum foil.

"You want something to drink?" he asked her. "I have wine and beer, as well as sparkling water. Pick your poison."

Percy froze. In Hugh's book, *Love on the Run*, Igor, the villain, poisons Sophie's wine. Fortunately, Sophie is onto him and pours the wine into a plant when Igor isn't looking. But still.

"Are you okay?" asked Hugh, seeing the look on Percy's face.

"Sorry, it's just that in *Love on the Run*, Igor poisons Sophie's wine."

Hugh chuckled.

"I promise, I'm not trying to poison you."

"Good to know."

"Though I know at least a half-dozen nearly untraceable poisons if I wanted to," he said with a grin.

"Not making me feel better!" said Percy.

"Sorry. But I promise you, I only kill people in my books."

Percy gave him a look that let him know she didn't quite believe him.

"Here," he said, going to the refrigerator and removing

a bottle of rosé. He uncorked it and poured some into a glass. Then he took a sip. "See? Perfectly fine." Just to prove his point, he drained the glass. "Nothing to worry about, except maybe a hangover if we drink too much. Shall I pour you some?"

Percy nodded and then watched as he filled her glass. She looked at him and then took a sip.

"It's good, right? Elizabeth and I had this wine in Provence a few years back, and I wound up ordering a case."

Not for the first time, Percy wondered if Hugh was still hung up on his late wife. Not that she would blame him. She often thought about Jim. But she didn't want to date someone who was still in love with someone else.

"Penny for your thoughts," Hugh asked her.

"I was just spacing out," Percy replied. "I probably need to eat something."

"Coming right up!"

Percy insisted on helping Hugh clean up after dinner, though there wasn't that much to clean. Then she asked him to drive her home. He had wanted her to stay, but Percy said it had been a long day, and she wanted to go home. Besides, she had work tomorrow.

Lucy's car was in the driveway, which Percy assumed meant that she was home.

"I had a really nice time today," Hugh told her.

"I had a nice time too."

They sat in Hugh's SUV looking at each other. Then Hugh moved his head closer to Percy's. Percy closed her eyes as Hugh's lips gently kissed hers. She kissed him back and heard herself sigh. Hugh knew how to kiss. They continued to kiss like teenagers, Percy wishing there wasn't a console between them.

Finally, they pulled apart.

"I should go," said Percy.

"Do you want to invite me in?"

"Not tonight. Lucy's home." Though Lucy would probably be thrilled to see Hugh. "Another time."

"Okay."

He sounded disappointed.

"Will you let me know if you hear anything from your source?"

"I will."

Percy gave him a quick kiss on the cheek and thanked him for dinner. Then she got out of the car. Hugh waited until she had unlocked the front door. Then he slowly backed out of the driveway.

"So?" said Lucy, startling Percy. Percy hadn't seen her there.

"So, what?" said Percy.

"Did you have a good time with Hugh? You were in his car a long time."

"Were you spying on us?"

"I wasn't spying. I just saw him pull in and… Did he kiss you?"

"Maybe." But Percy's face confirmed that he had.

Lucy grinned.

"And is he a good kisser?"

Percy felt her face grow hot.

"I'll take that as a yes."

"How was your day?" Percy asked her daughter.

"Good."

"I thought you were having dinner with friends?"

"I did. And then I came home. So you had a good time with Hugh? Did he like the house?"

"He did."

"You grill Dr. Rob's brother?"

"We didn't grill him. Hugh and I just asked him some questions."

"Uh-huh. Hugh still think he shot Dr. Rob?"

"No. Ed has an alibi."

"So, who does Hugh think did it?"

Percy wondered if she should tell Lucy about Carol and Joanna.

"If I tell you, do you promise not to say anything to anyone?"

"I promise."

"He thinks it was either Carol or her daughter."

"He thinks Carol shot Dr. Rob?"

"Or her daughter."

"Why does he think they shot him?"

Percy told her daughter what she had learned.

"Whoa. Well, if that's true, I don't blame either of them for shooting him."

"We must never condone violence, Lucy."

"You know what I mean. So, do you think one of them did it?"

"Unfortunately, I do." And the more Percy thought about it, the more she was sure she knew who killed Dr. Rob.

CHAPTER 36

Percy was on her way to the library Monday morning when she heard sirens. She watched as two police cars pulled up outside the building that housed the Wellness Center. She saw Detective Russo get out of one of the cars, accompanied by Officer O'Brien. They were joined by two more police officers, a man and a woman, who stood guard by the entrance to the building.

Percy watched as Detective Russo and Officer O'Brien went inside. Were they going to the Wellness Center?

Percy continued to watch, not caring if she was late for work for once. People had stopped on both sides of the street, no doubt wondering what was going on. Maybe five minutes later, Detective Russo and Officer O'Brien emerged from the building with Carol, who was in handcuffs. Joanna was right behind them, screaming at them and crying.

Had the police arrested Carol for Dr. Rob's murder? It sure looked that way. Percy continued to watch as Detective Russo opened the back door of the first police car for Carol, and she got in. Joanna rushed over, but Officer O'Brien held her back. Percy wondered where Ella was.

She watched as the two police cars drove away and then immediately called Hugh.

"Percy," he began. But Percy cut him off.

"I'm pretty sure the police just arrested Carol."

"How do you know that?"

"I'm standing across the street from the Wellness Center. I was heading to the library when I heard sirens. Then two police cars stopped in front of the building, and Detective Russo and Officer O'Brien got out. I waited, and maybe five minutes later, they brought Carol out in handcuffs. And you should have seen Joanna. She ran out after them and was hysterical."

"It sure sounds as though the police arrested her."

"Can you check with your source and confirm?"

"I'll get back to you."

The call ended, but Percy didn't move. While she had been on the phone with Hugh, Dr. Richardson had come out of the building and had led Joanna back inside. A part of Percy wanted to follow them. But she had a job. And she was already late.

She stood staring at the Wellness Center building for a few more seconds, then she turned and headed to the library.

"You're late," Bonnie said to Percy. "Is everything okay?"

Percy shook her head.

"What's up?"

"I'm pretty sure the police just arrested Carol."

Bonnie stared at her friend.

"For Dr. Rob's murder?"

Percy nodded.

"I saw her being escorted out of the building that houses the Wellness Center by Detective Russo. She was in handcuffs."

"Wow. So you were right."

Percy had called her the night before and told her what she and Hugh had learned and that, as much as she hated to think it, she now believed Carol was the killer.

"The one time I wish I wasn't."

"Elyse will be devastated."

Percy looked at Bonnie.

"Elyse? Why will Elyse be devastated?"

"She and Carol were close. Though now she'll have something new to gossip about."

"Well, I'm more concerned about Joanna and little Ella than Elyse right now."

"Right. Sorry. I don't know what I was thinking."

"I called Hugh. He has a source, I believe in the police department. I asked him to confirm that the police were arresting Carol, that she wasn't just a person of interest."

"Though do they handcuff persons of interest? Anyway, let me know what Hugh says."

"Enough gossiping, ladies. The library's about to open." It was Carmen.

Just then, Mary Beth came hurrying over.

"You'll never guess what I just heard!" Carmen, Bonnie, and Percy waited. "The police just arrested the office manager at the Wellness Center for Dr. Rob's murder!"

"How do you know that?" Percy asked her.

"Bruce just phoned me. He was there when the cops took her away."

No doubt, all of Stonebridge would soon know about Carol, Percy thought. Indeed, that was all anyone at the library could talk about that morning and afternoon. And Percy lost track of how many times she and the other librarians had to tell patrons to keep it down.

Percy had kept her phone on her, albeit with the ringer off, in case there was more news. But she didn't hear anything from Hugh that morning. She texted him as soon as she left to grab lunch. He wrote her back, saying he was still waiting to hear back from his source.

As Percy headed to the health food store, she made a detour and headed to the Wellness Center instead. However, when she got there, she saw a sign on the door saying that it was closed.

Percy called their number, but she got a recorded message saying that the Wellness Center was closed until further notice and to call 911 if this was a true medical emergency. Otherwise, you could leave a message and someone would get back to you.

Percy thought about leaving a message but decided not to. The mailbox was probably full anyway. She would wait until she heard from Hugh.

She still hadn't heard from Hugh by the time she left work. But from the gossip flying around the library, it sure sounded like the police had the killer, and that the killer was Carol.

Finally, after dinner, Hugh called her. She immediately picked up.

"Did you hear back from your source?"

"I did."

"And did he confirm that the police arrested Carol for Dr. Rob's murder?"

"He did."

"So did they find the gun? And were her prints on it?"

"I don't know. But Carol confessed."

"What? Carol confessed to killing Dr. Rob? Why did she do that?"

"I think she was afraid the police would pin his murder on Joanna."

"Why would she think that? Unless Joanna killed him. Were the police planning on arresting her?"

"I don't know for sure. My source said that the police had gone to the Wellness Center to speak with Joanna, not necessarily to arrest her, and while they were there, Carol confessed."

"Do you think Carol confessed to protect her daughter?"

"Maybe. But I think she was telling the truth."

"What makes you say that? What exactly did she say to the cops?"

"I don't know exactly what she said. All I know is that when Carol learned that Dr. Rob was Ella's father and that he refused to acknowledge her and admit what he had done, she confronted him."

"With a gun?"

"With a gun. But she claimed she didn't mean to kill him. She didn't realize the safety was off. And she pulled the trigger by accident."

"Do you believe that?"

"I believe in giving people the benefit of the doubt."

"But if it was an accident, why didn't she tell the police that right after she shot him?"

"She might have been in shock or too scared to."

Percy thought back to that day. Carol had definitely seemed to be in shock.

"But why did the police want to speak with Joanna?"

"They received a tip."

"Probably from Arianna."

"We don't know that for sure."

Percy made a face.

"Does Carol have a lawyer?"

"I don't know."

"I went to the Wellness Center earlier. It's closed until further notice."

"That doesn't surprise me."

"Do you think it will close permanently?"

"I don't know. But I can't see this being good for business."

"I suppose not. I wonder what will happen to Dr. Richardson, and Dr. Yates, and all of their patients."

"I don't know. I suppose we'll have to wait and see."

Three months later...

The Wellness Center had reopened after Labor Day, after being closed all summer. Percy had been surprised by the news, having thought the center had closed for good. There was an article in the paper about the reopening, with quotes from Drs. Richardson and Yates. They had both felt strongly that the center should reopen. They owed it to their patients. However, Percy wondered how many patients they would still have after all that had happened. Then again, as the center was one of the few practices in or around Stonebridge that accepted insurance, they would probably get some new patients to replace some of the ones who had left.

Percy decided she would make an appointment to see Dr. Yates. She wasn't sure if she would start therapy again, but she wanted to speak with someone objective about Hugh. The two of them were officially dating, but Percy had been feeling conflicted. A part of her felt as though she was betraying Jim, even though she knew that wasn't the case. Jim and Hugh were so different. And, as Lucy said, Jim wouldn't have wanted her to become a nun.

Lucy had gone back to school at the end of August, excited (and nervous) about her senior year. And Percy didn't feel it was right to burden her daughter with her relationship issues, even though Lucy had been the one to encourage her to take her relationship with Hugh to the next level.

And while Percy had talked about Hugh with Bonnie, she was careful about how much she shared, in part because Bonnie was dealing with her own relationship issues. Despite her seemingly extroverted nature, Bonnie liked having her personal space and alone time, and Harry didn't seem to understand that. And she had spent the summer wondering if she should break up with him.

As for Carlo, he had been gone a good chunk of the summer, first going to visit Barney in Provincetown in early July and then closing the gallery most of August to go to Italy, surprising Percy and Bonnie. Apparently, Carlo had an aunt there who was turning 90, and he had decided last minute to attend the big party his family was throwing for her, and then spend some time there, reconnecting with his roots.

When Percy had told Hugh about Carlo's trip and how she'd love to go back to Italy, Hugh had suggested they plan a trip there. Something else to discuss with Dr. Yates.

As for Hugh, he had finished the first draft of his new thriller, *Shot Through the Heart*, and had sent it to his agent. Percy had asked to read it, but Hugh said she would have to wait for the advanced reader copy (ARC). She had tried to convince him to let her read it sooner, but he had been adamant. So, she would have to wait.

Percy waited until the light turned green to cross the street. She was nervous about going back to the Wellness Center. A part of her felt responsible for Carol's arrest. Though she had had nothing to do with it.

She had heard that Carol had gotten a good lawyer and was out on bail, awaiting trial. Had she returned to the Wellness Center? Percy didn't know how she felt about that. She knew that people were considered innocent until proven guilty, but Carol had confessed. Albeit, she said it was an accident. And a part of Percy still thought Carol could have been covering for Joanna.

The light turned green, and Percy crossed the street. She thought she heard sirens in the distance, but it was probably just her imagination. Or else they could have been headed elsewhere. She waited outside the building for a few seconds, just in case a police car or an ambulance pulled up, but nothing did. Then she went inside.

She was surprised to see Joanna at the front desk.

"Joanna?" she said. Trying not to stare and failing.

Joanna smiled at her. Percy was relieved to see that Joanna wasn't angry with her.

"Dr. Yates should be out in a couple of minutes," she informed Percy. "Won't you have a seat?"

Percy remained standing.

"Are you working here?" Percy asked her. Though obviously, she was.

"Part-time while I'm in school."

"So you're back in school? Still planning on getting your MSW?"

"That's the plan."

Percy wondered how she could look so calm.

"And Ella? How is she?"

"She's good. Though I think she's starting to teethe."

"I remember those days. So, do you have help?"

Joanna smiled.

"My mom. Ella adores her."

"How is your mom?"

"Good. She loves that she gets to spend time with Ella. She says, 'Before you know it, Ella will be a teenager, and then out of the house. Enjoy her while you can.'"

Joanna said it in a voice that sounded like Carol's, and Percy felt a twinge of sadness. What if Carol were found guilty and sent to jail? She might not get to see Ella grow up.

"And you're okay working here, after what happened?"

"I admit, I wasn't sure about it at first. Mostly, I was worried that patients wouldn't be comfortable. You know, because of the whole Dr. Rob thing. But Dr. Richardson and Dr. Yates insisted I come back and that it would be fine. They've both been wonderful to me. And they were right. I mean, I have gotten some curious looks, but no one's said anything, at least to my face."

Percy was glad to hear it.

Just then, Dr. Yates appeared.

"Percy, are you ready?"

Percy looked over at her.

"Yes," she said. "I think I am."

To be continued...

ACKNOWLEDGMENTS

First, thank you for reading this book. If you enjoyed it, and I hope you did, please consider leaving a review or rating it on Amazon and/or Goodreads.

In addition, a big THANK YOU to my first readers: Sue Lonoff de Cuevas, Robin Muth, Anna Salo-Markowski, Kenny Schiff, and Amanda Walter. Your feedback and error spotting have made *An Obsession with Murder* a better book.

For the great cover, my thanks go to Dunya Ivanovic. And for making all of my books look as good on the inside as they do on the outside, my thanks to Jason Anderson at Polgarus Studio.

ABOUT THE AUTHOR

Jennifer Lonoff Schiff is the author of the popular Sanibel Island Mystery series and the novels *Tinder Fella*, *Something's Cooking in Chianti*, *Finding Gemma Lovegood*, and *A Mocktail for Murder*. Before becoming a full-time author, Jennifer worked as a writer and/or editor for multiple magazines and book publishers and founded a boutique marketing communications agency that helped companies tell their stories, for which she won several awards. When not plotting how to kill people (fictionally, of course), Jennifer can be found reading, planning her next vacation, taking long walks, or playing with her two cats.

For more information about Jennifer and her books, visit https://www.shovelandpailpress.com.